# LEE'S FERRY

## DESERT RIVER CROSSING

# LEE'S FERRY

## DESERT RIVER CROSSING

### W.L. Rusho

*With contributions by*
**C. Gregory Crampton**

**Tower Productions**
Salt Lake City • St. George, Utah

**1998**

Library of Congress Cataloging in Publication Data

Rusho, W.L.

LEE'S FERRY
Desert River Crossing

Bibliography: p.
Includes Index
1. Lee's Ferry, AZ - History

ISBN 0-9656645-1-1

(Previously published as ISBN 0-9630757-0-5)

First Printing - 1992
Revised Edition - 1998

Layout & Design by DataMax
St. George, Utah

Printed in the United States of America

# ACKNOWLEDGMENT

In addition to history gleaned from books, articles, and old records, much information was obtained from still-living participants—many of whom, in 1991, are now deceased. Their histories, given through interviews and correspondence, provided much background on Warren M. Johnson, James S. Emett, Charles H. Spencer, Buck Lowrey, and Art Greene. Many years ago, in researching this book, I talked with the following, all now deceased: Frank Johnson, St. George, Utah; Arthur C. Waller, Seattle, Washington; Albert H. Jones, Elizabeth, Colorado; Charles H. Spencer, Riverside, California; Albert Leach, Kanab, Utah; William H. Switzer, Flagstaff, Arizona; Bill Wilson, Clarkdale, Arizona; and Emery Kolb, Grand Canyon, Arizona. Art "Bill" Greene provided details about activities of his father, Art Greene. More recently, the author also talked with Jane Foster, Virginia Lowrey Greer, and Mamie Lowrey concerning Marble Canyon Lodge and Buck Lowrey. Jerry Cannon, bridge designer, provided valuable data and background on the new Navajo Bridge.

Original documents touching on Lee's Ferry history were made available by the Historical Department, Church of Jesus Christ of Latter-day Saints, Salt Lake City; the Utah State Historical Society, Salt Lake City; the Southern California Edison Company, Los Angeles, California; Northern Arizona University, Flagstaff, Arizona; Museum of Northern Arizona, Flagstaff, Arizona; Phoenix Public Library, Phoenix, Arizona; and Arizona Department of Archives and Library, Phoenix, Arizona..

Special acknowledgment is due to Otis "Dock" Marston, now deceased, who was a noted authority on Colorado River history, for providing documents and photographs, and for making significant corrections. In my personal investigations at Lee's Ferry and environs, I was ably assisted by Don Cecala of St. George, Utah , who contributed time, effort, and motorized equipment. Cecala also provided thoughtful suggestions, as well as physical exertions, that helped locate historic trails.

The late Professor C. Gregory Crampton, long a professor of History at the University of Utah, merits special thanks for his cheerful and generous—as well as important—contributions concerning the history of the Colorado Plateau canyon country. Don Cecala and I will always remember the delightful exchange of knowledge, laughter and wine on our many field trips with Greg. Crampton also made helpful corrections on manuscripts in 1975 and again in 1992.

Photographs uncredited in the captions were taken by the author.

—*W.L. Rusho*

# LEE'S FERRY

## DESERT RIVER CROSSING

The Colorado River, flowing left to right, breaks through the Echo Cliffs at Lee's Ferry. The Paria River flows from lower right past Lonely Dell Ranch. The sharp river bend at left was the main ferry site, used from 1873 to 1928.      *Bureau of Reclamation*

# FOREWORD

Thirty-five years ago this summer it was my privilege to be accepted as a member of an expedition down the Green and Colorado Rivers that was led by the late Norman Nevills of Mexican Hat, Utah. Although Nevills' boats were far lighter and more maneuverable than those used by Major John Wesley Powell on his pioneering transit of the river in 1869, and although much had been learned about the river in the intervening years, from the outset of our trip we shared some of the spirit of adventure that had characterized the Powell voyage.

On Thursday, August 1, 1940, we came to Lee's Ferry, our twenty-third camp after I had joined the eight-person party at Green River, Utah. I shall never forget that day. After three weeks in the upper canyons we were back in my native Arizona.

There were many factors to make the day so significant. We were now at Mile Zero on the Colorado, the point from which all distances on the river system are measured, upstream and downstream. For practical purposes this is the division point between the upper and lower basins of the drainage area.

As Will Rusho points out admirably in this book, Lee's Ferry was the crossroads and also the center of the riverman's world. It was the gateway into the promised land of refuge for many pioneer Mormons, who found new hope and a brighter future for their families in Arizona Territory. Some of these were "called" to their missions, while others sought to increase the distance from increasing pressure of prosecution faced by the Latter-day Saints in Utah for their plural marriage practices.

For some who found the arid lands of northern Arizona too difficult for colonization, Lee's Ferry was a memorable place on the return to home and family in Utah. Here the settled Arizona colonists crossed the river on the Honeymoon Trail leading to St. George, Utah, for ordinations and marriage in the LDS Temple there. For Navajos and Utes, as well as for all manner of white travelers, Lee's Ferry was the only acceptable crossing point along hundreds of miles of the turbulent Colorado.

In modern times, it has marked the start for river journeys through the lower gorges of the Colorado, one of the last memorable adventures still available in a shrinking world.

This book occupies a unique place in the annals of the Colorado River; none other has dealt directly with the long series of fascinating historical events that occurred at Lee's Ferry.

Beautiful, historic, restful, Lee's Ferry always has been one of my favorite spots in my native, my favorite state.

*Senator Barry M. Goldwater*

# TABLE OF CONTENTS

# INTRODUCTION... A POINT OF VIEW

In its long plunge to the sea, the Colorado River has cut its canyons through one upraised plateau after another, like deep grooves down through a giant staircase. In some places, where the river exits one canyon and before it enters another, a relatively short open area appears. Such a place is Lee's Ferry, located between Glen Canyon upstream, and Marble Canyon downstream.[1] For a stretch of about two miles at Lee's Ferry one can reach the river's edge from either bank.

In spite of this available access to the river, Lee's Ferry is far from being a level place. Visitors are confronted with a magnificent, but bewildering array of cliffs, rocky pinnacles, rough mesas and gulches that seem to defy pattern or understanding.

All of the massive exposures of rock strata are sedimentary in origin, having been laid down as water deposits, or solidified from arid sand dunes. Geologists say that the rocks visible about Lee's Ferry were formed during the Paleozoic and Mesozoic eras about 250 to 150 million years ago. For example, the highway into Lee's Ferry runs across the Kaibab limestone formation that is 225 million years old, a period of time that is almost beyond human comprehension.[2]

If the age of the rocks is mind-boggling, it may be a little easier to understand that it has taken the Colorado River, its antecedent streams, and its tributaries only about 20 million years to cut through the sedimentary strata to form the present landscape.

And what a landscape! Nearly every first-time visitor to Lee's Ferry is left breathless by the engulfing grandeur of the scenery. Steep, rough, and broken cliffs soar to heights of two to three thousand feet above the river. Between them the desert river, the Colorado, dramatically breaks through the long wall of the Echo Cliffs, tumbles over the broad boulder delta at the mouth of the Paria River, then plunges into the jagged gorge of Marble Canyon. Lee's Ferry is one of the most starkly beautiful places in the entire canyon country of the Colorado River.

None has appreciated it more than Theodore Roosevelt, who rode through on a pack trip in 1913:

> The landscape had become of incredible wildness, of tremendous and desolate majesty. No one could paint or describe it save one of the great masters of imaginative art or literature, a Turner or Browning or Poe.
>
> The sullen rock walls towered hundreds of feet aloft, with something about their grim savagery that suggested both the terrible and the grotesque. The cliffs were channeled into myriad forms–battlements,

---

1. In *Sixth Report of the United States Geographic Board: 1890 to 1932* (Washington: Government Printing Office, 1933) the name was decreed to be "Lees Ferry (not Lee nor Lee's)." Such a decision, however, is both poor grammar and poor history, since no person named "Lees" was ever involved. Hence, the author consistently inserts an apostrophe in Lee's Ferry.

2. The geology of the Lee's Ferry area is included in Herbert E. Gregory and Raymond C. Moore, *The Kaiparowits Region: A Geographic and Geologic Reconnaissance of Parts of Utah and Arizona* (Washington: Government Printing Office, 1931) U.S. Geological Survey, and in Charles B. Hunt, *Cenozoic Geology of the Colorado Plateau* (Washington: Government Printing Office, 1956) U.S. Geological Survey, and in Charles B. Hunt, "Geologic History of the Colorado River," The Colorado River Region and John Wesley Powell (Washington: Government Printing Office, 1969) U.S. Geological Survey Professional Paper 669. In David A. Phoenix, *Geology of The Lees Ferry Area, Coconino Country, Arizona* (Washington: Government Printing Office, 1963) U.S. Geological Survey, the emphasis is on stratigraphy and possible deposits of uranium ore.

spires, pillars, buttressed towers, flying arches; they looked like the ruined castles and temples of the monstrous devil, deities of some vanished race. All were ruins, ruins vaster than those of any structures ever neared by the hands of men, as if some magic city, built by warlocks and sorcerers, had been wrecked by the wrath of the elder god.... At Lee's Ferry, once the home of the dark leader of the Danites, the cliffs, a medley of bold colors and striking forms, come close to the river's brink on either side; but at this one point there is a break in the canyon walls and a ferry can be run.[3]

Individuals react differently to the almost overpowering cliffs, crags, peaks, and mesas, to the desert, and to the desert river. Some see the terrain as bleak and hostile, but most, like Theodore Roosevelt, see an heroic landscape of radiant beauty, capable of elevating thoughts and ennobling deeds of both men and women. From the pages of history, this diversity of reactions is expressed:

It has an agreeably confused appearance.            *Fray Velez de Escalante, 1776*

[Lee's Ferry] is desolate enough to suit a lovesick poet.
                                         *Jack Sumner of Powell's 1869 Expedition*

Oh, what a lonely dell!                              *Emma Lee, 1871*

I saw the constricted rapids, where the Colorado took its plunge into the box-like head of the Grand Cañon of Arizona; and the deep, reverberating boom of the river, at flood height, was a fearful thing to hear. I could not repress a shudder at the thought of crossing above that rapid.
                           *Zane Grey, in* THE LAST OF THE PLAINSMEN, *1908*

We dropped down over a lot of hills that seemed made out of all the scrapings of the Painted Desert and saw a big copper line like a badly twisted snake crawling along below with the greenest fields I ever saw beyond it and the reddest cliffs behind them... It was as beautiful as it was wild and strange and I doubt if there is a wilder, stranger spot in the Southwest.            *Sharlot Hall, Arizona Territorial Historian, 1911*

Lee's Ferry is, however, far more than a river channeled through a myriad of spectacular cliffs. One writer summed it up in these words:

Geographically our 42nd and Broadway lies exactly in the center of [the Colorado River Basin]. Like Times Square, it has its popular name, Lee's Ferry. For nearly four centuries everybody has eventually showed up here at the confluence of the Colorado and the Paria.
                                         *Frank Waters in* THE COLORADO, *1946*

---

3. Theodore Roosevelt, "Across the Navajo Desert," *Outlook* 105 (October 1913).

# LEE'S FERRY

## DESERT RIVER CROSSING

# THE
# FIRST PEOPLE

Thousands of years ago the first men and women reached the banks of the Colorado River, but no one can say exactly where, or when, this occurred. Evidence of early human inhabitants, perhaps the first in the area, has been found in the canyon country not far from Lee's Ferry. About thirty miles downstream, in Marble Canyon, river runners and archaeologists years ago unearthed a number of small animal figurines made of split willow twigs. When radiocarbon dated, these figurines were discovered to be an astonishing four thousand years old. Lack of any associated material, however, has left many questions about their makers.[1]

Artifacts from a still older Indian culture have been found near Navajo Mountain, about forty miles to the northeast. During the early 1960's, archaeologists from the Museum of Northern Arizona, sifting through the floors of shallow caves, unearthed woven sandals, made from yucca leaves, that registered an age of between seven and eight thousand years. These early dates surprised even the scientists. Discovered with the sandals were projectile points, knives, grinding slabs, and other artifacts. These items, together with an associated large number of small mammal bones, have enabled archaeologists to conclude that this group of Indians subsisted on wild plant foods and small game, with large game serving as a rare treat. To these ancient inhabitants of Navajo Mountain, and to their artifacts, scientists have bestowed the

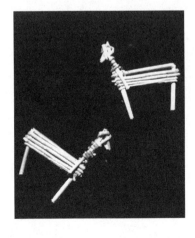

Split twig figurines,

made by prehistoric

Indians 4,000 years

ago, were found in

Marble Canyon caves.

---

1. Split twig figurines and prehistoric life in the Colorado River canyons are discussed in Robert C. Euler, "The Canyon Dwellers," *The American West* (May 1967). The succession of Indian cultures is treated in Robert C. Euler, *Southern Paiute Ethnohistory* (Salt Lake City: University of Utah, 1966) Anthropological Papers No. 78, Glen Canyon Series No. 28.

name Desha Complex.[2] The people of the Desha Complex and those who made the split twig figurines found in Marble and Grand Canyons probably both belonged to what is known as the Desert Culture. More abundant evidence of Desert Man has been found in the Great Basin portions of Utah and Nevada, but Desert Man seems to have disappeared. Either his descendants evolved into later Indian cultures in the same area or he migrated to other regions.

By the dawn of the Christian Era, (on the other side of the world), a new group of Indians was living on the mesas near Lee's Ferry. These were the Basketmakers and their lineal descendants, the Pueblos, differentiated principally by their knowledge of pottery-making. The Basketmakers and the Pueblos are collectively called Anasazi, from the Navajo word for "ancient ones." Anasazi Indians did not depend exclusively on hunting and wild food gathering, but obtained much of their subsistence from cultivated crops, such as corn or squash.

From physical evidence, it would appear that the Anasazi population was light at first; then their numbers increased dramatically beginning about 1000 AD. For the next 150 years this group built many stone and adobe structures to serve as dwellings, storage bins, and ceremonial rooms. Some of these structures were built as cliff dwellings within the canyons, but the greater number were constructed on the high rimlands.

To judge from evidence so far uncovered, Anasazi occupation of the immediate Lee's Ferry area, despite the easy availability of water and farm land, was light. During the 1960's, archaeologists from the Museum of Northern Arizona located two

---

2. The Desha Complex is discussed in Alexander J. Lindsay, Jr. et al, *Survey and Excavations North and East of Navajo Mountain, Utah, 1959-1962* (Flagstaff: Museum of Northern Arizona, 1968) Bulletin No. 45, Glen Canyon Series No. 8.

Typical small Anasazi ruin on the Paria Plateau.

small ruins near the mouth of the Paria River. These were dated about 1100 to 1150 AD.[3] On top of a hill near the Paria, known locally as Lee's Lookout, a circle of rocks appears to be of prehistoric origin. Petroglyphs, symbols or art work incised on rock surfaces, have been found in some number along the Paria River within three miles of its mouth. Perhaps additional evidence of Anasazi occupation of the Lee's Ferry area will be found, but no competent, systematic investigation has ever been made.

Even if prehistoric ruins are scarce at Lee's Ferry, several Anasazi ruins can be found on the high Paria Plateau, outlined by the spectacular Vermilion Cliffs immediately to the west. Due to almost total absence of surface water on the plateau, however, the population density of the Anasazi on the Paria Plateau must have always been low, certainly lower than on the Kaiparowits Plateau, a similar, but higher and better watered highland to the northeast, where archaeologists have found ten Anasazi dwelling sites per square mile.

Near the turn of the thirteenth century the Anasazi abandoned the canyon country. Either suddenly or over a number of years, a mass exodus took place. For what reason no one can say with certainty, but geologists have pointed to an intensive soil erosion cycle that began about the year 1250. A long drought, verified from tree ring data, probably dried the streams and fields. Natural vegetation withered and died, leaving the land open to the devastating force of brief, but torrential cloudbursts. Cornfields were slashed by deep gullies as the topsoil was washed into the Colorado River.

Other factors, such as pressure from encroaching Indian tribes moving in from the north, may have given additional reason for vacating the region. Most authorities believe that the Anasazi bands then in northern Arizona and southern Utah moved south, where their descendants are now known as Hopis.

Possibly a hundred years after the departure of the "ancient ones" from the canyon country, the ancestors of modern Indians moved in. These were the Southern Paiutes, close relatives of the Utes. It is even possible that the Southern Paiutes may have helped force the Anasazi into exodus. Fragmentary evidence indicates that by the fourteenth century Paiutes were in the vicinity of Lee's Ferry, although their numbers were few. Primitive in the extreme, the Paiutes did little else than spend their entire waking hours searching for food: seeds, rabbits, mice, or birds. Even insects were part of their diet. Deer were occasionally hunted on the plateaus.

Only on rare occasions would the Paiutes' hunting forays have taken them to the mouth of the Paria. If they desired to cross the Colorado River, which was probably seldom, they would have chosen a place where swimming or wading was a little safer. Such places were to be found farther upstream.

Sometime before 1500 AD. Navajos moved in from the north, settling in the Chuska Mountains near the present Arizona-New Mexico border. From this base they gradually extended their domain eastward into present-day New Mexico and westward to the Colorado River. Although Lee's Ferry today borders on the Navajo Reservation, no evidence indicates that Navajos lived along the Colorado River prior to about 1850.[4]

Neither Utes nor Paiutes live beside the Colorado River today, but a small Paiute Reservation, the Moccasin Indian Reservation, lies near Colorado City, about 60 miles northwest of Lee's Ferry.

---

3. *Arizona Daily Sun* (Flagstaff: 24 July 1963), article by william Hoyt.
4. James J. Hester, *Early Navajo Migrations and Acculturation in the Southwest* (Santa Fe: Museum of New Mexico, 1962) Papers in Anthropology No. 6.

# THROUGH AN UNKNOWN LAND

**B**ecause they had located a spring of cool water at the base of a desert cliffside, they had named their camp San Fructo. Winter was not far away, and the night winds were already cold. Early the next morning they were on their way again, urging their horses through the rolling sands and gravel at the base of the lofty cliff, heading northeast toward what they hoped would be an exit from the valley. Only when they neared the supposed exit, and when they descended toward the river, did they realize that the valley was virtually surrounded by steep, arid cliffs of broken red rock. There appeared to be no way out.

Thus did the first white men of European ancestry see what would later be called Lee's Ferry. The date was October 26, 1776.[1]

Leading the group of horsemen were two Spanish priests, Fray Francisco Atanasio Domínguez and Fray Silvestre Vélez de Escalante. Domínguez was nominally in charge, but Escalante kept the written journal, a fact that caused people, for many

Fray Domínguez, Fray Escalante, and Captain Miera y Pacheco examine a sketch map prepared by Miera, Cartographer for the 1776 expedition.

*Darrell Hatch*

---

1. Four major translations of the Dominguez-Escalante diary have been made. The first, W. R. Harris, *The Catholic Church in Utah, 1776-1909* (Salt Lake City: Intermountain Catholic Press, 1909), was a loose translation that generalized details. A good translation was Herbert S. Auerbach, "Father Escalante's Journal, 1776-77," *Utah Historical Quarterly* 11 (1943). The first interpretive study that attempted to relate the Escalante narrative to present-day topographic names was Herbert E. Bolton, "Pageant in the Wilderness," *Utah Historical Quarterly* 18 (1950).

years, to erroneously call it the "Escalante Expedition." Since more recent research has shown that the two priests were actually co-leaders, we now call it the Domínguez-Escalante Expedition.

Late in July 1776 the explorers left Santa Fe hoping to find a northern trail that would connect the New Mexico settlements with the California mission headquarters at Monterey. They knew that their late departure might not allow them time enough to reach their objective, but they would at least learn something about the geography of the land and about the culture and strength of the northern Indian tribes. And, of course, they could determine possible sites for new missions.

Because they expected that their route would soon be followed by settlers, soldiers, and priests, they provided details in their diary on directions, distances, and landmarks. Even today, over two hundred years later, one can still follow the route with an astonishing degree of accuracy.

Traveling northwest into present-day Colorado, they left previously explored routes to venture forth into *tierra incognita*, heading generally north, then west into what is now Utah. At Utah Lake they turned south to reach the latitude of Monterey before continuing on a westward course. As they plodded through the rough land near present-day Cedar City, they were struck by an early winter storm. They realized that hundreds of miles still lay between them and the Pacific coast, yet already snow was in the air. Conferring only with each other, the two priests decided that they had gone far enough, but it required a dramatic "casting of lots" (a drawing of destination names from a hat), to convince their followers that the expedition should return to Santa Fe. Since they had reached their location by a circuitous route, they chose to return by a more direct and shorter, but unexplored route.

Traveling south beyond the Virgin River, the Spaniards then turned east across the present Arizona Strip, [that part of Arizona north of the Grand Canyon], hoping to find a ford across the Colorado River. With no one to guide them, they had to rely on vague information supplied by whatever itinerant Indians they could catch. Most of these Paiutes, probably terrified by the strange visitors, simply ran away or hid themselves. No Indian would serve as a guide. About all Domínguez or Escalante could learn was that somewhere to the northeast a ford did exist.

When they reached what we now know as Lee's Ferry, they quickly realized that it was not the ford that had been described to them by Indians. After all their weary struggles, the expedition had indeed arrived at the bank of the Colorado River, but here the river was too deep to ford. Even worse, they suspected that they had ridden into a giant cul-de-sac, a place with no easy escape. With a touch of grim humor, they named their camp "San Benito"–a monk's robe of penance–then added "Salsipuedes," which means "get out if you can!" Located beside the Colorado at the base of a high rock, their campsite is easily identifiable today (see Tour Section, Site No. 8). The nearby Paria River was given the name Rio Santa Teresa.

Even if this was not the ford the Spaniards were looking for, they felt that perhaps a crossing could be made. Two of the men, naked, carrying their clothes on their

(1 continued): The newest, and probably the most accurate translation, was done by Fray Angelico Chavez, *The Dominguez-Escalante Journal*, Ted J. Warner. ed., (Brigham Young University Press: 1976). This 1976 translation and editor's notations had the assistance of several scholars and Government agency officials who carefully mapped out the trail and checked it in the field. A report of this field work is David E. Miller (ed.) *The Route of The Dominguez-Escalante Expedition, 1776-1777*, Utah State Historical Society (1976). All names supplied by the Spaniards were put on a map prepared by expedition cartographer Captain Bernardo Miera y Pacheco. Miera's was the first map to show a large section of the canyon country along the Colorado River that was based on actual exploration.

In 1776, at the future site of Lee's Ferry, Fray Escalante and two of the men try–and fail–to cross the Colorado River on a raft.

*Darrell Hatch*

heads, swam across, but the river was so swift and wide that they lost their clothes, then climbed from the muddy water too weak to explore the opposite bank. Although the men managed to recross, Domínguez and Escalante dismissed all further thought of swimming.

Several days later Escalante built a crude raft and set out to pole his way across the river. But he could not touch bottom with the pole, and contrary winds kept blowing him back to shore. Escalante probably did not know how close he came to becoming the first river rafter through the Grand Canyon! But with this failure the padres at last realized that they lacked both the knowledge and the equipment needed to cross their men at Lee's Ferry. Somehow, they must find a way out of this cliff-bound river bottom.

About three miles up the Paria one of the expedition members discovered a place where the rugged cliffs to the east might be climbed. Although Escalante and Domínguez were at first hesitant to try this arduous and hazardous ascent, they finally agreed that it was their only choice. On November 2, up they went, over the sometimes sandy, then steep and rocky, two thousand-foot high slope. In their journal, Escalante described the climb: "We spent more than three hours in climbing it because at the beginning it is very rugged and sandy and afterward has very difficult stretches and extremely perilous ledges of rock, and finally it becomes impassable" (see Tour Site No. 11).[2]

Before 1975 this pass over the cliffs had no official name, so I have named it Domínguez Pass, in honor of the nominal leader of the expedition. Domínguez Pass was used by many others in later years and will be mentioned again in this book.

When the expedition members finally crested the cliffs, they proceeded through rough gulches, then turned northeast across more open, sand dune country. That night they camped beside a small stream that was saline but fit to drink. Across from their camp Escalante noted "little mesas and peaks of red earth which at first sight look like the ruins of a fortress." The expedition was, in fact, on the banks of Wahweap Creek, near the place where Wahweap Lodge and Marina stand today. Across the

---

2. Since they successfully climbed the trail, the word "impassable" is not logical, but both major translations, Bolton and Chavez, include the word.

On November 7, 1776, the Domínguez-Escalante Expedition finally locates the ford across the Colorado River later known as Crossing of the Fathers.                    *Darrell Hatch*

bay, projecting from Lake Powell, are the rocky "ruins."

In desperation they spent two days trying to cross the Colorado at the mouth of Navajo Creek, only to fail and push on. Finally, on November 6, the long-sought ford was sighted, and on November 7, the expedition made its way down Padre Creek Canyon to the Colorado River, which was crossed diagonally without having to swim. In high spirits, Escalante wrote, "We praised God our Lord and fired off a few muskets as a sign of the great joy which we all felt at having overcome so great a difficulty which had cost us so much labor and delay."

With some further effort they traversed the intricate canyon country east of the river, but once past White Mesa they traveled through more open terrain by way of the Hopi villages and Zuni Pueblo. They arrived back in Santa Fe on January 2, 1777.

The ford that Escalante and Domínguez found had been used by Indians, perhaps for centuries. After 1776 it was used for about another 100 years, or until the ferry at Lee's Ferry became a reliable operation. The historic ford was eventually abandoned, but not forgotten. It went on the maps, appropriately enough, with two names: Ute Ford, which commemorates the Indian usage, and Crossing of the Fathers (as it is usually called), which commemorates Domínguez and Escalante. Crossing of the Fathers lies about forty river miles above Lee's Ferry and twenty-five miles above Glen Canyon Dam. It is now covered to a great depth by the waters of Lake Powell, in the center of what is known as Padre Bay. Wilderness closed swiftly upon the wake of the Domínguez-Escalante expedition. After 1776 the Spanish crown continued to ignore the region north and west of New Mexico. Due to a lack of settlers, soldiers, priests, and money, no effort was made to establish missions in present-day Colorado or Utah. Although one Mexican trading caravan on the way to California forded at Crossing of the Fathers in 1829, most travelers preferred less arduous routes.[3] After 1829, the Spanish Trail, (which should be called the "Mexican Trail"), and which headed the canyons through more open lands in central Utah, carried virtually all the traffic.

---

3. The diary of the Armijo Expedition of 1829 is found in LeRoy R. and Ann W. Hafen, *The Old Spanish Trail, Santa Fe to Los Angeles* (Glendale, Calif.: Arthur H. Clark Co., 1954), pp. 158-165.

## MOUNTAIN MEN

In the early 1800's the United States, having declared its independence in the same year that Domínguez and Escalante were in the field, was spreading its influence to the west. Among the first Americans to reach the Rocky Mountains were the beaver trappers, or mountain men, who worked mainly near the headwaters. But beaver were found and probably trapped along the Colorado clear to its mouth. It can be assumed that wherever there were beaver there were at least occasional visits by mountain men, even though few records indicate trapping along the Colorado.

Not all the mountain men were from American States to the east. Several of the men were Mexican, Frenchmen, or Americans that journeyed from Santa Fe or Taos. It should be remembered that almost all of the Colorado River Basin–including the Lee's Ferry area–was then a part of Mexico.

One recorded journey into the canyon country was made by James Ohio Pattie, who in 1826 traveled the rimlands of the Colorado from the Gila River north and east to the present state of Colorado.[4] Pattie's descriptions, however, are so imprecise that reconstructing his route is mostly guesswork; he may or may not have seen the site of Lee's Ferry.

Denis Julien, another enigmatic mountain man, "recorded" his presence in canyons of the Green and Colorado Rivers by cutting his name on the rock walls. His last inscription was placed in Cataract Canyon, 180 miles above Lee's Ferry. If Julien was boating, which is probable, and if he didn't drown in a rapid, he may have trapped beaver all the way through Glen Canyon.[5]

If for seventy years after Domínguez and Escalante, Lee's Ferry was seen by few, if any, non-Indians, by the 1850's new forces were shaping that would bring the lonely spot into historical prominence.

---

4. Timothy Flint, ed., *The Personal Narrative of James O. Pattie* (Cincinnati: John H. Wood, 1831).
5. Charles Kelly, "The Mysterious D. Julien," *Utah Historical Quarterly* 6 (1933) and Otis Marston, "Denis Julien" *Mountain Men and the Fur Trade*, 10 vols. (Glendale, Calif.: Arthur H. Clark Co., 1969), vol. 7.

# MORMON
# CROSSING

Expansion of the Mormon frontier outward from Salt Lake City after 1847 was the result of a determination by leaders of the Church of Jesus Christ of Latter-day Saints to extend the Mormon spiritual and temporal realm through all valleys and mountains still unoccupied by white men. Under the vigorous direction of Brigham Young, president of the Church, members participated in a cooperatively planned colonization. They were remarkably successful in extending their frontiers, even into the desert country of the Colorado Plateau.

Mormon colonization early developed a strong southward bent, a trend that continued for many years. Mindful of the importance of an ice-free river route to the Pacific, as well as of the desirability of colonization in warm climes, the Latter-day Saints founded the first permanent settlements in southern Utah, southern Nevada, and northern Arizona. Between 1850 and 1861, a cluster of settlements were made on the rim of the Great Basin and along the middle reaches of the Virgin River in southwestern Utah, including Parowan, Cedar City, Santa Clara, St. George, and others. These villages were then used as bases for Mormon settlers who pushed on southward into Nevada and California as well as eastward toward the Colorado River and into central Arizona.

In the Book of Mormon, Indians were called "Lamanites," an errant people who had fallen from the faith in the ancient past. One of the first Mormon efforts in any new area was therefore missionary activity to bring the Indian inhabitants back into the fold. Mormons believed that successful missionary work would not only save souls; it would lessen resistance to incoming settlers. But the often voiced Mormon conviction that peaceful conversion was better than violent confrontation turned out to be mostly complacent self-delusion, unrealized in reality. From a historical perspective, Utah Indians lost both land and lives just as inexorably, and in similar numbers, to Indians in other parts of the West.

Latter-day Saints' interest in propagating the faith among the "Lamanites" was not confined to nearby Utes and Paiutes; they also expressed interest in the Hopi Indians living southeast of the Colorado River. It had been reported to them that Hopis lived in towns, supported themselves by farming, and were peaceful. Perhaps they would favorably receive missionaries from the Mormon Church. In 1858 Jacob Hamblin, already known locally for his Indian mission activities, was sent by the Church to find out.

Jacob Hamblin, Mormon frontier explorer and Indian missionary. As leader of a group of missionaries to the Hopi Indians, Hamblin passed by the mouth of the Paria in 1858, 1859, and 1860. In 1864, his group made the first river crossing at what later became Lee's Ferry.

*Utah State Historical Society*

With a party of twelve men, Hamblin headed east for the Hopi villages, guided by a Paiute, Naraguts, who claimed he knew how to reach the old Ute Ford across the Colorado.[1] As they neared the river, Hamblin and his men unknowingly retraced Dominguez's and Escalante's footsteps. They too rode through House Rock Valley, looked up at the towering Vermilion Cliffs, and arrived at the mouth of the Paria River. Naraguts at length recognized his error; this was not the ford. The confused guide then led the party up the Paria to the only point where the cliffs to the east could be climbed, undoubtedly the same point reached in 1776 by the Spanish padres, Dominguez Pass (see Tour Site No. 11). When they finally located the Crossing of the Fathers, the Mormon missionaries forded the river and rode south to the Hopi villages without further trouble.

As it turned out, about the last thing the Hopis wanted was proselytizing missionaries from any outside religion. Preferring their own religion, the Hopis had, for over two hundred years, repeatedly turned deaf ears to preachments of Catholic fathers based in New Mexico, (including Escalante, on a trip in 1775), and had even excluded them from their mesa-top villages. Jacob Hamblin and his men were politely received by the Hopis, but these Indians gave no indication that they were ready to

---

1. Jacob Hamblin's missionary expeditions to the Hopis are recorded in James G. Bleak, "Annals of the Southern Utah Mission," typescript in L.D.S. Historical Department, Salt Lake City. Hamblin's autobiography is in James A Little, *Jacob Hamblin Among the Indians* (Salt Lake City: Juvenile Instructor Office, 1881). Two biographies of Hamblin are Pearson H. Corbett, *Jacob Hamblin the Peacemaker* (Salt Lake City: Deseret Book Co., 1952), and Paul Bailey, *Jacob Hamblin, Buckskin Apostle* (Los Angeles: Westernlore Press 1948). Corbett's book, although too laudatory, is superior.

embrace a new faith. After a visit of a few days the discouraged Mormons returned home.

A year later, in 1859, Brigham Young ordered another missionary attempt, again sending Jacob Hamblin and six others to the Hopis. Following the same route as the previous year, the party reached the mouth of the Paria where one of the members, Thales Haskell, took note of apparent natural resources. The Paria, he wrote in his diary, was a good-sized stream that might be used to irrigate crops planted along its banks. Camped that evening at the base of the cliffs, Haskell wrote, "We spread out our meat, ate a hearty supper–sang songs–hobbled the animals and went to bed. Plenty of water, grass, and cottonwood at this place."[2]

On this second mission the Hopis were noticeably less friendly and the Mormons accomplished little. Two men stayed through the winter, but the Hopis would not listen to their preachings. The undaunted Hamblin, however, made plans for yet a third trip to Hopiland in 1860. Because the Hopis had refused to supply even minimal sustenance to the uninvited Mormons, he carried along enough food and other essentials on the trip to last the missionaries a full year. Hamblin realized that if the men and their baggage could be ferried across the Colorado at the mouth of the Paria, they would eliminate much rough travel and would save considerable time. Accordingly, the expedition started out with a sixteen-foot boat loaded on a wagon. Both boat and wagon, however, were left behind on the Kaibab Plateau when the trail became too rough. Upon reaching the mouth of the Paria they constructed a crude raft, hoping to use it to ferry the Colorado. A few men barely made it across, a horse was drowned, and they concluded that it was too dangerous an undertaking. They mounted their horses and proceeded over Dominguez Pass toward the Crossing of the Fathers.

On this 1860 trip the Mormons had their first encounter with Navajo Indians–and it was a violent one. On November 1, 1860, near the present trading post at Tonalea, Hamblin's party was accosted by a group of defiant Navajos who finally agreed to leave the Mormons in peace if they would give up some

Thales Haskell, whose journal records the 1858 Mormon missionary expedition to the Hopi Indians.
*Utah State Historical Society*

of the trade goods originally intended for the Hopis. This done, the Mormons went on their way, all except young George A. Smith, Jr., who, having gone back to retrieve a horse, became separated from his party. Two Navajos rode up to Smith and asked to see his revolver. Smith complied, only to be shot three times with his own gun.

Hamblin and the others returned and rescued Smith, who was in great pain and

2. Juanita Brooks, ed., "Journal of Thales H. Haskell," *Utah Historical Quarterly* 12, no. 1-2 (1944).

Aerial of Crossing of the Fathers before it was covered by Lake Powell, looking downstream. The Dominguez-Escalante Expedition, on November 7, 1776, cut steps for their horses into Padre Creek (lower right), then followed the creek to the Colorado River. They crossed diagonally near the wide bend at right center. Mormon missionaries to the Hopi Indians crossed the river here in 1858, 1859, and 1860.

asked only that he be allowed to die in peace. Meanwhile the Indians gathered about in a threatening mood. Discarding all thought of going on to the Hopis, the Mormons turned back to Utah.

Smith managed to ride until sundown, when he asked Hamblin to stop. A few minutes later he died beside the trail. His body was wrapped in a blanket and hidden under a rock ledge, after which the surviving Mormons made haste for Utah, riding far into the night. A few months later, in mid-winter, Hamblin and a small group returned to the spot and recovered Smith's remains. George A. Smith, Jr. was the first casualty in a conflict of two expanding frontiers as Mormons moving south and east ran into Navajos moving northwest toward the Colorado River.[3]

As a result of their repeated raids on New Mexico settlements, Navajos in 1860 found themselves in a *de facto* war with the United States Army. To escape military expeditions sent against them, a few of the more recalcitrant tribesmen moved into the canyon country near the Colorado River. Warfare with the Navajos finally culminated in an intensive Army campaign in 1863 and 1864, (led by Colonel Kit

3. Bleak, "Annals."

16

Cathedral Rock, about one-half mile from Marble Canyon Lodge, on the road to Lee's Ferry. Except for a few river boaters, everyone who came to Lee's Ferry passed by this prominent rock–including Dominguez and Escalante. The "highway" in the foreground is now paved. Photo taken in 1962.

Carson), that concluded with a Navajo surrender. All Navajos that could be found were then marched to Bosque Redondo in central New Mexico, the so-called "Long Walk." Many of the more belligerent Navajos, however, escaped the round-up by fleeing to the remote canyons of the north, joining those that had gone there earlier. Also, in 1868, a treaty allowed the Bosque Redondo Navajos to return to their homeland.

For Utah's Mormon settlements, a growing population of Navajos just across the Colorado only spelled trouble. As had been feared, the Indians soon began making raids into Utah, driving off hundreds of cattle, horses, and mules. During this period, whenever southern Utah settlers had trouble with Indians, they called on Jacob Hamblin. Early in 1864, Hamblin was asked to warn the Navajos to stop making raids into Utah. Hamblin and his party of fourteen men reached the mouth of the Paria River on March 22, 1864. As in 1860, they built a raft, but this time they made it across the Colorado with all the men and baggage. They swam the horses behind the raft. Thus they made the first successful river crossing at the point later to become Lee's Ferry.[4]

As it turned out, this spring trip of 1864 was unfruitful, since no Navajos could be found. In the fall of the same year Hamblin tried again, once more rafting the river at Lee's Ferry, but this effort also failed to uncover Navajos. Although Jacob Hamblin couldn't find them, Navajos were certainly in the land, and close enough to continue raiding into Utah. Aware of their exposed southeastern frontier, Mormons in 1865 established Fort Kanab, but the fort helped very little. The situation became even more critical for these isolated settlers when nearby Paiute Indians also started making raids.

In 1866 widespread Indian raids and killings so alarmed Mormon authorities that they ordered the abandonment of remote outposts, including the new fort at Kanab. Travel between villages was cut to a minimum, while areas near the Indians were avoided altogether. Scattered fights occurred through the 1860s, but there were no major encounters.

One effect of the "war" was that Mormon militiamen, while on patrol, looked over much of the land to the east of their settlements, and, on occasion, found small areas suitable for farming. On one such military foray in March 1869, a force of thirty-six militiamen, approaching from the northeast, crested the Echo Cliffs near Dominguez Pass, and were afforded a magnificent view of cliffs, canyons, and river bottoms around the present Lee's Ferry. Although the campaigners did not descend to the Paria River, they later reported favorably on the area, stating that it might be a good place to cross the Colorado and that successful farming might be conducted beside the Paria.[5]

In October 1869, Jacob Hamblin, with a well-armed force of fifty-nine men, made another fruitless attempt to locate Navajos and give them a warning. More explicit this time, he states in his autobiography, "we crossed the Colorado where Lee's Ferry now is. Our luggage went over on rafts made of floatwood fastened together with withes." When he could find no Navajos he and his men went on to visit the comparatively friendly Hopis.

Later that same October, Hamblin posted Mormon guards at the Crossing of the Fathers and at the "Pahreah Crossing," as Lee's Ferry was then called, to watch for marauding Navajos. Throughout the winter of 1869-1870, Hamblin supervised the activities of sentries at both points. Guards at the Pahreah Crossing built a small stone building and a corral and named it "Fort Meeks," in honor of the elected leader of the camp, William Meeks. Situated against a high rock wall, Fort Meeks was probably quite close to the Escalante campsite of 1776 (see Tour Site No. 7).

In February and March, 1870, Jacob Hamblin roughed out a farm along the Paria.

---

4. Bleak, "Annals"

5. C. Gregory Crampton and David E. Miller, eds. "Journal of Two Campaigns By The Utah Territorial Militia Against the Navajo Indians," *Utah Historical Quarterly* 29, no. 2 (Summer 1961).

With the help of nine Paiutes, he cleared some land, dug an irrigation ditch a mile and a half from an upstream bend of the river, and sowed wheat seed. Much of the work was done, Jacob wrote, "with a gun strapped on my back in case of a sudden attack by Navajos."[6]

Apparently the venture did not succeed, for the farm was not mentioned in any other diary or journal for that period. Jacob Hamblin's account is all that is known about this first farming venture beside the Paria. By this time, however, Mormons had begun to realize the importance of Lee's Ferry, particularly in regard to their dealings with Navajos. But that same spot had seen other, quite dissimilar, activity less than a year before, for it was in the year 1869 that a group of men first boated through these canyons. Their leader's name was Major John Wesley Powell.

---

6. Details of the 1870 farm on the Paria and of Fort Meeks are found only in Corbett, *Jacob Hamblin*. Corbett, who is now deceased, cites an 1870 journal of Jacob Hamblin that was apparently loaned to him by the Hamblin family. The author made a search for this journal, but it does not seem to be among major library collections of Western Americana, and no member of the Hamblin family seems to know if it still exists.

# MAJOR POWELL
# DISCOVERS
# LEE'S FERRY

**T**hunderstorms played across the canyons around Lee's Ferry during the late afternoon of August 4, 1869, hurling wind, lightning bolts, and rain from a dark gray sky. But as evening came on, the clouds scattered and the wind stilled.

On an upstream bend of the river three dark shapes appeared. An observer might have made out three boats carrying nine strange-looking men. All were thin and haggard, their clothes merely a collection of torn and dirty rags. Near the mouth of the Paria, they pulled into shore on the right bank. A bearded, one-armed man stepped from his boat, looked around at the array of cliffs, and stated that camp for the night would be made at that point.

Leading the expedition was John Wesley Powell, then a professor of geology at Illinois Wesleyan University. As a Union officer in the Civil War he had lost his right forearm at the Battle of Shiloh. Although he was discharged with the rank of Brevet Lieutenant Colonel, he used the title of "Major" the rest of his life. In 1869 he was, as yet, little known, but his curiosity, solid competence, and driving ambition were soon to make his name known throughout the United States. One might say that his road to fame was the Colorado River.[1]

Powell had made summer expeditions to the Colorado Rockies in 1867 and 1868, and while there, had conceived a basic plan to study canyon geology by boating down the Green and Colorado Rivers. The purpose of the 1869 trip was only superficially scientific. Powell's real intent was to confirm his belief that men in boats could actually navigate the river. Rather than scientists, Powell chose for his crew bullwhackers, hunters, an army sergeant, and frontier newspapermen. These were men accustomed to outdoor hardships and who knew how to survive in the wilderness. Science could wait. Notably lacking among the crew were experienced boatmen.

On May 24, 1869, the party left Green River, Wyoming, in heavy, cumbersome boats that Powell imagined would be ideal. In the six hundred-mile long chain of river canyons above Lee's Ferry, they survived a two-month series of major and minor accidents.

---

1. Powell's highly readable report also served to spread his fame. Entitled *Exploration of the Colorado River of the West and Its Tributaries: Explored in 1869, 1870, 1871, and 1872, under the Direction of the Secretary of the Smithsonian Institution* (Washington: Smithsonian Institution, 1875), Powell's report ostensibly tells the story of the 1869 expedition only, yet events from the 1871- 1872 trips and from other explorations are mixed in without identification. Some recounted events are probably fictitious. For historical research, Powell's report is therefore somewhat undependable. Much better are the journals of Powell's men. See the Sumner and Bradley journals.

A woodcut from Powell's report depicts an 1872 lunch stop in Marble Canyon, a few miles
below Lee's Ferry.                                                                   *National Archives*

On the morning of August 4, while in the lower part of Glen Canyon, the voyagers passed the Crossing of the Fathers, recognized by Powell as the "Ute Trail." It was late afternoon of the same day when they reached the mouth of the Paria–today's Lee's Ferry. One of the men, Jack Sumner, climbed the hill known today as Lee's Lookout, on top of which he noted the remains of an "old Indian Fort" (see Tour Site No. 7). Of the entire area, Sumner wrote in his diary that it was "desolate enough to suit a lovesick poet."[2] Crewmember George Y. Bradley noted in his diary that at the "Pah Rhear River, [there is] a small trail where the Mormons have a ferry."[3]

Departing early the next morning, the voyagers began the long run through the Grand Canyon. Narrow escapes, continual hardships, and shortage of food culminated in the departure of three men who chose to climb out, hoping to reach the Mormon settlements rather than face what appeared to be certain death in the canyon. Brothers Oramel and Seneca Howland and William Dunn gambled and lost. The three were killed, reportedly by Indians, on the high Shivwits Plateau, not far from the rim of Grand Canyon. Meanwhile, reduced to six men, the boating party finished the trip through the canyon.

A year later, in 1870, Major Powell was back, not to boat the river but to plan a more extensive second voyage. He particularly wanted to find points along the river where supplies for the boaters could be brought in by pack train.

In Salt Lake City Powell met with Brigham Young, who not only pledged his cooperation, but who offered to explore part of the country with Powell. Their agreed-upon overland expedition got underway in early September, 1870, when Powell and Young, joined by about forty other Mormons, rode east across southern Utah high plateaus into the upper reaches of the Paria River. Jacob Hamblin was the guide.[4]

One of the important Mormons traveling with Young, Hamblin, and Powell was John D. Lee. During their week-long trip, Lee had many conversations with Young about Lee's future in the southern Utah settlements. Lee also talked frequently with Major Powell. A favorite topic of their discussions was the strange rock land through which they were passing. Brigham Young was disgusted at the general barrenness of the Paria Valley, declaring, "There is nothing here desirable for us." Apparently, he took little notice of the scenery.

From the Paria, Young's Party went to Fort Kanab, where the future town was laid out, then on to Pipe Springs, where Brigham and others made plans to construct a fort. The fort at Pipe Springs, today a national monument, was to serve both as a defensive post on the frontier and as headquarters for the operation of a Mormon livestock cooperative.

Leaving the large group at Pipe Springs, and accompanied by Jacob Hamblin, Major Powell headed southwest to learn the fate of the three men who had climbed out of Grand Canyon the year before. A few days later, at a campfire conference with the Paiute Indians, (probably of the Uinkarets band), Powell's inquiry was pressed by Hamblin, who acted as interpreter. As later reported by Powell, the tribesmen admitted

---

2. William Culp Darrah, ed., "John C. Sumner's Journal, July 6-August 31,1869," *Utah Historical Quarterly* 15 (1947).

3. William Culp Darrah, ed., "George Y. Bradley's Journal, May 24-August 30, 1869," *Utah Historical Quarterly* 15 (1947). There was, of course, no ferry in 1869. Bradley may have added those words in later years while editing his journal.

4. Details of the 1870 expedition to the upper Paria River are found only in Lee's diary, published as Robert Glass Cleland and Juanita Brooks, eds., *A Mormon Chronicle: The Diaries of John D. Lee, 1848-1876* 2 vols. (San Marino,Calif.. Huntington Library, 1955) 2:135-141.

killing the three men but claimed it was a case of mistaken identity.[5]

At least two writers have raised the possibility that Dunn and the Howland brothers may have been killed by a Mormon in one of the small southern Utah villages, and that Hamblin, at the 1870 Mt. Trumbull conference, concealed the crime by deliberately misinterpreting what the Paiute chief had said to Powell. Firm documentary proof of this possibility, however, has not yet surfaced.[6]

Meanwhile, two of Powell's men loaded lumber onto a mule train and headed for the mouth of the Paria. Their orders were to build a flatboat that could be used to cross the river. Christened the *Cañon Maid*, this scow was the first real boat used at Lee's Ferry as a ferryboat.[7]

Powell and Hamblin arrived at Lee's Ferry on September 30, 1870, and two days later, together with eight Mormon men, they boated across the river on the *Cañon Maid* and headed south. Powell must have realized at that time what a vital supply and access point Lee's Ferry would be to a future boating parties coming down the Colorado River.

Within the month of October, 1870, Powell and Hamblin visited the Hopi villages and went on to Fort Defiance, where Hamblin concluded a peace treaty with the Navajos. From Fort Defiance Major Powell boarded a stagecoach and headed east to make final arrangements for his next river trip.

Powell and his men embarked in May 1871 from Green River, Wyoming, for the

Major Powell and his men prepare to depart Green River, Wyoming, for the second exploration of the Green and Colorado Rivers. May 22, 1871          *National Archives*

5. John Wesley Powell, *The Exploration of the Colorado River and its Canyons* (New York: Dover Publications, 1961), pp. 320-322.
6. Otis "Dock" Marston, letter to W.L. Rusho. Also Scott Thybony, *Field Notes, Shivwits, 5/88*, unpublished, copy in possession of Arizona Historical Society, Tucson. See also "The Letter, or Were the Powell Men Really Killed by Indians?" Canyon Legacy, No. 17 (Moab, Utah, Spring 1993)
7. Powell, *Exploration of the Colorado River*, pp. 327-331.

Major John Wesley Powell, Government scientist, who headed exploratory expeditions down the Colorado River in 1869 and 1871-1872.

*National Archives*

second float trip through the canyons of the Green and Colorado Rivers. For the 1871 crew, instead of hunters and frontiersmen, Powell assembled a group of reasonably competent topographers, geologists, an artist, and a photographer, as well as a cook and general helpers. The only outstanding member, however, was Powell's own brother-in-law, Almon Harris Thompson, the chief topographer. Aside from Powell and Thompson, most of the men were green and inexperienced, but their skills later developed sharply under heavy demands of field work. As in 1869, none in the crew could claim any substantial experience as a boatman.[8]

Since Powell could count on bringing horses and supplies to the mouth of the Paria, his plan called for terminating the 1871 leg of the trip at that point. His men would spend the winter in southern Utah. Following this plan, the expedition moved slowly down the Green and Colorado, not arriving in lower Glen Canyon until October. Powell, impatient as usual, skipped part of the run on the Green River, rejoined his men, then left the trip at the Crossing of the Fathers while his men boated on down to the Paria.

On October 21, within sight of their goal, Thompson, Frederick Dellenbaugh, and Francis M. Bishop climbed the cluster of rugged peaks southwest of their camp. On top, Dellenbaugh tried to hit the distant river with a shot from his Remington 44 revolver. The deafening roar was followed by a silence of twenty-four seconds. Then,

---

8. Crewmember diaries from the 1871-72 expedition have been published in the *Utah Historical Quarterly* as follows: Almon Harris Thompson, 7, nos. 1, 2, 3 (January, April, July 1939); Francis Marion Bishop, 15 (1947); Stephen Vandiver Jones, John F. Steward, and W. C. Powell, 16-17 (1948-49). Frederick S. Dellenbaugh rewrote and expanded his diary, published as *A Canyon Voyage* (New Haven: Yale University Press, 1962), a reprint of the original 1908 edition. The latest diary published was Don D. Fowler, ed., *Photographed All The Best Scenery: Jack Hiller's Diary of the Powell Expeditions, 1871-1875* (Salt Lake City: University of Utah Press, 1972).

Dellenbaugh reported, the sound echoed back with a "rattle like that of musketry." Their perch was named on the spot–the Echo Peaks. From these high points a long line of cliffs runs from the lower valley of the Paria, is bisected by the Colorado, then extends southward about sixty miles to the Indian village of Moenave. Taking the name from the peaks, the line of cliffs became known as the Echo Cliffs (see Tour Site No. 19).[9]

From their vantage point 2400 feet above the river, the explorers enjoyed magnificent vistas of the canyon country all about them: to the southwest, the rugged Echo Cliffs, House Rock Valley, the jagged gash of Marble Canyon and the forest capped Kaibab Plateau; to the far south, the San Francisco peaks; to the northeast, Glen Canyon, Kaiparowits Plateau and Navajo Mountain; and to the northwest, directly in front of them, the spectacular Vermilion Cliffs bordering the Paria Plateau.

When Powell's men made camp in the tall willows at the mouth of the Paria on October 23, the 1871 leg of the second river trip came to an end. Five days later they used their boats to ferry Jacob Hamblin and his men, who were returning from another trip to the Navajo country. With Hamblin were nine visiting Navajos who entertained the whites all that evening with songs and dances.

Powell's men remained at the Paria, waiting for a pack train with supplies, which finally arrived several days late. Apparently the two men with the pack train knew of Dominguez Pass but couldn't recognize it from the top. They had wandered along the rim of the cliff overlooking the Paria for days before they finally found the trail. By then their animals were practically dead of thirst.

At the confluence of the Colorado and Paria Rivers, the supplies not needed until the next summer were cached, while the boats were taken above high water mark and concealed. On November 6, 1871, Powell's men left the mouth of the Paria, passed Jacob's Pools, (small ponds at the base of the Vermilion Cliffs), and proceeded to the north. Dellenbaugh describes how House Rock Valley got its name:

> [We found] two large boulders which had fallen together, forming a
> rude shelter, where... someone... had slept, and then had jocosely printed
> above with charcoal the words "Rock House Hotel." Afterward this
> had served as identification, and Jacob [Hamblin] and the others had
> spoken of "House Rock" Spring and House Rock Valley.[10]

At Kanab, Powell's men set up a base camp and headquarters, from which they conducted a winter survey of parts of southern Utah and the Arizona Strip. In June 1872, Thompson and some of the men made a difficult traverse across canyon tributaries of Glen Canyon from the upper Paria to the Dirty Devil River. Their central objective was to obtain geographical information about the intricately eroded canyon country, but they also sought to recover one of their boats that had been left for them at the mouth of nearby North Wash in 1871. After reaching the Colorado River, four men were detailed to take the boat down to the mouth of the Paria and to take photographs on the way. The others made their way overland. From the point of view of the four men who floated leisurely down the placid waters of Glen Canyon, perhaps the most eventful part of the trip occurred at their destination, for at the mouth of the Paria they met the mysterious John D. Lee.

---

9. Dellenbaugh, *A Canyon Voyage*, p. 151.
10. Ibid. p.160

John D. Lee had served an important role in early-day southern Utah. As noted earlier, Lee was one of the select group to accompany Brigham Young, Major Powell, and Jacob Hamblin to the banks of the upper Paria River in 1870. During that trip, Lee noted in his diary that Brigham Young had asked him if he would like to establish a mission on the Paria. Appalled by the suggestion, Lee recorded his reply: "I would want no greater punishment than to be Sent on a Mission to the Pahariere. I would turn out Indian at once & take no woman to such a place."[11]

Powell's men little realized how ironic it was to find Lee, in 1872, living on the banks of the Paria. Moreover, on the Lee's Ferry Ranch now lived one of Lee's wives, Emma, and their children. Lee <u>had</u> taken a woman to such a place.

The actual "House Rock" from which House Rock Valley takes its name. Located at House Rock Springs, it sheltered a couple of Powell's men in 1871, when they camped overnight. It was jokingly referred to as the "Rock House Hotel." Greg Crampton investigates the sleeping quarters.

11. Cleland and Brooks, *A Mormon Chronicle*, 2:138.

Major Powell and Jacob Hamblin (right side of campfire), confer with Paiute Indians on the Arizona Strip, north of the Grand Canyon.                    *National Archives*

# THE LEE OF
# LEE'S FERRY

John Doyle Lee, scapegoat for the Mountain Meadows Massacre and founder of Lee's Ferry, photographed about 1865.
*Utah State Historical Society*

**I**f the matter were judged dispassionately, perhaps Lee's Ferry should not have been so named. It was Jacob Hamblin who used the crossing first, and it was his interest and initiative that led to the establishment of the ferry by the Church of Jesus Christ of Latter-day Saints. When service was actually started, John D. Lee was on hand only long enough to convey a few travelers across the river. Nevertheless, Lee was the first operator and the first settler. Furthermore, his commanding personality and his notoriety insured the perpetuation of his name.

John Doyle Lee, one of the leading colonizers of southern Utah, helped establish the towns of Parowan and Harmony. Later he pioneered further south into Utah's "Dixie," in the present St. George area. A man of wide abilities, Lee served variously as farmer, miller, judge, legislator, tavern keeper, and ferryman. In earlier years he had worked as a clerk for Brigham Young. On many occasions the Mormon leader expressed or demonstrated his affection for Lee, even calling Lee his "adopted" son.[1]

In religious matters Lee often revealed a touch of the fanatic. He was quick to voice righteous indignation at those Mormons whose conduct was tinged with human weakness. To Lee, what the Church or Brigham Young said was law, regardless of conflict with secular statutes. Given the example by high Church leaders, Lee zealously embraced the doctrine of polygamy, eventually marrying nineteen women. Lee's inflexibility and intolerance toward wayward Mormons left him unpopular among his own people. Yet he commanded respect. He was aggressive and industrious, and when a difficult job had to be done, Lee was often given the assignment.

Lee's trail to Lee's Ferry was a long one, covering a full fourteen years of his life. It all hinged on the Mountain Meadows Massacre back in 1857 and on the role Lee played in that tragedy.

To be understood, the Mountain Meadows Massacre must be put into the context of the times. In 1847 and 1848, thousands of Mormons moved west to free themselves from harassment and persecution at the hands of punitive neighbors in Missouri and Illinois. Once settled in Utah, the Saints labored hard to gain sustenance, if not prosperity, from the wilderness. Their political leaders, however, headed by Brigham Young, were obviously trying to establish an independent theocracy. Consequently, as the Great Basin commonwealth of Mormons grew and seemed to thrive, their relations with Federal authorities sent to administer the Territory of Utah deteriorated to an alarming degree.

Tension mounted to critical pitch when, in 1857, President Buchanan sent a military force of 2500 men under Colonel Albert Sidney Johnston to depose Brigham Young as Territorial Governor, put down any armed resistance, and enforce Federal authority. As the army approached, excitement and emotion among the Saints ran high. Feeding on the emotion to unify the Saints, Brigham Young and his Councilors were guilty of gross excesses of rhetorical invective that inflamed mob passions, and that precipitated actual preparations for war. If anything, unchecked emotionalism was more intense in the outlying settlements, where slow communication compounded rumor and fact, creating an atmosphere of hysterical uncertainty.[2]

Into this explosive atmosphere, in the late summer days of 1857, came the Baker-Fancher Train, an emigrant group of about a hundred and forty men, women, and children, most of them from Arkansas. After leaving Salt Lake City, the emigrants headed south over the all-weather route to southern California.

Apparently the Baker-Fancher Train encountered trouble soon after leaving Salt Lake City. When Mormons along the way refused to sell them provisions, some of the

---

1. Lee's life and character are summarized from Juanita Brooks, *John Doyle Lee, Zealot-Pioneer-Scapegoat* (Glendale, Calif.: Arthur H. Clark Co., 1962), a generally well-done study.

2. A more detailed account of the "Utah War" can be found in Norman F. Furniss, *The Mormon Conflict*, 1850-1859 (New Haven: Yale University Press, 1960).

emigrants countered with abusive language; some even boasted of having helped to drive the Mormons out of Missouri. Cattle were turned into fields, and some Mormons claimed that water supplies were intentionally fouled. Name calling was freely indulged in by both sides. The situation worsened as the train moved south. To local Mormons caught up in the hysteria provoked by the ominous approach of Johnston's army, the emigrants appeared to symbolize all injustices the Saints had suffered, past and present.

At this point, the local Paiute Indians became involved. Promising plunder, the Mormons convinced the local Paiutes that they should act as allies if war broke out with the Federal government. Observing Mormon belligerence toward the Baker-Fancher Train, the Paiutes were eager to launch an attack on the "enemy." In the past, Indians living along main-traveled roads had suffered from the thoughtlessness of passing emigrants, who often shot the natives on the slightest pretext, or none at all. Now the tribesmen would have a chance to get even.

In the southwest corner of present-day Utah, at the edge of the long desert road ahead, the Baker-Fancher party camped for several days in a green valley while their stock gained strength. Local settlers knew this valley as Mountain Meadows. The place had also been a vital stopping and resting point on the Spanish Trail.[3]

At Cedar City, about twenty miles east of Mountain Meadows, Mormon leaders, urged on by LDS Stake President Isaac Haight, resolved that the Baker-Fancher Train should "not be allowed to escape." But because the actual killing might be distasteful, they decided to turn the job over to their Paiute Indian "allies." Since Jacob Hamblin, the regular Indian sub-agent, was in northern Utah at the time, Haight sent for John D. Lee, the so-called Indian Farmer, to "manage the Indians."

Lee said later that he objected to the job but felt that he could not refuse. Not only was the Stake President Lee's religious superior, he was also Lee's military superior in the Nauvoo Legion, the Mormon militia.

Given Mormon acquiescence, the Paiutes eagerly rode down upon the emigrants, probably under John D. Lee's direction. Although startled by the attack, the emigrants rallied quickly and were soon returning a deadly fire that inflicted losses on the Indians. The Paiutes retreated, but kept the wagon train under siege.

Now the Indians felt betrayed; neither had the Mormon God protected them, nor had their Mormon "allies" come to their aid. As Lee reported later, he was told by the Paiutes that if the Mormons did not assist in another attack, the Indians might make war on the Mormons themselves. Considering the weakness of the Piutes, this sounds like a rationalization. Much more important, it was apparent to Haight, Lee, and other LDS leaders that the Indians were incapable of "finishing the job," i.e., killing the emigrants.

Educated guesses date the tragedy on or about September 11, 1857, early in the morning. About fifty Mormon men rode toward the emigrant train, but stopped some distance away while John D. Lee and a man named William Bateman rode on, under a flag of truce. Within the wagon circle, Lee and Bateman proposed to the emigrants that they surrender their arms, that they give their cattle to the Indians, and that the accused among them be taken to Mormon jails to be held for misdemeanor trials. Although the offer was not a good one, the frightened emigrants felt that it was the only way to escape with their lives. They accepted.

---

3. Hafen and Hafen, *The Old Spanish Trail*

Mountain Meadows, where, on Sept. 11, 1857, about 120 emigrants from Arkansas were killed by Indians and white men. Much of the massacre took place near the line of Lombardy poplars at right center.

The waiting Mormons then rode into camp, gathered the arms, sent the women and older children on ahead, and put the younger children in a wagon. A Mormon man walked beside each male emigrant until all were in line. Major John Higbee then crested the hill and shouted the order, "Do Your Duty!"

Upon this command each Mormon turned and killed the emigrant man next to him. A few hundred yards ahead, the women and children turned at the sound of gunfire only to see hundreds of Indians rushing at them from the tall bushes. Within a few minutes all emigrants were dead, excepting only eighteen small children who, earlier, had been taken by wagon over a nearby hill. Years later Lee stated that he tried to "do his duty," but that his gun fired prematurely, slightly wounding a fellow Mormon.

So ended the Mountain Meadow Massacre—a field of blood-spattered brush and grass, still-warm bodies in death's posture, a band of Indians systematically rifling corpses , eighteen frightened children crying for their parents, Mormon men suddenly aghast and revolted by the horrible scene.[4] During the 1850's, even though travel was tedious, communications were not as slow as one might imagine. In less than a month, on October 2, 1857, the *Los Angeles Star* reported the rumor of a massacre, and on October 10, 1857, the headline read *HORRIBLE MASSACRE OF EMIGRANTS!! OVER 100 PERSONS MURDERED!!*. Furthermore, reported details were fairly accurate. That the atrocity had indeed occurred was confirmed by a visit to the site by a U.S. Army detachment in May 1859. The soldiers buried a few scattered bones and put up a stone cairn, but they learned almost nothing about why or how the massacre took place. Several of the over fifty Mormon men who had participated were named as suspects, but remained free, protected by isolation and by their Church membership.

Even before the army visit to the site, the president of the Southern Utah Mission, George A. Smith, realized that outsiders would eventually learn much of the truth, and he hoped to keep blame from being attached either to Brigham Young or to the LDS Church as a whole. Smith therefore held a number of public hearings to obtain facts on the massacre. In August 1858, after one of the hearings in Parowan—one that John D Lee did not attend—a report was issued stating, "It is reported that John D. Lee and a few other white men were on the ground during a portion of the combat." From this first accusation, however tentative, can be traced Lee's growing role as

---

4. See Juanita Brooks, *The Mountain Meadows Massacre* (Norman: University of Oklahoma Press, 1962).

The burial square at Mountain Meadows, where 34 bodies were buried by the U.S. Army in 1859. This is the campsite of the Baker-Fancher party. The remains of the others killed were buried about one and one-half miles to the north.

scapegoat, resulting in his eventual banishment to the Colorado River as well as his final personal tragedy.

Lee had a few more years of comparative freedom from worry, for although he had been named as a participant and a warrant for his arrest had been issued, no Mormon would reveal Lee's whereabouts. Nevertheless, pressure on the Church continued to mount; Church leaders were accused of harboring a fugitive, if not of outright complicity in the crime.

In late 1870, just after his friendly association with Brigham Young and Major Powell on the trip to the upper Paria Valley, the Church shocked Lee by officially excommunicating him for his part in the massacre. In his diary Lee recorded that he rode to St. George, where he told Brigham Young that "I suffered the blame to rest on Me, when it should rest on Persons who's Names that have never been brought out & that if any Man had told to the contrary, his informant had lied like Hell." In spite of his protest, however, no formal hearing on his excommunication was held. Instead he was sent an unsigned letter stating, "Trust no one. Make yourself scarce & keep out of the way."[5]

Although Lee had married a total of nineteen wives, only seven were still with him in 1870, the others having died or left him in earlier years. Upon his excommunication, two of the seven remaining wives also left. Therefore, during the

---

5. Cleland and Brooks, *A Mormon Chronicle, The Diaries of John D. Lee,* 2:154.

The new memorial to the Baker-Fancher company overlooking Mountain Meadows. This memorial was dedicated in September, 1990, with descendant relatives of the victims—most of them from Arkansas—in attendance.

On Christmas Day, 1871, John D. Lee inscribed his name on the cliff near House Rock Spring, located about a day's ride northwest of Lee's Ferry

last seven years of his life, five women called Lee "husband." Of those five, three remained in Utah: Caroline Williams Lee in Panguitch, Utah; Mary "Polly" Young Lee and Lavina Young Lee (sisters) of Skutumpah, Utah. Rachel Woolsey Lee and Emma Batchelder Lee accompanied Lee into Arizona.

At the semi-annual Church conference held at St. George in the fall of 1871, Lee's future was apparently discussed. Almost certainly, Jacob Hamblin was the one who suggested that Lee be sent to the mouth of the Paria to establish a ferry crossing of the Colorado River. Brigham Young accepted the suggestion and sent the order to Lee, who, in spite of his being excommunicated, still considered himself a loyal member of the Church and therefore agreed to accept the order.

On December 4, 1871, Lee, with one of his sons and two other men, took fifty-seven head of cattle and left the village of Pahreah (now spelled Paria), heading south toward the Colorado River. Incredibly, they traveled right down the forty-mile long, narrow, twisting, canyon floor of the Paria River. Lee's diary comment sums up the ordeal.

> We concluded to drive down the creek, which took us Some 8 days of toil, fatuige, & labour, through brush, water, ice, & quicksand & some time passing through narrow chasms with perpendicular Bluffs on both sides, some 3000 feet high, & without seeing the sun for 48 hours, & every day Some of our animals Mired down & had to shoot one cow & leve her there, that we count not get out, & I My Self was under water, Mud & Ice every day... My Son & My self also carried 1 & 1/2 Bus. seed corn with us from the Setlement & it was Baptised as often as I was & one place it was under water 24 hours before I could find it, & had passed the place some 10 miles. Finally returned & found it.[6]

Lee reached the Colorado River, now Lee's Ferry, on December 12, finding the place deserted. Major Powell's men had just left to spend the winter in Kanab. Upset that many members of his family, traveling by wagon, had not arrived, Lee set out on the "supposed wagon road" to find them. But there was no road; no wagons had ever yet been taken across the Kaibab and through House Rock Valley to the mouth of the Paria. While searching for the "road" over the Kaibab Plateau, Lee and his son wandered into a region of rough gulches, taking five days to reach his wife Emma's house several miles northeast of Kanab.

After resting a few days, Lee and Emma loaded a wagon and headed for the mouth

---

6 Cleland and Brooks, *A Mormon Chronicle, The Diaries of John D. Lee*, 2:178-179

of the Paria. This time Lee made the Kaibab crossing at a better spot, passed House Rock Spring (where, on Christmas Day, he carved his name in the sandstone), and reached his destination without serious trouble.

By this time Lee's other family members–those Lee had searched for earlier–were there to greet him. Principal among them were Lee's wife Rachel and several children.

The next day Emma obtained her first real look at the barren cliffs that rose in profusion about her new home. Sensing the brooding isolation that separated her family from even the smallest settlement, she cried, "Oh, what a lonely dell." Struck by her remark, Lee decided that the name for the place should be Lonely Dell.[7]

For the rest of his life, Lee and his family always referred to the place as Lonely Dell. But to the world it was a hideout where the infamous John D. Lee lived and worked. It was Lee's Ferry. The dawn of a new year, 1872, found Lee and his sons building stone and wooden shelters for his families. For the first time Lee's Ferry had residents who intended to stay.

---

7. Brooks, *John Doyle Lee*, p. 307.

# FORGING THE VITAL LINK

**D**uring his first year at Lee's Ferry, Lee spent little time taking people across the river. In the first place he didn't have a ferryboat. What crossings he did make were more in the character of memorable incidents than routine business.

In January 1872, Lee obtained his first customers–a band of fifteen Navajos heading north to trade. For a makeshift ferryboat Lee found near the river bank, the flat-bottomed scow *Cañon Maid*, that Powell and Hamblin had used to cross the river in 1870. By caulking it, Lee made the craft serviceable enough to carry the Navajos across.[1]

But the *Cañon Maid* did not serve long as a ferryboat. One day in April, while Lee was on his cattle range in House Rock Valley, a prospector named Parker and his men rode up to tell Lee what had happened to the *Cañon Maid*.

Parker and his fellow prospectors had apparently been in the van of the first gold rush to reach these Colorado River canyons. Hearing that gold had been found in the river sands and nearby gravel bars, several groups of prospectors had set out for the few places where they could reach the river–including Lee's Ferry.

Lee had met Parker at Lee's Ferry in March, and since Parker carried letters of reference from leading Mormons, Lee knew that Parker would not expose him as a fugitive. Although they worked the river thoroughly at the mouth of the Paria, the prospectors could find only traces of gold, not the rich bars that they believed lay beside the river further downstream.

Parker's story to Lee was that the prospectors, wishing to investigate possible gold deposits downriver, took the *Cañon Maid* and floated down into Marble Canyon! They also took along a crude raft to carry supplies. Apparently they reached Badger Creek Rapids, and possibly Soap Creek Rapids, when both the *Cañon Maid* and the raft were smashed against rocks and destroyed. Somehow all the men escaped with their lives, though they lost their gear and some of Lee's tools.[2]

A few days later seven Navajos, returning from a trading trip to Kanab, showed up at Lee's Ferry and asked Lee to take them across the Colorado. Lee told them he had no boat, but the Indians had seen the *Nellie Powell*, one of Powell's three boats that had been cached in 1871. These Navajos insisted that Lee take them over in this boat. Lee finally agreed, but with the stipulation that the Navajos first work on the

---

1. Cleland and Brooks, *A Mormon Chronicle: The Diaries of John D. Lee*, 2:181. Although Lee does not name the *Cañon Maid*, his description fits. His description would not fit any of Major Powell's river boats, which were cached at the time at Lee's Ferry.
2. Further identification of the *Cañon Maid* can be surmised from Parker's reference to it as "Jac. Hamblin's Boat," (Cleland and Brooks, *A Mormon Chronicle*, 2:185). Powell could have given the craft to Hamblin when the two used it as a ferryboat in 1870.

dam and irrigation ditch until water flowed to his ranch house. This they did, but their help turned out to be worse than none, for they were lazy, they frequently stole potatoes and other food, and in general they were, in Lee's words, a "Band of low Maraders from the chief down." When the time for river crossing arrived, Lee had to buckle on a revolver in order to back up his commands. The incident ended with the Navajos and Lee shouting insults to each other as the latter rowed back across the river.[3]

Lee used the *Nellie Powell* once more during 1872 when he conveyed Powell's former photographer, E.O. Beaman, across the river in August.[4]

## LEE AND MAJOR POWELL - 1872

While Lee was plowing a field at the Lee's Ferry Ranch, the four Powell men who, having retrieved their cached boat at the mouth of North Wash, floated through Glen Canyon, and arrived on July 13. A few days later the group that had traveled overland from the mouth of the Dirty Devil also arrived. The meeting of these men with John D. Lee was no surprise to either party, since both had knowledge of each other's activities.

The youthful boatmen could even find humor in Lee's status as a fugitive from justice. Dellenbaugh, relating a story about Andy Hattan, the cook, and Lee, says that:

> *Brother Lee... called to give us a lengthy dissertation on the faith of the Latter-day Saints (Mormons), while Andy, always up to mischief, in his quiet way, delighted to get behind him and cock a rifle. At the sound of the ominous click Lee would wheel like a flash to see what was up. We had no intention of capturing him, of course, but it amused Andy to act in a way that kept Lee on the* qui vive.[5]

Major Powell did not arrive for the voyage through the Grand Canyon for another month, so the men, with little to do, helped Lee on the grueling task of putting in an irrigation system. In return, Lee and Emma frequently had the "boys" over for dinner.

Major Powell's arrival on August 13 was the occasion for the second meeting between Powell and Lee, the first having occurred on the trip to the upper Paria valley in 1870. Lee greeted Powell as an old friend.

On August 17, after Emma had served breakfast to the entire crew, Powell and his men departed for their voyage through the Grand Canyon—actually the second leg of Powell's second trip. For three weeks during 1872 Powell and his six men fought rocks, unusually high water, and unwieldy boats until, at the mouth of Kanab Creek, the Major called it quits. Although a supply train was on hand to meet him, he decided to abandon the boats and leave the river.

John D. Lee and Major Powell never met again. Whereas Lee had not long to live, Powell went on to become a giant in governmental science programs. By 1871, Powell already had his own Congressional mandated land survey, while in later years he headed the U.S. Geological Survey, the Irrigation Survey, and the Bureau of American Ethnology. And his persuasive influence helped to create the Bureau of Reclamation. He was also one of the leaders in the establishment of the National Geographic Society.

---

3. Cleland and Brooks, *A Mormon Chronicle*, 2:196-197.
4. Ibid., pp. 208-209.
5. Dellenbaugh, *A Canyon Voyage*, p. 212

## THE FIRST FERRYBOAT

Brigham Young and other leading Mormons had long considered Arizona within their territory. Years before, Arizona had been included in the ambitious projections for the huge State of Deseret that was proclaimed by Young but largely ignored by Congress. Jacob Hamblin's missionary efforts to the Hopis were not totally religious in nature; he was also assessing prospects for Mormon settlements.

Hamblin's unfavorable early reports on hostile Navajo and Hopi Indians and on the rugged topography of northern Arizona held up colonization efforts until the southern Utah towns were free of Indian wars and strong enough to support more remote settlements. By 1872 the potential looked good enough in the Little Colorado Valley to organize a colonizing expedition. To travel to the south, however, colonists would have to cross the Colorado River and would require a sturdy ferryboat at Lee's Ferry. The ferry was indeed regarded as a vital link in plans to extend the Mormon frontier into Arizona Territory.

In the fall of 1872, lumber, sent by the Mormon Church for the first real ferryboat, arrived at Lee's Ferry. Built largely by a crew of Mormons sent from St. George, this first ferryboat was launched on January 11, 1873. It was 26 feet long, 8 1/2 feet wide,

First photograph ever taken of the Lee's Ferry area. Looking across the Colorado River to the Lonely Dell Ranch and on up the valley of the Paria River. Taken by Timothy O'Sullivan of the Wheeler Expedition, using a glass plate negative, in 1873. Two small ranch buildings are barely visible at the far left. *National Archives*

and was named by Lee *Colorado*. A small skiff named *Pahreah* was also launched.[6]

Within a few days a Mormon exploring expedition led by Lorenzo W. Roundy and Jacob Hamblin arrived and was taken across the river in the new ferryboat. On this exploratory trip, Roundy and Hamblin and their men rode south to the San Francisco Peaks and east through part of the Little Colorado River Valley, which they declared on their return was suitable for settlement. Church authorities thereupon put out a "call," instructing selected men and their families to move to Arizona.[7]

While awaiting the colonists, Hamblin and Lee argued about the actual placement of the ferry crossing. Jacob noted correctly that if the crossing were made below the Paria, it would take only a short dugway to reach the general level of the valley floor, the Marble Platform. While agreeing with Hamblin, Lee pointed out that the south side river bank was practically a sheer cliff, and the narrow rock landing would be submerged during periods of high water. Furthermore, a crossing right at the head of

The first major expedition to colonize "Arzonia" found no suitable land and so returned to Utah, much to John D. Lee's disgust. As attested by this inscription at House Rock Spring, they "busted"

---

6. Cleland and Brooks, *A Mormon Chronicle*, 2:219.

7. The history and early use of Lee's Ferry by Mormons as well as the colonization of the Little Colorado River country may be found in James H. McClintock, *Mormon Settlement in Arizona, A Record of Peaceful Conquest of the Desert* (Phoenix: Manufacturing Stationers, 1921). A summary of early expeditions to Arizona, as well as the use of Lee's Ferry, appears in Charles S. Peterson, *Take Up Your Mission: Mormon Colonizing Along the Little Colorado River, 1870-1890* (Tucson: University of Arizona Press, 1973).

Marble Canyon might place the ferryboat and its passengers in danger. Lee wrote in his diary , "I would expect to hear of the Boats being carried away & Some Persons drownded."[8]

A far safer crossing, Lee said, could be made about one-half mile above the Paria, below the big bend in the river. One big drawback to this site would be expense, since longer and more costly approach roads would be necessary, particularly on the south side. Also, once across the river travelers would be forced to ascend the steep rough ledge of Shinarump Conglomerate later referred to disparagingly as "Lee's Backbone" (see Tour Site No. 15). Stake President Joseph W. Young and Bishop Edward Bunker, after inspecting the sites, agreed that safety was paramount; the ferry would cross the river at Lee's preferred site.

## THE FIRST ARIZONA EMIGRANTS - 1873

In May 1873, the colonists began arriving. About seventy wagons with emigrant families, plus their horses and cattle, were in the three separate contingents. Horton Haight was the overall commander of the wagon train. After the first two groups of about fifty wagons had been taken across the river, the river rose and became more swift, forcing Lee to move the *Colorado* further upstream, around the bend.

Since no approach roads had been built to reach this revised site, it was difficult for travelers to get their wagons to and from the ferryboat. Henry Day, the leader of the third contingent, complained angrily to Lee that "it was a Poor Shitten arrangement & that this company never Should have been Sent on a Mission until a good Road & Ferry had been Made first." Lee replied sharply, giving Day a stern lecture on the duties of a pioneer. According to Lee's diary, this seemed to silence Mr. Day.[9]

Other emigrants at Lee's Ferry that day seemed to take a different view of John D. Lee. Andrew Amundsen, a Norwegian missionary who used inimitable spelling, wrote in his journal:

> when we got ther we found John DeLee working at the boat and two
> others. efter dinner we crosed ouer animalls and one Wagon. Dealee was
> very jocky, and jovele, full of fun. . .The Morning wass very calm no
> wind, and the Rivver still, the Wether pretty and clear, birds singing and
> all injoyed a good spirrit. we then comenst crosing ouer Wagons, all over
> sef and sound.[10]

The colonists did not stay long in Arizona Territory. In early June 1873, the sound of gunfire brought Lee to the river bank where he saw two of the Arizona colonizers. They reported to Lee that the large expedition had "busted" and that they were returning to Utah. "Nothing but sand and rock, and crooked cottonwoods" in the Little Colorado Valley, they told Lee. Disgusted at their lack of faith and persistence, Lee nevertheless ferried the two travelers back across the river.

Before the main expedition arrived, however, a violent thunderstorm toppled a large cottonwood into the mooring of the ferryboat. By the time Lee got to the scene, the *Colorado* had broken loose and had disappeared into the depths of Marble Canyon. When the would-be settlers arrived at the south bank, Lee was able to convey them

---

8. Cleland and Brooks, *A Mormon Chronicle*, 2:232.
9. Ibid., p. 240.
10. Andrew Amundsen, "Journal of a Mission to the San Francisko Mountains, Commenced March 26th 1873," manuscript in L.D.S. Historical Department, Salt Lake City.

Rachel Lee's first desert home was but a shanty at Jacob's Pools, a desolate spot at the base of the Vermilion Cliffs.                                    *Utah State Historical Society*

across in the small skiff, the *Pahreah*. No mention is made of the of the wagons, but they were probably dismantled, and a few pieces at a time carried over in the skiff. The wagon boxes would then have been floated and towed across.

### LEE'S HOME AT MOENAVE

As useful as he was in his new role as ferryman, John D. Lee was still a fugitive. When told the rumor (unfounded, as it turned out), that troops from Camp Douglas in Utah were on their way to Lee's Ferry to set up a military post, Lee had no choice but to flee. Following the route of the recent emigrant train, he headed south, further into Arizona following the Echo Cliffs. On the cliffside about sixty miles from Lee's Ferry, he found a good spring, called by the Hopis "Moenave," where he set up a small ranch.

Jacob Hamblin had already made a claim on this spring at Moenave, so Lee made a trade with him. In return for Lee's outpost ranch in House Rock Valley called Jacob Pools, Hamblin turned over the Moenave property to Lee. Lee's wife Rachel, who had been living at Jacob Pools, then moved to Moenave.

Late in 1873 Mormon workmen from the St. George Stake again journeyed to Lee's Ferry to build another ferryboat. Its immediate purpose was to convey a new colonizing expedition across the river in 1874.[11]

11. Cleland and Brooks, *A Mormon Chronicle*, 2:312.

Rachel Woolsey Lee, sixth wife of John D. Lee, was steadfastly loyal to her husband throughout his ordeals. *Utah State Historical Society*

# LEE'S FERRY
# FORT

Of the present Lee's Ferry buildings near the river, only one stands out as an obvious relic of the past. A small structure of rough-cut, random-sized rocks holding a thatched roof of sticks, willows, and mud, it blends into the landscape and holds its secrets in mute decay. Referred to as Lee's Ferry Fort (or erroneously as Lee's Fort), its thick walls and narrow windows imply that violence, or the threat of it, was once reality itself along this river of the West. (See Tour Site #4)

Yet the fort is not so much a monument to violence as to frustration, for the building symbolizes the year 1874, when Mormon plans to colonize northern Arizona were blocked by the malevolence and misdeeds of men.

It was early January, 1874. A hundred miles north of Lee's Ferry, four young Navajo men rode south on their return from a trading trip to the Ute country. On their way they passed into Grass Valley, (near present-day Bryce Canyon National Park), which had been settled by Mormons and a few "Gentiles" the previous year. At one of the ranch houses they stopped, probably in hopes of obtaining food.

Apparently entering without knocking, they found William McCarty and his sons cooking breakfast. A visitor named Clinger was also in the kitchen. The Navajos, although ordered to leave, placed themselves between the white men and the guns stacked in a corner. The Indians then forced McCarty, his sons, and Clinger to leave, but the settlers took refuge in the barn while the Navajos ate the breakfast in the house.

McCarty and Clinger then realized that the guns in the house were useless to the Navajos, since all available ammunition was in the gun belts the white men still wore. Devising a plan, the McCarty boys gathered some hay, tied it into a bundle, and began rolling it toward the house, perhaps preparatory to setting it on fire. Seeing this, the Navajos panicked and ran. Two of them jumped on Clinger's horse, while the other two took their own horses.

Immediately, the white settlers obtained their guns from the house and opened fire. The two Indians on their own horses were killed, but those on Clinger's horse rode out of sight. Within a few minutes the McCartys saddled up and gave chase. When they finally caught the Navajos they killed one of them, wounded the other, and shot Clinger's horse. The wounded Navajo, on foot, escaped into a rough canyon and hid out until oncoming darkness finally forced the McCartys to give up the search and return home.[1]

---

1. Probably the best account of the 1874 shooting of Navajos in Grass Valley appeared in Peter Gottfredson, *History of Indian Depredations in Utah* (Salt Lake City: Skelton Publishing Co., 1919), pp. 330-332.

The wounded Navajo, Ne-Chic-Se-Cla, then began his long wintertime walk south. Somehow the youthful Indian covered the distance, crossed the river at Crossing of the Fathers, and reached his home near Moenkopi. Upon hearing his version of the story, the Navajo leaders were outraged, many of them demanding all-out war on southern Utah settlers. Two of the Navajos killed were sons of a leading chief in the tribe.[2]

Unimportant to the Navajos, but a vital point to the Mormons was the fact that William McCarty was not a Mormon. McCarty and his sons, Tom, Bill, and George, had just moved to the area. In later years, Tom and Bill became notorious western outlaws, associating with a group known loosely as the Wild Bunch. They were often led by another man from southern Utah, Robert LeRoy Parker, also known as Butch Cassidy.

While many Navajos were calling for bloody revenge, a Hopi chief named Tuba who had befriended whites in the past learned of the Indian war council and rushed a warning to the nearest white settler, who happened to be John D. Lee. Lee was on another of his periodic departures from Lee's Ferry, and was working on his new ranch at Moenave. Told of the imminent Indian War, Lee immediately saddled up and rode north to Lee's Ferry on a cold and foggy night. When he reached the ferry the next day his sons carried the message on to the town of Pahreah, and then to Jacob Hamblin at Kanab.

About a week later, Lee was out on his cattle range in House Rock Valley when he met Jacob Hamblin heading for the ferry. Hamblin, acting on telegraphed instructions from Brigham Young, was on his way to meet with the Navajo chiefs and, hopefully, to prevent a Mormon-Navajo war. Lee returned with Hamblin as far as Moenave where he found that Rachel had converted the ranch house into a virtual fortress, complete with sand bags and rifle ports.[3]

About February 1, 1874, Hamblin did meet with the chiefs in a grueling twelve hour session where he was accused of lying and deceiving the Indians. Tension within the large hogan was so intense at times that Hamblin believed the Navajos intended to kill him. At last the Indian leaders allowed Hamblin to leave, but only after he promised to seek reparations in the form of cattle and other stock and to meet again with the Navajos in twenty-five days.[4]

But Hamblin did not keep his word. He knew that the struggling settlements of southern Utah could not afford to send hundreds of cattle and horses as reparations. Furthermore, he felt that the Mormons were not to blame. When he failed to keep his appointment, however, the Navajos' irritation and anger only increased.

Into this explosive atmosphere John L. Blythe led a small company of Mormon colonists south from Lee's Ferry toward Moenkopi. In his diary, Lee dates the occasion as March 14, 1874, when he ferried them across the river. Although the Mormons reached Moenkopi without incident, they were soon harassed by Navajos, who rode wildly through the village each day yelling and taunting the settlers.

Since Hamblin had failed to keep his appointment with the chiefs, the Navajos

---

2. John R. Young, "The Navajo and Moqui Mission," *Improvement Era* 17, no. 3 (Jan. 1914).

3. Lee's role in the 1874 Navajo uprising appears in his diary, Cleland and Brooks, *A Mormon Chronicle* 2:320-323

4. See James A. Little, *Jacob Hamblin Among the Indians*, (Salt Lake City: Mutual Improvement Association, 1959), which is Hamblin's autobiography. Hamblin's highly colored account of his meeting with Navajos in early February 1874, and of the meeting's aftermath, is obviously over-dramatized.

demanded that Blythe and Ira Hatch come to their council hogan and "talk things over." Reluctantly, Blythe and Hatch complied, only to find themselves virtually on trial, with their lives in balance. Many hours later it was finally decided to release Hatch and to burn Blythe at the stake. Blythe's steadfast refusal to show fear, however, turned the odds in his favor, and both men were released.

When word reached Kanab that missionaries to Moenkopi were being held hostage, a rescue force of fifty men was organized under John R. Young. This group crossed at Lee's Ferry and rushed south in time to prevent an expected attack on Moenkopi.[5] For the time being, however, the mission to Moenkopi was finished. Settlers could not live peacefully in the midst of a hostile Indian land, nor could they garrison a village adequately for defense. Their only choice was to return to Utah Territory.

In May 1874, Hamblin and other Mormons sent a letter to all Navajo chiefs that included the following:

> *If a few of your good men will come over the Colorado, with a good Spanish interpreter, we will meet you at our Ferry Boat, where we will be happy to see you, and satisfy you that what we have said is true. But should any attempt to cross the Colorado above our Ferry Boat we shall look upon them as enemies.*[6]

In other words, Lee's Ferry was to be the only point of friendly Navajo-Mormon contact.

Anticipating that the Navajos would come to Lee's Ferry to negotiate, Hamblin was anxious to make the place important to them, not only as a place to talk but as a place of trade. At the May semi-annual Mormon conference, held in 1874 at St. George, Jacob therefore proposed that a trading post be built at Lee's Ferry. A useful

Lee's Ferry Fort is inspected by some of Charles H. Spencer's mining men in 1910. Spencer later built an addition onto the west end and converted the fort into a cook house for his men.

*Albert H. Jones*

5. Young, "The Navajo and Moqui Mission."
6. Reprinted in Corbett, *Jacob Hamblin, the Peacemaker*, p. 374

Lee's Ferry Fort, photographed from the rear by Julius Stone (who was on a river trip), in 1909.

*Utah State Historical Society*

trading post would mean that Navajos would not have to journey into the Utah settlements to trade, which would be easier for the Indians and considerably safer for the Mormon villagers. Brigham Young agreed to the suggestion and ordered construction of the post.

In June 1874, a group of at least fifteen men, led by Andrew Gibbon and Thales Haskell, began work on the building "a little above the Lee Ferry on the Colorado."[7] Although called a trading post, it was also referred to as a fortification, giving it a dual purpose. By July the small rock structure was finished, ready for the Navajos. But the attitude of the Navajos continued hostile, keeping them from any peaceful contact with Mormons. The Grass Valley affair was simply another in a series of Navajo grievances against whites in general and against the Indian Bureau in particular. Agent W.F.M. Arny at Fort Defiance sided strongly against the Mormons, blaming them for the Grass Valley killings, but the reasons for his hasty accusation seem unclear. The matter was, however, one of the subjects he proposed to bring up with administration leaders when he escorted a group of Navajo chiefs to Washington. In September 1874, Arny and the traveling chiefs met with President Grant, but what they discussed was not recorded. If Grass Valley came up at all, the President did nothing about the matter.[8]

So few of the Navajo demands were acceded to by government officials that the tribesmen considered the Washington trip to have been virtually a waste of time and money. They placed blame on Agent W.F.M. Arny, which helped contribute to his early dismissal from the post. In this way Arny became the scapegoat for many Navajo dissatisfactions–including the Grass Valley killings–indirectly bringing peace to the Mormon-Indian borderlands.

Of some value also was the inspection trip–at Jacob Hamblin's urging–of Navajo

7. Bleak, "Annals of the Southern Utah Mission."

8. The intervention of Navajo Agent W.F.M. Arny is discussed in Lawrence R. Murphy, *Frontier Crusader–William F.M. Arny* (Tucson: University of Arizona Press, 1972), and in Frank McNitt, *The Indian Traders* (Norman: University of Oklahoma Press, 1962).

Chief Hastele to the Grass Valley area. Hamblin reported that Hastele was satisfied that Mormons were not involved in the killings. In a late summer conference at Fort Defiance, Hamblin and Hastele spoke to a group of tribal leaders. According to Hamblin, "The truth was brought to light, and those who wished to throw the blame of murdering the young Navajos upon the Saints were confounded."

The small trading post now called Lee's Ferry Fort thus began operations, although how much business it handled is not known. Jacob himself worked as a part-time trader during the winter of 1874-75. Other Mormons also served as traders during the next two or three years. It is doubtful that the post continued operations into the 1880s.

In 1910 a miner-promoter named Charles H. Spencer, who planned a big operation at Lee's Ferry, added a wing onto the west end of the old fort and converted the whole structure into a mess hall. But by 1913 the miners had departed. Spencer's additional wing was later either partially torn down or gradually collapsed. (For more details of Spencer's operations, see Chapter 12.) The original 1874 fort remains virtually intact (see Tour Site No. 4).

## THE LAST DAYS OF JOHN D. LEE

Although John D. Lee, by carrying the first warning of Navajo unrest from Moenave to Lee's Ferry, became involved in the Mormon Navajo disputes of 1874, he apparently played no further role. He continued to operate the ferry from time to time and to farm at both Lee's Ferry and Moenave. He made at least one trip with some prospectors to the San Francisco Mountain region of Arizona. While on this trip he met some friendly Havasupai Indians, who may have invited him to visit their canyon village. Since Lee's diary for most of 1874 is missing, it can only be said that

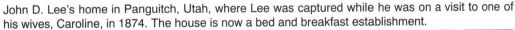

John D. Lee's home in Panguitch, Utah, where Lee was captured while he was on a visit to one of his wives, Caroline, in 1874. The house is now a bed and breakfast establishment.

John D. Lee, (seated, center) and trial officials pose during Lee's trial for murder, Beaver, Utah, 1875. (L to R) William W. Bishop, Judge Jacob S. Boreman, Enos D. Hoge, Wells Spicer, extreme right, unidentified, John D. Lee center front.          *Utah State Historical Society*

he spent little time at Lee's Ferry. According to certain stories he spent considerable time visiting the Indians in Havasu Canyon. Perhaps the stories are true.[9]

In November 1874, Sheriff William Stokes of Beaver, Utah, acting on the still valid warrant for Lee's arrest, heard that Lee was somewhere in the Utah settlements. After receiving more reports, Stokes concluded that Lee must be at Panguitch, perhaps visiting his wife Caroline. Upon reaching Caroline's house and questioning Lee's family, Stokes guessed that Lee must be hiding in the chicken coop that was covered with straw. Peering through a hole in the straw, Stokes saw Lee holding a Smith and Wesson five shooter. Several times Lee was ordered out by Stokes and his four deputies until Stokes said, "If he makes a single move, I'll blow his brains out!" Lee quickly replied, "Hold on boys. Don't get excited. I'll come out."[10]

Thus on November 7, 1874, Lee was captured and taken to the jail in Beaver to await trial. At the trial, which began in July 1875, many details of the Mountain Meadows Massacre were aired. It appeared that Lee had indeed played a significant role, but that he had probably acted under orders—and certainly not alone. Yet the jury was split, with the eight Mormons being for acquittal and the four Gentiles for conviction. Another trial would be required.[11]

In August, 1875, Lee was moved to the Utah Prison in Salt Lake City, By this time Lee's imprisonment and forthcoming trial had become national news, with stories

9. Alfred F. Whiting, "John D. Lee and the Havasupai," *Plateau* 21, no. 1 (July 1948).
10. *Arizona Sentinel*, 28 November 1874. Microfiche at Arizona State University, Arizona Historical Foundation, Tempe.
11. Details of Lee's trials and his execution are taken from Brooks, *John Doyle Lee.*

in *Harper's Magazine*, and in several national newspapers. Lee himself was treated with unusual respect, and was allowed, under guard, to work daily outside the prison. The Warden even treated Lee to a buggy ride tour of the city. During the winter, Lee conducted a prison school, teaching other convicts to read and write

When Lee was released on bail in May 1876, he rode south as a man growing embittered at the scapegoat role he saw being forced upon him. Still he clung to the frail belief that the Mormon Presidency, as well as other leaders, would speak in his behalf and that he would be acquitted. Until his second trial, which was set for September, he could visit those few friends that continued to stand by him. Although his diary for the period is missing, he evidently divided his time among his

Artist's drawing of John D. Lee writing his "Confessions," while jailed at Ft. Cameron, Utah.

wives and families, going to Lee's Ferry, Skutumpah, Panguitch, and Moenave.

When urged to jump bail and to take refuge in Mexico, Lee refused. After he had left on his return to the Beaver jail, a messenger reportedly arrived at Lee's Ferry with advice from the Church authorities suggesting that Lee should leave the country. The Church would apparently assume responsibility for the bail bond. But the messenger missed Lee, and Lee was back in jail before he received a report about the messenger.

Behind the scenes, authorities were comspiring to make Lee the scapegoat, or "fall-guy," for the massacre. Although no documentary proof exists, it is clearly apparent that U.S. Attorney Sumner Howard met with Church authorities, probably Brigham Young himself, and threatened to indict several Mormon participants–unless he could get a conviction in the Lee trial. To escape further damaging publicity, the Church officials agreed.

When Lee learned that the jury members for the second trial would all be Mormons, he realized that he was to be sacrificed. "Just one Gentile!" he pleaded, but it was not to be; the jury had already been selected. Resigned to his fate, Lee sat in his prison cell and wrote his confessions, which praised the LDS faith, but which strongly dammed the leaders who had turned their backs on him.

And at the second trial, the tone had certainly changed. Appealing to emotions, the prosecution presented hearsay evidence, innuendoes, and apparent contradictions– all without challenge. Jacob Hamblin, who was in northern Utah at the time of the massacre, even gave damaging hearsay evidence. Later, in a letter to Emma, Lee spilled forth his anger at Hamblin:

> *Six witnesses testified against me, four of whom pergured themselves by*
> *swearing falsehoods of the blackest character. Old Jacob Hamblin, the*
> *fiend of Hell, testified under oath that I told him that two young women*

At Mountain Meadows, March 23, 1877, John D. Lee sits on his coffin awaiting execution by a firing squad. At his left the Deputy U.S. Marshall reads the death warrant. The execution was conducted by a twenty-three man U.S. Army unit from Fort Cameron under the direction of 2nd Lt. George T.T. Patterson. The photograph was taken by James Fennimore, who, when sick, had stayed with Lee at Lonely Dell for three weeks in 1872. *Library of Congress*

> *were found in a thicket, where they had secreted themselves, by an Indian chief, who brought the girls to me and wanted to know what was to be done with them. That I replied that they was to old to live and would give evidence and must be killed...that I then cut her throat and the Indian killed the other. Such a thing I never heard of before, let alone committing the awful deed.*[12]

Yet Lee presented no defense, possibly because of threats to his family by LDS authorities. His worst fears were realized when the all-Mormon jury found him guilty. He was sentenced not only to be shot by a firing squad, but shot at the scene of the crime--Mountain Meadows. Although the Territorial Governor offered to commute Lee's sentence if he would make a full confession, Lee refused.

On the early morning of 21 March 1877 a detachment of U.S. Army soldiers under the command of 2nd Lt. George T.T. Patterson, left Ft. Cameron, at Beaver, under great secrecy, to convey Lee to Mountain Meadows. They arrived on the morning of March 23rd. A coffin for Lee had been hastily nailed together, and it was on this coffin that Lee sat for his final photograph, the photograph taken by an old friend, James Fennimore.

Before being blindfolded, Lee stated, "It seems I have to be made a victim; a victim must be had, and I am the victim. I studied to make Brigham Young's will my pleasure for thirty years. See now what I have come to this day! I have been sacrificed in a cowardly, dastardly manner. I do not fear death; I shall never go to a worse place than I am now in. I ask the Lord my God, if my labors are done, to receive my spirit."[13]

The sound of five shots signaled the death of John Doyle Lee. His body was conveyed to Cedar City, where it was turned over to Lee's sons, who took it on to Panguitch for burial.

---

12. Letter of John D. Lee to Emma Lee, 21 Sept 1876. Reprinted in *Journals of John D. Lee, 1846-47 and 1859*, ed. by Charles Kelly (Salt Lake City: University of Utah Press, 1984)
13. Hubert Howe Bancroft, *History of Utah,* Bookcraft, Salt Lake City, 1964, p. 570

For the next seventy-three years the Mormon Church maintained that Lee was solely responsible for the massacre. Then in 1950 a courageous Mormon lady named Juanita Brooks published a book, *The Mountain Meadows Massacre*, that detailed much of the true story. In 1961 Church authorities reinstated Lee to membership in the Church. Lee family descendants placed a marker on his grave, reading:

"Ye Shall Know the Truth,
And the Truth Shall Make You Free."
John 8:32

The grave of John D. Lee at the Panguitch, Utah Cemetery. The horizontal tablet was placed by the Lee family in 1961 after Lee's excommunication by the LDS Church was rescinded.

# ON TO
# ARIZONA

**L**ong before Lee was actually captured, Mormon Church authorities realized that Lee's Ferry, the vital link between Mormon settlements in Utah and Arizona, should not be controlled by a fugitive who spent much of his time in hiding. James Jackson was sent to help, but he was not physically up to the task and he died from exposure in January 1874.

Another man, stronger than Jackson, more mature, and proven in wilderness trials was needed. The man picked for the job was Warren M. Johnson, then a school teacher in Glendale, Utah, but a man who had served well on the rugged pioneering mission to the Muddy River, Nevada. A Mormon convert, Johnson was sincere, hard-working, and dependable–just the type of man needed for the job.[1]

After receiving the "call" in October 1873, Johnson moved the older of his two wives, Permelia, to Lee's Ferry in March 1875. Since Emma Lee was still living at the ranch house, Johnson moved into the cabin vacated the year before by James Jackson. Johnson finally moved his younger wife, Samantha, to the river early in 1876. Samantha and her young child were housed in the trading post, Lee's Ferry Fort. Later he moved both families into the fort.

Failure of the Haight mission in 1873 had been compounded by the Indian unrest of 1874, but Church leaders persisted in their efforts to colonize Arizona Territory. A scouting expedition headed by James S. Brown crossed the ferry and headed south in 1875, traveling up the valley of the Little Colorado. Brown's favorable report again set serious colonizing in motion, with about two hundred missionaries "called" from many parts of Utah.

The first settlers crossed the river without mishap and arrived at their destination on the Little Colorado March 23, 1876, but the migration continued for many weeks thereafter.

As the widow of John D. Lee, Emma Lee continued to have a proprietary interest in the ferry. In this connection, Warren Johnson would have been Emma's employee, but what financial arrangements they had are unknown. Some emigrant diary accounts suggest that Emma, at least on occasion, actually rowed the ferryboat herself. Indeed she was said to be quite competent.

---

1. Details on Warren Johnson, his families, and their long tenure at Lee's Ferry were obtained from an interview with his son, the late Frank Johnson of St. George, Utah. Other descendants of Warren Johnson also provided information. A brief but valuable article is P.T. Reilly, "Warren Marshall Johnson, Forgotten Saint," *Utah Historical Quarterly* 39, no. 1 (Winter 1971).

Warren Marshall Johnson (center) operated Lee's Ferry and the Lonely Dell Ranch from 1875 to 1896. He is shown with his wife, Permelia (left), and some of his children. In the doorway holding the baby is Vina Brinkerhoff, wife of Johnson's assistant David Brinkerhoff. *Frank Johnson*

Imaginary picture of Lee's Backbone. from *In Desert Arizona,* S.C. Richardson, (Independence, MO., 1938) p.81

Emma Lee, however, had little reason to remain at this isolated and remote river crossing. In May 1879, the Mormon Church bought the ferry rights from her for $3,000, paid mostly in cattle.[2] She then moved south, farther into Arizona, where she married again and lived until 1897.

The successful colonizing expedition of 1876 led to larger and more ambitious emigrations in following years. From 1876 to about 1890, use of Lee's Ferry was most intensive, for it served as the critical river crossing for many hundreds of Mormons heading into Arizona.

In spite of boating safety precautions, the river remained an ever-present danger, especially when the ferry was operated by inexperienced persons. On May 28, 1876, Daniel H. Wells, Counselor to the LDS President, arrived at the river with Erastus Snow, Jacob Hamblin, Bishop Lorenzo Roundy, and other high-placed Mormons, all on their way to Arizona.

William Lee, age 15, Emma's son, who was operating the ferry that day, warned them that the river was too high to cross safely on the large boat. He recommended instead that they disassemble the wagons, float them across, and transport the men in the skiff. Lee recounted the incident years later:

> ...*they disregarded my warning and spurned my judgment... when they loaded the big boat I refused to take any responsibility, but stood by with the skiff ready for the emergency call.*[3]

To compensate for the strong flow of the river, they towed the big boat further upstream that usual, then tied it to a large rock that projected out into the river while they made ready to leave. Unnoticed, the bow of the boat, rising and falling on the current, gradually worked itself under the rock, until suddenly the water began filling the boat. In an instant:

> *The flood swept over it and washed buggies and men into the raging stream... I rushed with all haste to the middle of the river and had just time enough to rescue the two men. I watched my good friend [Bishop Roundy] sink in the muddy water at the head of the rapids and as he went down the third time he waved his hand three times as if to say farewell.*[4]

Lorenzo Roundy, who was wearing two cartridge belts and a holstered revolver, disappeared in the swift flowing river. The ferryboat floated on down the river into Marble Canyon and was never seen again. The party finally completed its river crossing by carrying its disassembled wagons over in the skiff.[5]

During these early years, if passengers were lucky enough to escape the river unharmed, they still faced the terrible piece of road known as Lee's Backbone, a one and one-half mile route through tortuous rock gullies of the Shinarump ledge which rises sharply from the river on the left bank. The steep, hard rock surface defied leveling attempts; a road of sorts was dug, picked, and blasted into what still looks like giant rock stairs. Veteran wagon drivers, well-acquainted with frontier roads, called Lee's Backbone the worst road they had ever traveled.

---

2. Lee's Ferry file, Historical Department, L.D.S. Church, Salt Lake City.
3. Newspaper clipping dated 15 April 1936, of an account of the accident, as told by William Lee to his wife, Clara. Library, Archives and Public Records Division, State of Arizona, Lee's Ferry file.
4. Ibid.
5. Ibid. Also, an account that emphasizes Hamblin's heroics appears in Little, *Jacob Hamblin*. A third account is in the Lee's Ferry file of the Historical Department, L.D.S. Church.

Wilford Woodruff, future President of the LDS Church, on March 14, 1879, crossed on the ferry and then rode a wagon over Lee's Backbone. His journal entry stated:

> *[Lee's Backbone] was the worst hill Ridge or Mountain that I Even attempted to Cross with a team and waggon on Earth. We had 4 Horses on a waggon... we Could ownly gain from 4 inches to 24 with all the power of the horses & two men rolling at the hind wheels and going Down on the other side was still more Steep rocky and sandy which would make it much worse than going up on the North side.*[6]

When a wagon finally reached the summit of Lee's Backbone heading south, the driver had to face a frightening, teeth-jarring descent of 350 feet to the Marble Platform. Frequently the trip from the river over the Backbone and down to the Platform would consume an entire day. If a wagon was damaged enroute, the trip took even longer (see Tour Site No. 15).

Since the worst of Lee's Backbone lay at its lowest part, nearest the ferry, Warren Johnson traced out an alternate route through softer formations above the Shinarump. Working by hand, it took Johnson and his occasional assistants from 1885 to 1888 to complete the bypass, which joined the old Backbone road about half-way up. Although quite steep in places, the bypass offered the advantage of a smoother surface, and was probably preferred.

Wagon ruts cut into solid rock on Lee's Backbone. Being inspected by W.L. Rusho.     *Don Cecala*

---

6. Wilford Woodruff, *Wilford Woodruff's Journal*, Edited by Scott G. Kenney, (Midvale, Utah: Signature Books, 1985), 7:473

Dugway leading to the lower, or winter ferry site below the mouth of the Paria, on the south side of the Colorado. This site and the dugway, much preferred to the alternative of surmounting Lee's Backbone, was used from 1878 to 1896 during times of low flow of the Colorado.

Of more value perhaps to passing emigrants was the alternate ferry site, located below the mouth of the Paria. A crossing made here completely bypassed Lee's Backbone by way of a quarter-mile long dugway on the left bank leading from the river up an almost sheer precipice to the Marble Platform. This was where Hamblin wanted to put the main ferry site in 1872, but was overruled. In 1878 the Church sent a quarryman to construct the dugway, which was completed late in the year. From that time until 1898, the lower ferry site was used continually except in times of high water, when the south side landing was submerged (see Tour Site No. 18).

After 1878, arriving ferry passengers always hoped that the lower ferry would be in operation. If this crossing site happened to be closed due to high water, it meant they would have to traverse Lee's Backbone, and they frequently complained bitterly to the ferryman.

Ferryboats could be used for only a limited period. Sometimes boats were lost in accidents, but more often they became waterlogged and unwieldy and had to be replaced. In 1881, Church officials decided that a large boat capable of holding two

The first emigrants bound for Mesa, Arizona, paused along Lee's Backbone to chisel this inscription.

wagons would be ideal. Apparently they did not ask an opinion of Warren Johnson, who would have to propel the boat with 12-foot sweeps. Once across the river, he would then have to drag it upriver to the starting point. Eventually the large boat was built, but Johnson could make little use of such an unwieldy craft. During this period, most of his crossings were made by skiff.

Fortunately for Johnson, the Church sent him assistants, the best of whom was Johnson's own brother-in-law, David Brinkerhoff. Brinkerhoff stayed from 1881 until 1886, when he was appointed bishop at Tuba City. Other assistants came and left at frequent intervals.

After completion of the Mormon temple at St. George in 1877, a new class of travelers began using the Utah-Arizona road. Young Mormon couples, married by civil authorities in the Arizona settlements, began traveling north to have their marriages solemnized in the temple. So many couples did this that the road was referred to as the "Honeymoon Trail." It has been reported that many couples, having visited the temple, were seen heading back home to Arizona, apparently in no hurry whatsoever.[7]

---

7. Will C. Barnes, "The Honeymoon Trail", *Arizona Highways* 10 (Dec. 1934).

# OUTLAW GANGS

**A**n important river crossing like Lee's Ferry is eventually visited by a full share of humanity, including those on the wrong side of the law. Just how many known or unknown criminals used the river crossing can never be determined. Two stories, however, are worthy of retelling.

In the early 1880's, a trio of outlaws, Tom McCarty, Matt Warner, and Josh Sweat, met in a saloon at Fort Wingate to make plans. All three were from villages in southern Utah. Tom McCarty, in fact, had been involved in the Grass Valley shootings of 1874 that led to the Mormon-Navajo friction and to the building of Lee's Ferry Fort.

Their plan was simple. They would steal a few hundred head of horses in Mexico, drive them north, then sell them to ranchers. Their plan worked once, but when they tried it again, their trail was followed by U.S. deputy marshals who reached the outlaw camp one morning just before dawn. In the shoot-out that followed, Josh Sweat was severely wounded in the chest, arm, and leg. The marshals, however, withdrew after the outlaws killed four of the seven lawmen present. A posse was soon organized to follow the outlaw trail, which headed north toward the Colorado River.

In spite of his wounds, Sweat was able to ride in what turned out to be a three hundred-mile horse race to Lee's Ferry. At one point the posse got ahead and prepared an ambush at a spring, but the outlaws detected the trap and slipped on by. At another point a marshal rode close enough to shoot one of the trio's extra horses.

When they reached the crest of Lee's Backbone the outlaws could see the posse only a couple of miles to the rear. They knew by then that they could reach the river in advance of the lawmen, but where would the ferryboat be? If they had to signal for the ferry, then wait for the boat to reach them, they would surely be apprehended.

Galloping their horses the final distance they reached the river to find that the boat was in the middle of the river moving slowly in their direction. One of the outlaws hollered to the ferryman (probably Warren Johnson), "I'll bet you fifty dollars you can't make it the rest of the way in two minutes."

Johnson yelled his acceptance of the bet and put his back to the big sweeps. He won the money, but just as the trio led their horses aboard, Johnson looked up the trail and said, "Let's wait awhile. I see a dust up the road. It might be someone that wants to go over and I can take you all at once." At Johnson's innocent remark the three pulled their guns on the boatman, stating, "Get going. We don't wait for nobody."

By the time the posse reached the riverbank, Johnson and the outlaws were halfway across the river. The marshals yelled for Johnson to return, but with three guns on him he couldn't very well comply. Furthermore, the marshals couldn't shoot for fear of hitting the ferryman.

Once across, McCarty, Warner, and Sweat felt quite secure. With the river too wide to shoot across, and with Johnson as their captive, they relaxed, took a bath, ate a hot meal, and had a good night's sleep—all within sight of the helpless marshals.

Next morning they saddled up and rode north, taking Johnson with them. About five miles from Lee's Ferry they released the unfortunate boatman, but one report says they tied his hands behind him and close-hobbled his feet. It took Johnson two days of rolling and falling to return to Lee's Ferry. With this time lead over the officers, the three outlaws made good their escape into Utah, where they split up, McCarty and Sweat going to Nevada and Warner heading for the Vernal area.

Details of the story were provided by Josh Sweat and Matt Warner years later in separate interviews. Although their versions differed on some minor points, they agreed closely on major details.[1]

Before the decade of the 1880's was out, another group of outlaws tried to escape across Lee's Ferry, only this time they were not so lucky.

On the cold, snow-filled night of March 20, 1889, four masked men took command of the eastbound express of the Atlantic and Pacific Railroad when the train stopped briefly at remote Canyon Diablo in the desert east of Flagstaff. Within a few minutes the four had forced an employee to open a safe, from which the outlaws scooped up all the money in sight, plus a substantial amount of jewelry, and had ridden off into the night, apparently heading south.

The four, John J. Smith, Dan Harvick, Bill Stiren, and John Halford, were lately tough cowhands of the famous Hashknife outfit of northern Arizona. Winter boredom had given them an itch for action, which resulted in the train robbery. Smith was apparently the leader.

After dividing the meager bundle of stolen cash they split up, agreeing to meet again in Wyoming. In pairs they rode off, Stiren and Harvick together and Smith and Halford together. From Canyon Diablo they traveled south to throw off pursuers, but they soon turned north toward the Colorado River.[2]

Little did the four know that they were being followed even before the robbery. On their way to Canyon Diablo they had broken into a ranch house, helped themselves to supplies, and made a general mess. When Will C. Barnes, the ranch owner, discovered the break-in, he set out to follow the thieves. Barnes and one of his cowboys, William Broadbent, were able to track the outlaws south, then north, across the Little Colorado River and all the way to Lee's Ferry.[3]

At Lee's Ferry, Barnes was told that no one had seen any suspicious horsemen, whether in groups of two or four. Not until the capture of the outlaws days later was it learned that Stiren and Harvick had bribed a passing traveler to cross on the ferry, then after dark take the boat back to the south side of the river where it was left waiting. With the hooves of their horses muffled by cloth, Stiren and Harvick had quietly crossed the river and headed north. One or both of them must have been familiar with the trails around Lee's Ferry, for they had headed up the hard-to-find Dominguez Pass over the Echo Cliffs.

With their horses nearly spent, Barnes and Broadbent gave up the chase at Lee's

1. See Harvey Hardy, "A Long Ride with Matt Warner," *Frontier Times*, October-November 1964, and Matt Warner, *The Last of the Bandit Riders*, as told to Murray E. King (New York: Bonanza Books, 1940).
2. Primary source for details of the robbery, the chase, and the final capture is Keithley, Ralph, *Buckey O'Neill* (Caldwell, Idaho: Caxton Printers, Ltd., 1949).
3. Barnes recounts his involvement in Will Croft Barnes, *Apaches & Long-horns* (Los Angeles: Ward Ritchie Press, 1941).

Will C. Barnes, of Arizona, photographed about 1884. Barnes was the first to track the train robbers in 1889.

*Arizona Historical Foundation*

Ferry, but as they rode south they met a posse headed by the energetic young sheriff of Yavapai County, William O. "Buckey" O'Neill. O'Neill had also followed the dim trail, and although he was still two days behind the outlaws, he was closing in fast.

O'Neill predicted that the outlaws would have to visit at least one of the isolated communities in southern Utah, probably either Cannonville or Pahreah. He and his men crossed on the ferry, followed up the Paria to Dominguez Pass, and headed directly for Cannonville. So fast was O'Neill traveling, however, that he unknowingly passed the outlaws and reached Cannonville before they did. Puzzled as to how he had missed them, he headed back south trying to pick up the trail.

Soon after O'Neill left, Stiren and Harvick rode into Cannonville, posing as itinerant cowhands. They asked a local inhabitant if they could spend the night, were shown into a house, and were surprisingly confronted with the sight of their two fellow outlaws, Halford and Smith. Although they pretended not to know each other, the Mormon residents were suspicious.

After the four strangers had gone to bed, a group of Mormon men surrounded the house. Capturing three of them was simple, but Smith pulled a hidden gun and took charge. Instantly the Mormons laid down their arms while the four saddled up and rode, laughing, out of town.

A messenger who caught up with O'Neill and his posse told them that the outlaws had been captured in Cannonville, so the sheriff headed back north, arriving soon

William O. "Buckey" O'Neill, sheriff of Yavapai County, Arizona, relentlessly pursued train robbers across Lee's Ferry and into Utah in 1889          *Arizona Historical Foundation*

after the train robbers had escaped. Now Buckey O'Neill was on a hot trail, which led again to the south, astonishingly back toward Lee's Ferry. He passed a camp where the fire was still burning, and realized that his quarry was not far ahead.

On a barren, rocky point over Wahweap Canyon the outlaws had become rimrocked. Just as they were starting to backtrack to find a place to descend, O'Neill and his men came riding up. Confronted by the lawmen, the outlaws opened fire but hit no one. Realizing the desperate situation, Smith attempted to charge through the line on his fast horse, but O'Neill shot the horse dead. At this point Halford and Stiren surrendered. Harvick and Smith, however, jumped over the edge of the rocky point and ran headlong down the steep talus slope. O'Neill and his men fired at them many times, but without effect. O'Neill's posse found a way to descend on their horses, and spent the rest of the day and part of the night following occasional boot tracks in bits of soft ground between the rocks. The next day they began to find tracks of bare feet, then traces of blood. Apparently, long distance hiking in cowboy boots was so painful that the fleeing men chose to go barefoot over the rough rocks.

Smith and Harvick were approaching Dominguez Pass above Lee's Ferry when they found the small water hole known as Willow Tanks. They stopped, soaked their feet, and managed to put on their boots. Just as they were about to continue on down into the Paria Canyon, a rifle cracked and a bullet hit the rocks. Although the outlaws took cover and opened fire, O'Neill was not to be denied. The sheriff rode his big roan right toward Smith, firing as rapidly as possible. Under the onslaught, Smith couldn't even take proper aim. Suddenly the sheriff was almost on top of him, and Smith found himself looking up a rifle barrel at Buckey O'Neill. Naturally, Smith surrendered.

With Smith in custody, O'Neill turned to the other outlaw. "You're next," he yelled to Harvick. A few shots were fired, but with the sheriff and his men advancing, Harvick realized the hopelessness of his situation and threw up his hands.

O'Neill had a difficult time getting his prisoners to Prescott. He took them first to Kanab, then to Milford, where he boarded a train for Salt Lake City. The rest of the way was by train through Denver, south into New Mexico, and finally into Arizona. It was late at night when the train neared the Colorado-New Mexico border. O'Neill and his deputies had dozed off in their chairs. Smith managed to slip a shackle off one leg and to jump off the train as it was climbing a hill. O'Neill and his men were quickly awakened by the cold air from the window, but Smith had escaped in the darkness. Smith made it into Texas, but he "borrowed" a horse that didn't belong to him and was jailed for horse stealing. After a bit of checking, he was found to be the escaped train robber. O'Neill personally went to Texas to bring Smith back.

Thus ended Buckey O'Neill's most celebrated outlaw chase. The epilogue, however, had an ironic twist. Because he had conducted much of the chase in Utah, where he had no jurisdiction, the Yavapai County Board of Supervisors, backed by a court decision, forced the sheriff to pay over two thousand dollars of his own expenses.

Strangest of all, not even O'Neill realized that robbers Smith and Harvick had actually returned to Arizona when they were captured on the mesa above Lee's Ferry. O'Neill's case was better than he knew.

In 1897, Bucky O'Neill was elected Mayor of Prescott, Arizona. While serving as a Captain in the Rough Riders during the Spanish-American War, O'Neill was killed by a sniper at Santiago, Cuba 1 July 1898. He was buried at Arlington National Cemetery.

# JIM EMETT AND ZANE GREY

Outlaws could be troublesome, but they were such infrequent visitors that Warren Johnson probably thought little about them. Ordinary life at Lee's Ferry involved enough hardship and worry to occupy a man's time. Maintaining the roads and keeping a leaky ferryboat in operation were only parts of Johnson's responsibility. The ranch also demanded his time. Labor required on the diversion dam, on the long ditch and flume, and in the fields was endless. Although growing children could and did help out with some of the work, Johnson and his two wives endured much toil and trouble. (See Chapter 16, Lonely Dell Ranch).

The LDS Church agreed that Johnson's "mission" at Lee's Ferry was completed in 1895. After some negotiation, Johnson at first decided to buy some land in Fredonia, but this was canceled when Johnson broke his back in a fall from a wagon. Nonetheless, in November, 1896, Johnson sold his interests at Lee's Ferry to the LDS Church for $6,500. Johnson, his wives, and their children moved first to Kanab. Then, in spite of being paralyzed from the hips down, he decided that they should pioneer in a new settlement opening up in the Big Horn Basin of Wyoming.

Passengers were always relieved when the ferryboat completed the dangerous river crossing.
*Southern California Edison Company*

Warren Johnson's move to Wyoming was a disaster. Harsh winter weather and lack of adequate food took its toll, and Johnson died on March 10, 1902. He was buried at Byron, Wyoming.[1]

## JIM EMETT TAKES OVER

Church authorities replaced Johnson with a rugged veteran of frontier life named James S. Emett. Born in a covered wagon, he was ever the outdoorsman, uncomfortable in houses, strong, and resilient. Zane Grey, who met Emett in 1907, once wrote a story about the tough ferryman entitled "The Man Who Influenced Me Most," in which he stated,

> *[Emett] stood well over six feet, and his leonine build, ponderous shoulders, and great shaggy head and white beard gave an impression of tremendous virility and dignity... He had a grave, kindly countenance, rugged and strong.*[2]

Grey thought that Emett possessed "a strange gift of revelation... connected with his profound psychic and religious powers." Like Warren Johnson, Emett was a practicing polygamist; his two wives bore him eighteen children. Emett had been a rancher and at one time was superintendent of the Canaan Cooperative Stock Company operating on the Arizona Strip.[3]

At the time he was given the Lee's Ferry assignment, Emett was forty-six. His three grown sons and their wives moved with him and assisted him in the ranching and ferry operation. While no longer a youth, Jim Emett was still in his prime both physically and mentally. Arriving in 1896, he quickly concluded that many modifications were needed at Lee's Ferry. With the help of his sons, he did everything, whether it involved carpentry, blacksmithing, leather tanning, stone masonry, or farming. Among other tasks he built a new ferryboat.

For twenty-three years at Lee's Ferry, the ferryboat was simply a flat bottom barge that was actually rowed across. The oars were made of 2" x 6" boards, bolted together, with a 2" x 10" board on the end that dipped into the water. Frank Johnson, son of Warren, said that it was agony to have to pull on these oars, or sweeps, for very long. Of course the current would push the boat downstream as it crossed, so that the ferryman, after letting off his passengers, would have to tow the boat back upstream with great labor for about a quarter mile before he could start back across.

A track cable was the natural answer. Why it was not put in during the earlier years remains a mystery. When properly rigged with connecting ropes or cables and when angled slightly upstream, the current would actually push the boat across. Also, the boat would not drift downstream.

In 1896 Emett convinced Church authorities that a track cable was necessary. A big two-inch diameter cable consisting of only six strands was brought in, and several men were hired to stretch it across the river. But the cable was simply too big and too heavy for them to handle. Therefore they carefully removed three of the strands–half of the cable–and managed to put it across and to anchor it firmly in rock. On the gently-sloping north bank, the cable was hung across a low tower of cribbed logs. As

---

1. Pat Reilly, "Warren Marshall Johnson, Forgotten Saint," *Utah Historical Quarterly,* Winter, 1971
2. Zane Grey, "The Man Who Influenced Me Most," *American* 102, no. 2 (August 1926).
3. Larson, Andrew Karl, *I Was Called to Dixie: The Virgin River Basin: Unique Experiences in Mormon Pioneering* (Salt Lake City: Deseret News Press, 1961) pp. 238, 243.

A team and wagon crossing at Lee's Ferry in the early 1900's. The boat was angled so that the force of the current would drive it across the river. *Phoenix Public Library*

expected, the cable made crossing the river much easier and safer. (See Tour Site #1).

Warren Johnson had long thought about building a dugway (a road notched into a steep slope) on the southern approach to the ferry so that travelers would not have to cross either Lee's Backbone or the steep, tortuous bypass Johnson had built. Just before he left, Johnson had laid out the dugway and had even performed some work on it, but it was far from finished.

When Emett arrived, he shortly concluded that completion of the dugway was a necessity and asked the Church to provide it. Undoubtedly, one of his arguments was that the ferryboat was by then locked onto the track cable at the upper ferry site, making the lower ferry site virtually useless. Emett was apparently persuasive, for a contract to build the road was let in 1898 to a construction firm in Richfield, Utah, for about $1200. The final product wasn't much of a road, being only ten to twelve feet wide, but it served as the main highway for the next thirty years.

Built in soft earth, the dugway was always subject to washout and rock-falls from above, as an account by some state officials on an automobile trip in 1915 indicates:

> *[We] encountered serious difficulty in going down the dugway into Lee's Ferry. Heavy storms had washed the road considerably, requiring much work to make it passable. The most serious setback was a large boulder, weighing a couple of tons, that had been dropped in the middle of the ten foot dugway. It was necessary to blast this in order to get past.*[4]

Apparently dynamite had to be included in ordinary automobile supplies!

---

4. A.M. McOmie, G.G. Jacobs, and O.C. Bartlett, *The Arizona Strip Report of Reconnaissance of the Country North of the Grand Canyon* (Phoenix: Arizona Board of Control, 1915).

Unused since 1928, the dugway is still clearly visible as a line beginning at the gauging station and rising slowly until it reaches the Marble Platform about one and a half miles away (see Tour Site No. 17).

Emett was also active in the ranching business, keeping his stock in House Rock Valley. He occasionally received stock in payment for ferry services, but he may have also acquired cattle illegally. In House Rock Valley he competed for the range with the Grand Canyon Cattle Company, led by B.F. Saunders and Charles Dimmick. Even though the valley was mostly public domain, the company acted aggressively to control water holes and available grazing land. Jim Emett was not a big cattle operator, but he was nonetheless such an irritation to the company that the Bar-Z built a long, barbed wire fence across the north-south axis of the valley to keep the stock separated.

In his memoirs, cowboy Rowland Rider, who worked for the Bar-Z, states that Emett and his sons would frequently stampede the Buffalo Ranch buffalo into the fence. By the next day, with a big tear in the fence, Bar-Z cowhands would find Emett's cattle grazing on the Bar-Z range. Rider adds that, "Emett would increase his herd by twenty-five or thirty calves at a time by shooting the mothers and stealing their calves... "[5]

In 1906 the company filed a complaint against Emett charging him with cattle theft. Charles Dimmick was the chief accusing witness. In a noted jury trial in Flagstaff, Emett denied the charge, stating that he was not in House Rock Valley at the time specified, and that, at any rate, the cattle in question were his own. In April 1907, the jury found Emett not guilty.[6]

## ZANE GREY - FIRST VISIT

It was at the Flagstaff trial that Zane Grey first met Jim Emett. Grey waited out the verdict, then rode with Emett back to Lee's Ferry.

Also in the group was Charles Jesse Jones, known generally as "Buffalo" Jones. It was Jones who had encouraged Grey to come out west to participate in a mountain lion hunt on the Kaibab Plateau. At that time, Buffalo Jones was a famous hunter, adventurer, lecturer, and wildlife expert. Among more routine exploits, he had founded Garden City, Kansas, hunted musk ox during a Yukon winter, and served as game warden at Yellowstone National Park. In House Rock Valley he had established a buffalo ranch to experiment with "cattalo," the hybrid offspring of buffalo and cattle. The cattalo experiment failed, however, because of persistence of the buffalo hump in the fetus, which made for a difficult, if not impossible, birth. By 1907 Jones had concluded his experiments and had sold his buffalo to his partner, James "Uncle Jim" Owens.[7]

From these experiments has evolved today's Buffalo Ranch, located in southern House Rock Valley twenty-two miles from U.S. 89a, and run by the Arizona Game and Fish Commission. The present herd is maintained at about two hundred buffalo.

Uncle Jim Owens, who left the Buffalo Ranch soon after the cattalo experiment

---

5. Rider, Rowland W., *The RollAway Saloon*, (Logan, Utah, Utah State University Press: 1985) p. 48.
6. District Court Criminal Trial No. 294. Record now at Superior Court, Flagstaff, Arizona.
7. Zane Grey's first major book about the West was a biographical treatment of Buffalo Jones. See Zane Grey, *Last of the Plainsmen* (New York: Outing Publishing Co., 1908). More detail on Buffalo Jones and on the "cattalo" experiment in House Rock Valley is in Robert Easton and Mackensie Brown, *Lord of Beasts: The Saga of Buffalo Jones* (Tucson: University of Arizona Press, 1961)

failed, epitomized the paradox of frontier mentality common to the time. He was reportedly a gentle man with people, especially children, and he loved the small animals of the forest so much that he often talked to the white-tailed Kaibab squirrels. Yet he made his reputation as a killer, a Government "animal control agent", hired to literally exterminate all mountain lions, bobcats, and other predators. And he was good at it, killing hundreds of mountain lions, on special hunts for dignitaries such as Zane Grey, or simply as a part of his everyday operations. Furthermore, almost everyone applauded his efforts to rid the forest of "varmints."

Owens could not have foreseen the tragic consequences of his work. By the 1920's, the reduction of predators had allowed the deer population on the Kaibab Plateau to multiply so tremendously that, during the winter, all the reachable bark was stripped from the aspen trees. Thousands of deer simply died of starvation.[8]

Zane Grey first saw Lee's Ferry about twilight on that April day in 1907, when he and Emett rode in from Flagstaff. Grey awoke the next morning ready to explore:

> *Dawn opened my eyes to what seemed the strangest and most wonderful place in the world. Emett's home was set at the edge of a luxuriant oasis, green with foliage and alfalfa, colored by bright flowers, and shut in on three sides by magnificent red walls three thousand feet high. The thundering Colorado formed a fourth side and separated the oasis from another colossal wall across the river. Paria Creek ran down from the cliffs to water this secluded and desert-bound spot. The low long cabins, crude and picturesque, were shaded by a grove of old cottonwoods, spreading and gnarled, like the oaks of the Druids.[9]*

The rock range cabin built by the Grand Canyon Cattle Company at Jacob Pools. Vermilion Cliffs in the background. Theodore Roosevelt stayed in this cabin in 1913. The confrontation of Jim Emett and Charlie Dimmick, witnessed by Zane Grey, occurred in front of this cabin in 1907.

8. A good description of Owens is in Hall, Sharlot, *Sharlot Hall on the Arizona Strip*, (Flagstaff, AZ: Northland Press, 1975), edited by C. Gregory Crampton, p. 78-85
9. Grey, "The Man Who Influenced Me Most."

Zane Grey poses with two Navajo citizens at The Gap Trading Post in northern Arizona, probably about 1923.                                         *Jane Foster, Marble Canyon Lodge*

Later that day, Emett, Buffalo Jones, and Grey rode off toward the Kaibab Plateau for the scheduled lion hunt. On their second day out they reached a spring in House Rock Valley (apparently Jacob Pools), where the Grand Canyon Cattle Company had built a small rock cabin. As they were dismounting in front of the cabin, Grey heard Emett utter a "deep, fierce imprecation." Grey turned and saw Emett holding his six-gun on a man who had just emerged from the cabin. It was Charlie Dimmick, who had accused Emett of cattle rustling. In Dimmick's hands was a rifle.

Grey wrote that he acted instinctively, stepping out between the two men. "Don't kill each other," he said, "it'll spoil my trip."

Emett immediately sheathed his gun and walked away. Dimmick could only say to Grey, "Howdy, young feller! You shore took chances heah!" Later Buffalo Jones told Grey that Emett and Dimmick would someday kill each other if they ever met again. Fortunately, they never did.[10]

In another version of the confrontation, young Bar-Z cowboy Rowland Rider kicked a pistol (not a rifle) out of Dimmick's hand before he could fire. Then Zane Grey begged Emett not to shoot Dimmick.[11]

Emett predicted that the untamed desert country around Lee's Ferry would capture Zane Grey's imagination, that the land would form a backdrop for many stories Grey would write. The "revelation" was, to say the least, highly accurate, for in the Arizona Strip, Grey had stuck gold—a vast and rugged landscape, cut off from most of the world and largely unknown.[12] In many of his books, Grey seems to be describing House Rock Valley, the Kaibab, or the red-rock canyons to the east. In his first book about the West, *The Last of the Plainsmen*, nonfiction, Grey wrote a biography of Buffalo Jones. In a later fiction work, *Heritage of the Desert*, he centered the story about a place easily recognized as Lee's Ferry—with a white-bearded patriarch thrown in!

What the Grand Canyon Cattle Company could not accomplish with court action they did with money. In August 1909, the company bought the ferry from the Church of Jesus Christ of Latter-day Saints, thus putting Emett out of business. Emett

---

10. Grey, "The Man Who Influenced Me Most."
11. Rider, Rowland, *The Rollaway Saloon,* (Logan, Utah, Utah State University Press: 1985), p. 58.
12. Kant, Candace C., *Zane Grey's Arizona*, (Flagstaff: Northland Press, 1984), p. 18

acceded the next month by selling his ranch and other holdings at Lee's Ferry to the company.

Lee's Ferry had been a key link between Mormon settlements in Utah and Arizona, but by 1900 most people who had to travel a long distance between these states went by railroad. The train trip through either Colorado or California, though much longer in miles, was much shorter in time. By 1909 traffic along the historic wagon road and across the ferry was almost entirely local in character. The once-vital link that had served Church interests for so long was no longer needed.

Zane Grey was to return to the Arizona Strip and Lee's Ferry for a short visit in 1911. During the 1920's, he was involved in the filming of a number of his novels, on location, in northern Arizona. It was a time of spontaneous experimentation in the motion picture industry, where changes in weather, such as rain or wind, merely required filming a few new scenes for the film, a procedure that certainly "added a touch of freshness."[13]

*Heritage of the Desert*, filmed at Lee's Ferry in October, 1923, was an elaborate production that required a crew of 70 from Hollywood, plus 50 Indians and 2,000 horses. The silent film starred Bebe Daniels, Noah Berry, Sr., and James Mason. Considering the rough roads, the primitive accommodations, and the isolation from cities, it must have been a gargantuan undertaking.[14]

Another of Grey's books was adapted to silent film at Lee's Ferry and at The Gap in 1927. The change to "talkies" in 1930, however, made films so expensive that producers asserted artistic control to hold down costs. In 1931, for instance, *Heritage of the Desert* was remade as a talkie, but all the location shots were simply copied from the 1923 film. With this technological and financial restructuring, Zane Grey's role as writer or advisor was severely restricted, causing Grey to lose interest in further film-making.

13. Kant, Candace C., *Zane Grey's Arizona*, (Flagstaff: Northland Press, 1984), p. 147
14. Ibid. pp. 141-142

# THE ENGINEER-
# ROBERT B. STANTON

## STANTON - THE RAILROAD SURVEY

Let us now backtrack a few years to midsummer 1889, the first of July. Warren Johnson was still operating Lee's Ferry. On that day sixteen men in three boats seemed to come out of nowhere, descending the river from Glen Canyon. At Lee's Ferry they tied up, got out, and made plans for their next move. One of the group, Frank Mason Brown, apparently rented a team and wagon from Johnson and drove away toward Kanab for supplies.

During the week-long wait for Brown to return, the other men told Johnson the incredible story of this expedition. In a nutshell, this group was the working nucleus of the newly-formed Denver, Colorado Canyon, and Pacific Railroad Company. Their mission on the river was to survey for a possible railroad route right through the canyons from Grand Junction, Colorado, to the lower Colorado River, then across southern California to San Diego.[1] The object was to transport Colorado coal to the Pacific coast where it could be used in industrial plants or shipped overseas.

The chief engineer, engaged to survey and design the railroad, was Robert Brewster Stanton, a civil engineer who had specialized in building difficult mountain railroads and who was convinced that the "water level" route would prove feasible. Although Stanton directed all field operations, the man actually in charge was Frank M. Brown, the company president.

Robert B. Stanton planned to build a railroad through all of the Colorado River canyons, from Grand Junction to Yuma, then overland to San Diego. He later dredged for gold in Glen Canyon.

*Utah State Historical Society*

---

1. Primary sources for information on the railroad survey are Robert B. Stanton, *The Colorado River Survey–Robert B. Stanton and the Denver, Colorado Canyon and Pacific Railroad,* Dwight L. Smith and C. Gregory Crampton, eds., (Salt Lake City: Howe Brothers, 1987), and Robert Brewster Stanton, *Down the Colorado*, ed. Dwight L. Smith (Norman: University of Oklahoma Press, 1965).

Robert B. Stanton (left, at end of table) and his men eat Christmas dinner, 1889, beside the Lee's Ferry Fort, before resuming their railroad survey through the canyons of the Colorado River.
*Utah State Historical Society*

On their voyage down the river toward Lee's Ferry, the Brown-Stanton party had suffered many accidents, most of them in the wild rapids of Cataract Canyon. Two of their five boats had been sunk, and they had lost most of their supplies.

In his journal, Stanton complained about the "light, brittle, cedar hunting and pleasure boats" that Brown had supplied them with. What Stanton didn't mention was that the round-bottom boats were dangerously unstable in white water. Yet with only three of these inadequate boats left, the party was preparing for an even more hazardous voyage through Marble and Grand Canyons. To make matters worse, they carried no life preservers!

Brown finally returned with supplies, and on July 9, 1889, the group left Lee's Ferry to continue the survey. They didn't get far before tragedy struck. Somehow the boats made it through Badger Creek and Soap Creek Rapids, but just below the latter rapid, Frank Brown and crewman Harry McDonald were caught by an eddy current in midstream. Without warning the cross current flipped the boat over, spilling the men into the water. Without a life preserver, Brown sank quickly to his death. McDonald, who managed to reach the left bank, ran for help. Stanton, close behind in another skiff, could do nothing more than retrieve Brown's notebook, which bobbed to the surface. This quick and fateful accident happened just twelve miles downstream from Lee's Ferry.

Probably not realizing that his round-bottom boats were dangerously inappropriate, chief engineer Stanton made a major error by deciding to continue on into Marble Canyon.

On July 15, two crewmen, Peter M. Hansbrough and Henry Richards were caught in a current that welled up against a rock wall at Mile 25.2. In their efforts to push away from the wall, the two men capsized the boat, and both were quickly drowned.

After this second tragic accident, Stanton decided to abandon the voyage. Near Vasey's Paradise, thirty-two miles below Lee's Ferry, the boats and supplies were cached. Then Stanton and his men climbed out to the west by way of a narrow side canyon. Reaching the floor of House Rock Valley, they walked north to the VT Ranch at the base of the Kaibab Plateau. From there they traveled to Kanab and finally reached Denver.

Undaunted by the tragic deaths, Stanton was completely sold on the idea of building a watergrade railroad down the canyons. His enthusiasm convinced the New York financiers, who agreed to back him on a second voyage. Stanton even bought an interest in the company. Exceptionally heavy boats were constructed with watertight compartments. Furthermore, life preservers were included among the supplies.

Stanton's second expedition put into the river at the mouth of North Wash, near the head of Glen Canyon, on December 10, 1889, with the group expected to spend the winter months on the Colorado completing the survey.

Traveling in three boats, Stanton and his eleven men arrived at Lee's Ferry on a windy afternoon, December 23. There they made camp near the old fort, rested, and began preparations for the next part of the trip. For Christmas dinner they set up a table in front of the fort and had a regal feast: turkey, beef, ox heart, chicken, Colorado River salmon, plum pudding, cake and pie—some of it courtesy of Warren Johnson and his two wives.

Three days later they shoved off, and by December 31 had passed the point where Frank Brown was drowned. But they were to have troubles of their own. The next day, January 1, 1890, photographer Franklin A. Nims, while trying to climb high enough to include all three boats in a photograph, fell from a ledge, breaking his leg

Unlike the disastrously inadequate boats of the Stanton's first expedition, the *Bonnie Jean* (shown here), and the others used by the second expedition, 1889-1890, were heavy and unwieldy, but they were sturdy and were employed with success. *University of Utah*

and cracking his skull. Obviously Nims had to be taken out of the canyon. Through a side canyon, Stanton ascended to House Rock Valley and proceeded to Lee's Ferry, where he arrived about midnight. The next morning, Warren Johnson, accompanied by his son Frank, hitched up his team and wagon for the rough trip to the rim of Marble Canyon. Meanwhile Stanton's men slowly and painstakingly lifted Nims, on a makeshift stretcher, up the steep, rough west side of House Rock Canyon (a Marble Canyon tributary). Occasionally the stretcher had to be swung along by ropes around and over vertical drops.

Finally, with Nims sent off with Johnson and his son, and with Stanton himself now acting as photographer, the expedition resumed its voyage. Although there were many more adventures, including a smashed boat, no lives were lost. Stanton felt his trip was a complete success. With the initial survey for the D.C.C.& P. Railroad completed, the results, in the opinion of the doughty engineer, were highly favorable. Possibly Stanton could almost hear the steam engines rumbling through the canyons, carrying coal from Colorado to the industrial plants of the Pacific Coast.

New York financiers might have been intrigued by Stanton's dream, but when it came

Franklin A. Nims, photographer for the Stanton expedition, in front of Lee's Ferry Fort, Christmas, 1889. A week later, on January 1, 1890, Nims fell from a ledge in Marble Canyon and had to be lifted out of the canyon on a stretcher.          *University of Utah*

Stanton (far right), and his expedition after successfully completing their voyage and railroad survey down the Grand Canyon. Photographed at Needles, California, March 24, 1890.

*Utah State Historical Society*

time to put up millions of dollars for railroad construction, they backed out. Perhaps they could discern that Stanton's enthusiasm had overcome his judgment, that he was dismissing such difficulties as removing lofty, nearly vertical cliffs, as "minor rock removal." Stanton campaigned for funds throughout the 1890's, but finally turned his attention to other enterprises.[2]

## STANTON - MINING IN GLEN CANYON

While in Glen Canyon, Stanton had noticed fine particles of gold in the sand of the river bed. Attracted by the placer gold possibilities, he began planning construction of a massive dredge to extract this gold. Even before the dredge was actually built in 1900, (near present-day Bullfrog Marina), Stanton boated up and down Glen Canyon, staking out claims he expected to mine with a whole fleet of such dredges.[3]

Some of Stanton's claims were located just upstream from Lee's Ferry, one of the few places that he could reach by land. In 1899 Stanton had his men put in a road along the left (south) river bank from the ferry upstream about one and one-half miles. The road, which goes nowhere and serves no purpose, is still visible today. Stanton's only reason for building it was to "prove up" his claims in the area by doing required assessment work (see Tour Site No. 13)

Unfortunately for Stanton, his big dredge operation was a failure. Gold was certainly present, but in such fine particles that it would not settle on the amalgamators. In late 1901 Stanton ceased all operations, abandoned his dredge, and placed his company in receivership.

Although Robert B. Stanton's mining operations were the most extensive at the time, much prospecting and mining occurred in Glen Canyon and in the San Juan River Canyon in the 1880's and 1890's. During these years many prospectors passed Lee's Ferry, either on their way in or out of the canyon. Several entered upper Glen Canyon at Hite, 140 miles upstream, and worked their way downstream to Lee's Ferry. Most of their efforts were concentrated on gravel bars lying several feet above the river. Some gold was found, but few, if any, struck it rich. Most prospectors soon discovered that expenses almost always exceeded income. By 1900 only an occasional prospector was seen along the river above Lee's Ferry.[4]

A few men, like Stanton, believed that the gold in the sands of the Colorado could be recovered with better technology and equipment. Stanton found that even with his big investments, the technology of 1900 was not equal to the task. A few years later, however, another man even more visionary perhaps than Stanton, felt he had the answer. His name was Charles H. Spencer.

2. Stanton's detailed railroad building proposal appeared as Robert Brewster Stanton, "Availability of the Canyons of the Colorado River of the West for Railway Purposes," *Transactions of the American Society of Civil Engineers* No. 26 (April 1892), pp. 283-361.

3. C. Gregory Crampton and Dwight L. Smith, eds. *The Hoskaninni Papers: Mining in Glen Canyon, 1897-1902* (Salt Lake City: University of Utah, 1961) Anthropological Papers No. 54.

4. C. Gregory Crampton, *Historical Sites in Glen Canyon–Mouth of San Juan River to Lee's Ferry* (Salt Lake City: University of Utah, 1960) Anthropological Papers

# THE PROMOTER— CHARLES H. SPENCER

$C$harles H. Spencer is an enigma in the history of the canyons. Although he pursued the quest for gold, he seemed to enjoy the pursuit more than the gold, especially when he was spending other people's money. A product of the wilderness, Spencer obviously had a thirst for adventure, a love for wild scenery, and a passion for freedom. Virtually unschooled himself, Spencer's attitude toward so-called "experts" bordered on disgust, a conviction that they lacked imagination.

Charlie Spencer could and did endure harsh weather, lack of food, and hostile Indians. He performed heavy, backbreaking toil, and, above all, he did almost everything as well, if not better, than any of his men. Following him into the wilderness with only a vague promise of future pay, they eagerly pursued his schemes, and, when all had failed, they spoke well of him.[1]

In 1909, Spencer and his men set up a crusher and amalgamator on the San Juan River, about 125 river miles above Lee's Ferry. Their object was to extract gold from rocks of the Wingate formation, a deep red, broken sandstone frequently exposed in the canyon country. After some laborious testing, however, someone discovered that the Chinle formation, lying just below the Wingate, contained as much, if not more, gold. Moreover, the purple and gray banded Chinle was easily loosened with water and could be sluiced with high pressure hoses. Their only question then was where to find sufficient fuel to run the pumps.

At this point two wandering prospectors appeared, discussed the problem with Spencer, and suggested moving the operations to Lee's Ferry, where access was much easier. The Chinle shale, they pointed out, was also exposed at Lee's Ferry. Furthermore, coal deposits were known to exist in the cliffs a few miles to the northeast. Quickly realizing that the coal could fuel boilers that would power pumps to sluice the Chinle, Charlie headed for Lee's Ferry.

Spencer and some of his men were led by a Navajo over an old Indian trail across rugged country near Navajo Mountain to the eastern side, near the top, of the Echo Cliffs. Then they followed the trail across a succession of deep, dry gullies just south of the Echo Peaks, and finally, within sight of the Colorado River, crested the ridge just east of the peaks. At this point the Navajo guide picked up a stone and tossed it on a large pile of stones. He said that every passing Navajo added a stone in commemoration of a battle between the Utes and Navajos in this vicinity years ago.

---

1. Albert H. Jones, "Spencer Mining Operations on the San Juan River and in Glen Canyon," original manuscript in possession of W. L. Rusho.

Charles H. Spencer promoted large sums of money to bring mechanized mining to Lee's Ferry.
*Charles H. Spencer*

Someone remarked that this old Indian trail was the "Buzzard's Highline." The name caught on and was applied to the trail which was so known for many years.[2] Today this trail is all but forgotten, and except at certain points, it is so faint that it is almost impossible to follow (see Tour Site No. 20).

From the crest of the Echo Cliffs, Spencer and his men obtained their first view of Lee's Ferry, about two thousand feet below. From that point the Buzzard's Highline trail wound down the immense sand slope to the river bank, which the men followed a mile and a half downstream to the ferry. Arriving in May 1910, Spencer immediately studied prospects of the Chinle shale, here exposed as a wide strata about three hundred yards from the river behind the old fort. The river would provide water. A boiler and pumps could be installed to convey water under high pressure to sluice the shale. Charlie's only question at this point was fuel: where were the reputed seams of coal?

After examining several dry but rugged canyons, Spencer's men finally located a sizeable vein of coal on a distant branch of Warm Creek, a tributary of the Colorado that joined the river twenty-eight miles upstream in Glen Canyon. Eager to test the gold prospects, Spencer began his experiments at Lee's Ferry even before he obtained coal, using driftwood for fuel.[3]

First he experimented with a "pipe dredge," a device that injected air and water under high pressure directly down into the ground, forcing sand and fine particles up through a casing. Spencer tried the pipe dredge on a gravel bed near the river bank, but he had great difficulty making it work. Just below the surface the dredge hit coarse rock and would sink no further. The experiment was given up as a failure.

Undaunted, Spencer went ahead with his plan to recover gold from the Chinle by sluicing the shale over an amalgamator filled with mercury. If everything works correctly, the mercury in the riffles of the amalgamator will absorb the gold particles. Then the mercury itself can be boiled off, leaving free gold. Spencer's men activated a

---

2. Arthur C. Waller to W.L. Rusho, 15 November 1962.
3. Jones, "Spencer Mining Operations."

Setup for the Lovett pipe dredge at Lee's Ferry, American Placer Company. The framework, ladder, winch, etc., mark the position of the dredge pipe. Probably used a centrifugal riffle in the square box at right with amalgamators arranged in the sloping box beneath. Pipelines in the foreground run to the boiler. This dredge was unsuccessful in penetrating the coarse gold-bearing gravels near bedrock. Taken in 1911 *Kolb Bros. Collection, Northern Arizona University*

High-pressure hose is used to sluice the Chinle Shale at Lee's Ferry. Water is pumped from the Colorado River in background. Sluiced material is then carried by a flume to an amalgamator setup for attempted removal of the gold.     *Charles H. Spencer*

big boiler and pumps near the river's edge, thereby pumping water through hoses to high pressure nozzles aimed at the shale. The water dissolved the soft Chinle and carried it down a long flume back toward the river where an amalgamator was set up.

It should be mentioned here that the Chinle shale does in fact contain small amounts of gold in the form of "dust," or microscopic particles. In terms of value the gold runs only a few cents for each cubic yard of shale. Spencer, of course, was either a victim of erroneous assays, or he was working on his own wishful thinking that the values would actually prove to be much higher.

Spencer's first "runs" of shale over the amalgamators were made in the spring of 1911. At first everything worked fine, but it soon became apparent that the mercury in the amalgamators was becoming clogged. Instead of being absorbed by the mercury, the gold was passing on out with the tailings. The plates were scraped, new mercury was applied, and more material was sluiced across them. The same result. What in the complex Chinle formation was causing a film to form on the mercury? Tests were suspended until a chemical analysis could be run.

Numerous efforts were made to solve the problem, but nothing was successful. Several of Spencer's chemists made tests, and samples were sent to outside experts. Spencer said later that he even sent samples to the famous Madame Curie in Paris, who reported the presence of a foreign element that could not be identified.[4]

Even with this setback Spencer would not admit the possibility of failure. While chemists and mining engineers wrestled with the problem, he shifted his crew to bringing coal to Lee's Ferry.

## THE SPENCER TRAIL

At first Spencer thought that mules might be used to haul coal from the mines on Warm Creek. With this in mind he ordered his men to build the incredible trail up the steep Echo Cliffs immediately east of his mining operations at Lee's Ferry. Spencer and his men knew about and frequently used Dominguez Pass, (which they called the "Old Mormon Trail"), but it was difficult. In addition, the trail to the pass started two and one-half miles up the Paria. Certainly a good trail right above the work site would be a marked improvement.

---

4. Interview with Charles H. Spencer, 22 August 1962.

Spencer's trail was actually built during the late summer and fall of 1910 by men using shovels, picks, and crowbars.[5] On at least one occasion, Spencer used the trail construction to promote his enterprise financially. He told the men that a group of investors from Chicago was coming for a visit and asked his workmen to put on a good and noisy show. When these officials crossed on the ferry and arrived at the river bank, the workmen high on the trail began setting off sticks of dynamite, one every few minutes. When the investors left they were apparently quite satisfied that Spencer's workmen were earning their money, and that the project was progressing satisfactorily.[6]

Spencer later claimed that the trail was laid out by his white mule, Pete. "I just told him what to do and he started up the cliff. I followed him, marking the trail."[7] While admitting that Pete was a superior mule, none of the workmen could recall later that Pete had anything to do with laying out the trail.

In spite of booming displays for visiting dignitaries, the trail was eventually finished to the top. Spencer and his men used it in preference to the Dominguez Pass trail, but the Spencer trail was rarely used to carry coal. Nevertheless, it is one of the more spectacular reminders of Charles H. Spencer's mining operations at Lee's Ferry. Although eroded in places, it may still be traversed to the top of the Echo Cliffs (see Tour Site No. 2).

## THE STEAMBOAT

Despite the new trail up the cliffs, Spencer was reluctant to decide on mules to transport coal. If his mining operation were ever to get beyond the experimental

A pack train headed for the Warm Creek coal mine, heads up the Spencer Trail above Lee's Ferry in 1910, just after the trail was built.                                                                    *Arthur C. Waller*

5. Arthur C. Waller to W. L. Rusho, 27 March 1965.
6. Interview with Albert Leach, Kanab, Utah, 18 February 1961.
7. Interview with Charles H. Spencer, 22 August 1962.

state, he would need far more coal than could be provided by such a slow, inefficient system. But there was another way–transportation by water.

The coal vein that had been located on a high branch of Warm Creek Canyon lay about twenty miles north of the Colorado River. Normally Warm Creek was dry, carrying water only for brief periods after storms. A wagon road, Spencer surmised, could be built down Warm Creek canyon to the river. From there the coal could be moved by boat twenty-eight river miles to Lee's Ferry.

While some men opened the mines, others began building a crude road down Warm Creek. Still others began construction of a barge at its mouth. Sometime during the early fall days of 1911 the first load of coal was taken by ox-drawn wagon down the dry canyon to the Colorado and loaded on the barge. Three or four men took the coal-laden barge from Warm Creek through Glen Canyon to Lee's Ferry, using green aspen poles to push it away from the cliffs.[8]

The obvious question was how to get the barge back upstream for another trip. Logically, a tug boat was needed. A twenty-six-foot launch, christened the *Violet Louise*, was purchased and brought to Lee's Ferry to do the job.[9] Unfortunately, the *Violet Louise* was far too underpowered to push a big barge up a river current or to pull away from shallow sandbars that lay hidden in the murky brown water.

Sharlot Hall, the Arizona Territorial Historian, happened to be visiting at Lee's Ferry on August 7, 1911, when the *Violet Louise* arrived on an ox-drawn wagon. She

Sharlot Hall, Arizona Territorial Historian and tireless promoter of Statehood, traveled the Arizona Strip by wagon in 1911, crossed at Lee's Ferry, talked with Charlie Spencer, and took remarkably good photographs.

*Phoenix Public Library*

---

8. Interview with Albert Leach, 23 October 1962.
9. Interview with Charles H. Spencer, 22 August 1962.

wrote that:

> *The new gasoline boat was too long to go round the sharp turns of the*
> *"dug way"; it was unloaded and launched at the foot of the grade and*
> *came up over the half mile of rapids like a seabird.*[10]

Even before the *Violet Louise* arrived, one of the Chicago officials from Spencer's company, Dr. Julius Koebig, came up with a novel suggestion: Why not build a big steamboat to carry the coal? Charlie Spencer said later he wasn't consulted on the steamboat idea and didn't even know about it until the boat had been ordered from a firm in San Francisco.

At any rate, the craft agreed upon was to be the largest boat ever afloat on the Colorado River north of the Grand Canyon. In length it was to measure ninety-two feet and in width twenty-five feet. It would have a large steam boiler that would power a twelve-foot wide stern paddlewheel.

Built during 1911 in San Francisco, the steamboat was dismantled, placed on railroad cars, and shipped to the railhead at Marysvale, Utah, fully two hundred miles from the mouth of Warm Creek. When it arrived in Marysvale in September, 1911, the parts were placed on a series of wagons for the rest of the trip.

Near Circleville, Utah, on a steep slope, the wagon road contained a tight elbow turn. All the wagons made this difficult turn except the last one carrying the heaviest load, the boiler. The wheels on this last wagon slipped off the road, the chains snapped, and the boiler rolled seventy-five feet down the embankment. It took an entire month and some ingenious methods to drag the boiler up and reposition it on the wagon.[11]

When all parts had finally arrived at the mouth of Warm Creek, the long process of reconstructing the boat was begun under the direction of a shipwright sent from the San Francisco firm.

10. Hall, Sharlot, *Sharlot Hall on the Arizona Strip*, p. 52.
11. Interview with Charles H. Spencer, 22 August 1962.

The hull of the steamboat *Charles H. Spencer* is reconstructed at the mouth of Warm Creek. November 1911.                    *Kolb Bros. Collection, Northern Arizona University*

Workman engaged in construction of the superstructure for the steamboat *Charles H. Spencer* at the mouth of Warm Creek. None are identified. Photographed in November 1911 by the Kolb Brothers on their trip down the river.          *Kolb Brothers Collection, Northern Arizona Unviersity*

The Steamboat *Charles H. Spencer* is almost completed at the mouth of Warm Creek. February, 1912.                    *National Archives*

In early November, 1911, Ellsworth and Emery Kolb, traveling by boat down the Colorado River, paused at Warm Creek to watch the men reconstruct the steamboat. Ellsworth wrote:

> On rounding a turn we saw the strange spectacle of fifteen or twenty men at work on the half-constructed hull of a flat-bottomed steamboat, over sixty feet in length... It was a strange sight, here in this out-of-the-way corner of the world. Some men with heavy sledges were under the boat, driving large spikes into the planking.[12]

Work was suspended during mid-winter but was finished early in the spring of 1912. Despite Spencer's professed lack of enthusiasm for the boat, the craft was christened the *Charles H. Spencer*, and the name was painted on the bow.

Finding a willing crew for the steamboat was not easy, for few of Spencer's workmen had ever done any boating of this type. Most had backgrounds in farming, ranching, mining, or carpentry, and few of them wished to tempt fate on a steamboat plying the treacherous Colorado River. Only one, Pete Hanna, who was designated captain, had ever operated a steamboat. Finally a group of reluctant individuals was persuaded to board the steamer for a run downriver to Lee's Ferry.

Bull-whackers, meanwhile, were each laboring to drive a five-yoke team of oxen (ten oxen) that pulled two wagons of coal—from the mine to the mouth of Warm Creek, where the steamboat was being assembled. On one occasion, having unloaded the coal and while returned up the creek, two scouts, far in advance of the wagons, heard a flash flood coming. They raced back to warn the drivers. Four of the five teams and wagons were able to reach high ground, but the fifth was too slow. The eight-foot high flood caught the back wheels of the last wagon, tipped it over, and dragged wagons and ten oxen into the maelstrom. Fortunately, the driver jumped clear just in time.

When the steamboat *Charles H. Spencer* was completed, about 3 or 4 tons of coal were loaded on the main deck of the steamboat. Hanna ordered the boiler fired, and when steam pressure was up, he sounded the whistle. The big stern paddlewheel began to turn. Now it was just twenty-eight miles to go!

About a hundred yards away from the launch point, however, the boat, ignominiously, ran hard aground on a hidden sandbar. Working with shovels, the men dug all day to free the unwieldy craft. Night was spent in a rocky cove beneath the cliffs of Glen Canyon.[13]

When they started off the next day, Hanna tried a different technique. He directed that the boat be turned around so as to head *upstream*, even though it would be moving *downstream*. In other words, it went backward down the river, with the paddlewheel serving to slow its downstream plunge. This method imparted maneuverability and helped avoid further mishaps.

Late that day the *Charles H. Spencer* backed its way into Lee's Ferry, where the workmen on shore cheered its arrival. It thus appeared that the boat had proven itself. However, Pete Hanna, being the cautious type, directed that only a small amount of coal be unloaded, for no one knew how much coal it would take to get back to Warm Creek.

---

12. Kolb, Ellsworth, *Through the Grand Canyon, From Wyoming to Mexico*, (New York: The Macmillan Co, 1914), p. 171.
13. Interview with Bill Wilson, Clarkdale, Ariz. 24 September 1961.

The *Charles H. Spencer* awaits cast-off time at the river bank at Lee's Ferry. On board are Pete Hanna, captain; unidentified crewman; "Rip Van Winkle" Schneider, "Smithy" Smith, Jerry Johnson, Bert Leach, and Al Byers. Photo taken in 1912.          *Kolb Brothers Studio, Grand Canyon*

The *Charles H. Spencer*, at Lee's Ferry Fort. Since the steamboat was used only on an infrequent experimental basis, it was generally moored to the river bank with no one on board.

*National Park Service,*
*Lee's Ferry*

Lee's Ferry, photographed in September 1962. The Fort and the Post Office are at right. The buildings at left were built by Charles H. Spencer and his men for use in the mining of Chinle shale. Initially, they were used for (l to r) laboratory, blacksmith shop, cook's quarters, main house, unknown (built subsequent to Spencer), and two bunkhouses. All the Spencer buildings, except one bunkhouse, were destroyed in 1967.

On the return trip it became apparent that the steamboat had to run full steam to make even slow progress against the current. When Warm Creek was reached a check showed that most of the coal had been consumed. Many people, including the author of this book (in the first edition), have repeated the humorous story that the boat consumed more coal than it could carry. It's a good story, but not true. A comparison with similar steamboats that plied the lower Colorado River a few years earlier reveals that, had the *Spencer* been equipped with large coal bins (which it was not), it probably could have carried up to 50 tons or more, while its consumption was probably no more than two tons per day.[14]

Hanna and his crew loaded on a few tons of coal, brought the craft back to Lee's Ferry, and tied it up at the bank. Except for Hanna, the crew quit or were assigned to other jobs. Coal, in quantity, was not yet needed, so the steamboat operation could wait.

At this point the record becomes more hazy. Witness statements confirm that a new crew was subsequently assigned to the steamboat, and this second crew is the one pictured on the deck in the accompanying photograph. A member of this second crew, Bert Leech, reported riding the *Charles H. Spencer* from Warm Creek down to Lee's Ferry. Some time later, he watched from the bank as some men tried to head upstream in the steamboat, but the craft had insufficient power to buck the current. "It was therefore beached and never ran again." Leech said.[15]

14. *Submerged Cultural Resources Site Report, Charles H. Spencer Mining Operation and Paddle Wheel Steamboat,* (Glen Canyon National Recreation Area, National Park Service, 1987) p. 98
15. Interview with Albert Leach, 18 February 1961.

Jerry Johnson, one of the Johnson family that operated the ferry, also worked for Spencer as a crewman of the steamboat. As a witness in the famous River Bed Case in 1929 (to determine ownership of the Colorado River bed), Johnson stated that the steamboat towed a barge up to Warm Creek and that the barge was then loaded with coal. Three or four men then free-floated the barge to Lee's Ferry, using poles to keep it from hitting the cliffs. The steamboat apparently followed.[16]

The record of exactly how many trips the *Charles H. Spencer* actually made will forever remain uncertain, a victim of incomplete, and often conflicting, recollections by witnesses. Probably the closest figure is five one-way trips, three with the first crew and two with the second.

But more coal was still not required. Spencer and his chemists were never able to extract gold from the Chinle. When they failed to discover why the mercury in the amalgamators quickly clogged and stopped absorbing gold, Spencer's entire operation was doomed. The big steamboat was never used again.

Three years later, in 1915, flood water forced driftwood under the boat. Then when the high water subsided, the boat settled on the driftwood, tipped on its side, and sank in a few feet of water.[17] In later years someone ripped off the superstructure, probably for the lumber. Today the weathered hull and boiler of the *Charles H. Spencer* lie where the steamboat sank, highly visible in today's clear water (see Tour Site No. 3).

A National Park Service study of the *Charles H. Spencer* in 1986 concluded:

> The steamboat was and has been characterized as a failure by association
> rather than by a careful examination of the facts. Charles H. Spencer
> became a scapegoat and was used as an excuse to help explain the collapse
> of a poorly-conceived mining operation. Charlie Spencer's steamboat

16. Testimony of Jeremiah Johnson in United States v. Utah, (Supreme Court of the United States, No. 14, October Term, 1929). Abstract in Narrative Form of the Testimony Taken Before the Special Master, 2 vols. (Washington: Government Printing Office, 1931), copy at Utah State Historical Society, Salt Lake City.
17. Interview with Bert Leech, 18 February 1961

In 1915, on the river bank at Lee's Ferry lies the steamboat *Charles H. Spencer*, abandoned by Spencer and his men when the mining venture failed in 1913.　　　　*U.S. Geological Survey*

was not abandoned because it was a technological failure, the steamboat was abandoned because the men and the mine were an economic failure.[18]

## SPENCER - OPERATION'S END

Directly north of the old fort about two hundred yards is the scar in the gray Chinle shale made by Spencer's hydraulic sluicing operation. An old boiler used by Spencer lies on the flat near the point where it was used.

While at Lee's Ferry, Charlie Spencer engaged in a number of related enterprises and side operations. For instance, another complete hydraulic and sluicing operation was carried out at the town of Pahreah, about 40 miles up the Paria River. The Pahreah operation also concentrated on the Chinle shale and also encountered the same difficulty—clogged amalgamator plates.

Usually, he operated as local manager for a Chicago-based company, the American Placer Corporation, but he worked with other companies, with different investors, including one called the Black Sand and Gold Recovery Company. Rarely was there enough money available to pay the workmen for their work. In lieu of wages Spencer promised his men a certain amount of acreage in an irrigation project, (in this case the name he used was the Arizutah Irrigation Company), that he said he was planning to build on the Paria River about thirty miles to the north. In his pitch to his men, Spencer would expound on the obvious fertility of the Lonely Dell Ranch, which

---

18. *Submerged Cultural Resources Site Report,* National Park Service, 1987

The Thomas Royal Flyer, first automobile to reach Lee's Ferry, broke an axle on the return trip and was towed back into Flagstaff by a team a team of oxen. *Charles H. Spencer*

obtained its water from the Paria. Thus many men continued on at their mining tasks without pay, dreaming of the day they would become rich landowners.[19]

Charlie Spencer also brought the first automobile into Lee's Ferry. It was a long convertible called a Thomas Royal Flyer, vintage about 1910, and for its day a very prestigious automobile. Since none of Spencer's men could drive, the company sent along an optional extra–a chauffeur.

To everyone's surprise the Royal Flyer came in from Flagstaff without trouble and was crossed on the ferry. The next day Spencer ordered the chauffeur to return to Flagstaff to pick up some needed chemicals. When days passed and the auto still did not return, Spencer sent out a search party, which found the car in a ravine near Flagstaff. The chauffeur had apparently abandoned the car after accidentally veering off the road and breaking an axle. A ten-yoke team of oxen was sent from Lee's Ferry to tow the auto into Flagstaff, where it was sold.[20]

Charlie Spencer even had a hand in operating the ferry. After Emett's departure in 1909, the ferryboat was operated by whatever cowhands of the Grand Canyon Cattle Company happened to be at the crossing. That this arrangement provided the public less than optimum service was obvious. Needing reliable ferrymen, the company called on the men most qualified–sons of Warren Johnson.

In February 1910, Jerry Johnson arrived from Wyoming and assumed the role of ferryman. In July Frank Johnson also moved to Lee's Ferry to assist his brother. From that time until the end of ferry service, Johnson family members held official responsibility for its operation.[21]

In June 1910, Coconino County bought the ferry from the cattle company because the county was concerned that the ferry remain a vital link in the highway system, yet the cattle company was reluctant to spend required funds for maintenance.[22]

19. Interview with Albert Leach, 23 October 1962.
20. Interview with Arthur C. Waller, 28 September 1962.
21. Interview with Frank Johnson, 28 October 1962.
22. "History of Lee's Ferry." *Coconino Sun*, McClintock file, Phoenix Public Library.

Even though the Johnson brothers were the official ferrymen, this did not mean that a Johnson was always on hand to help cross the river. A number of cowhands from the cattle company, as well as Spencer's workmen, often operated the boat. Charlie Spencer and his men even built a new ferryboat and when necessary made needed repairs to the ferry equipment.

Inexperienced hands, however, sometimes got into trouble. In March 1911, Spencer's men finished installation of a new track cable, and since one of the men had to make a trip to Flagstaff, they decided to take him across the river. No one bothered to summon one of the Johnson brothers from the ranch. Unfamiliar with the ropes and pulleys, the crew allowed the bow rope to become too slack, causing the boat to stop in mid-river and begin to nose under the water. Finally the boat lunged clear under, throwing a team, a wagon, and men overboard. One man, Pres Apperson, was drowned, while the other men reached shore only with great difficulty.[23]

## SPENCER - THE AFTERMATH

By 1913, almost everyone associated with Spencer had left Lee's Ferry. Spencer himself took on new enterprises in other parts of the country, yet he never forgot the Chinle shale. He eventually learned that what caused the amalgamators to clog up was rhenium, a rare metallic element completely unknown in 1912. Rhenium can be removed by simple procedures discovered long after Spencer left Lee's Ferry. Learning of these techniques in later years, Spencer returned to his still-valid claims at the ghost town of Pahreah in 1962 and 1963, when he was over ninety years old. His objective was no longer gold, but the rhenium itself, which is a highly valuable superconductor of electricity. He and his daughter, Mrs. Muriel Pope, set up camp at Pahreah and ran a series of chemical tests on the Chinle shale. Spencer, however, claimed his success was being blocked by international mining cartels that didn't want his vast body of ore to be put on the market.[24]

Whatever the true story, Spencer never struck it rich. During the years from 1914 to 1920, he devised an elaborate scheme to channel, store, and distribute water from the San Francisco Peaks to Flagstaff, Winslow, and the South Rim. Some of his planned features, such as short tunnels, canals, and pipelines, were actually built, but he ran into opposition from vested interests of some landowners, and the scheme had to be abandoned. Too bad. It might actually have worked![25]

Although Spencer is now dead, he will not soon be forgotten. The canyon country has never seen anything quite like him.[26]

In February, 1967, on orders from the Superintendent of the Glen Canyon National Recreation Area, a number of rock buildings that Spencer had erected at Lee's Ferry were bulldozed to oblivion. Ironically, the reason was to "protect them from vandalism." Secretary of the Interior Stewart Udall, who was a descendant of David King Udall, a pioneer Mormon emigrant who crossed at Lee's Ferry into Arizona in 1880, was so

---

23. Jones, "Spencer Mining Operations."
24. Interview with Charles H. Spencer at Paria ghost town, Utah, 22 August 1962.
25. Valeen Tippetts Avery, *Free Running–Charlie Spencer and His Most Remarkable Water Project*, (Flagstaff, AZ: Flagstaff Westerners, 1981).
26. Spencer died at age 95 in Los Angeles on February 10, 1968.

incensed by this unwise and unjustified action that he ordered the Superintendent shipped out, exiled, to another post. Today, local National Park Service officials, who of course had nothing to do with the incident in 1967, readily apologize for the mistake.[27]

## OTHER MINING NEAR LEE'S FERRY

Sporadic mining activity has occurred near Lee's Ferry at intervals throughout this century. During the depression of the 1930's, a few prospectors searched for gold in Glen Canyon, but their efforts soon proved fruitless.[28]

During the 1950's hopeful uranium seekers armed with geiger counters swarmed all through the canyon country, looking especially in Shinarump conglomerate, where uranium was often located in petrified wood. At Lee's Ferry, the Shinarump is prominent in Lee's Backbone and in the four hundred-foot high bench below the Vermilion Cliffs. A number of uranium claims were staked, mines were opened, and access roads were bulldozed, but in general, uranium mineralization in the Lee's Ferry area was found to be quite low. The only mine near Lee's Ferry ever to ship ore was the El Pequito, located northwest of the Lee's Ferry Ranch. Within a few years after uranium activity first began, all mines were abandoned and prospecting had entirely ceased.[29]

Lee's Ferry Fort, with an addition to the west end, was used as a cook house-mess hall by Charlie Spencer's crew, posing here in front of the fort about 1911.          *Charles H. Spencer*

27. Interview with Superintendent John Lancaster, Glen Canyon National Recreation Area, Page, AZ, 6 March 1991.
28. Crampton, *Historical Sites in Glen Canyon.*
29. David Allen Phoenix, *Geology of the Lees Ferry Area, Coconino County, Arizona* (Washington: Government Printing Office, 1963), U.S. Geological Survey Bulletin 1137.14

# THE DAM BUILDERS

Charlie Spencer once said that Glen Canyon Dam was bound to fail, primarily because it rests on layers of rock strata that contain the Chinle shale, the crumbly, slimy-when-wet formation that Charlie once worked for its gold content. In his nineties when he made the statement, Charlie was not dissuaded by the fact that the Chinle is sandwiched between solid rock layers several hundred feet below the concrete of the dam and that sheer pressure holds all strata in its place. "I don't care what the geologists say; the dam will fail when the water seeps down to the Chinle," Spencer declared.[1]

If the dam had been built where early Government engineers first recommended, Charlie might have been right, for the Chinle is exposed at Lee's Ferry, and their choice damsite during the 1920's was not far away. In fact the proposed dam was often referred to as the Lee's Ferry Dam.

Before 1914 the great plateau canyons of the river were largely unknown and unvisited by dam builders, who surmised that dams in the big canyons would be prohibitively expensive if not technically impossible.

Anyone with imagination, however, could see the great economic potential of the water then flowing to the sea. As far back as 1890, Major John Wesley Powell, writing of the lower Colorado, predicted:

> *If the waters [of the Colorado River] are to be used, great works must be*
> *constructed costing millions of dollars, and then ultimately a region of*

1. Interview with Charles H. Spencer, Riverside, California, 18 June 1961.

Laden with a wide variety of emergency equipment, a U.S. Geological Survey crew pauses on their adventurous automobile trip to Lee's Ferry in 1915. *U.S. Geological Survey*

Enroute from Flagstaff to Lee's Ferry in 1923 to map the Grand Canyon, the government survey crew has to stop and repair the road.                    *U.S. Geological Survey*

*country can be irrigated larger than was ever cultivated along the Nile,*
*and all the products of Egypt will flourish therein.*[2]

The art of designing and building dams advanced rapidly during the early 1900's until, by the time of World War I, engineers had gained enough confidence to consider placing a major dam in one of the Colorado River canyons. According to Eugene, "E.C." LaRue, of the U.S. Geological Survey, writing in an influential report in 1916, a number of storage reservoirs in the canyons and irrigation projects along tributary streams were potentially feasible.[3]

Irrigation possibilities were important, but so also was the need for main stream flood control, since the highly erratic Colorado had repeatedly devastated parts of California and Arizona. The high potential for hydro electric power generation also greatly interested urban officials in the larger cities–particularly those in Los Angeles.

In the first half of the twentieth century, the people of the United States, and particularly those in the American West, almost universally believed that anything that would help the economy and increase the population was, *a priori*, a good thing.

2. John Wesley Powell, "The Irrigable Lands of the Arid Region," *Century Illustrated Monthly Magazine* 39 (1890): 766-776.
3. E. C. LaRue, *Colorado River and Its Utilization* (Washington: Government Printing Office, 1916) U.S. Geological Survey Water Supply Paper 395.

A U.S. Geological Survey crew pauses during the installation of the river cable for the gauging station at Lee's Ferry in 1921.                    *U.S. Geological Survey*

Radio "set-up" and part of the Grand Canyon survey party at Lee's Ferry. South bank of the river. July 28, 1923.                                                    *U.S. Geological Survey*

Except for a few faint voices from people like John Muir in California, environmental preservation was unheard of. Thus when engineers set off down the canyons to appraise damsites, they did so with overwhelming public support.

Necessary to any detailed investigation of the canyons were high quality topographic maps that showed exact distances up and down the river. This job fell to the U.S. Geologic Survey, which sent survey crews into each of the major Colorado River canyons. These technicians, together with hydrologists and geologists, were ordered to delineate canyon topography, to examine potential damsites, and to obtain an accurate listing of mileages through each canyon.

Lee's Ferry was chosen as the key point in the mapping survey. Due to its unique accessibility, as well as its strategic location, it was given mile zero designation, with all mileages both up and down the stream shown as distances from Lee's Ferry.[4] (Actually, two separate Mile Zeros were used, one-half mile apart. See Tour Site No. 1)

The products of these surveys, the U.S.G.S. "profile" maps of the canyons, are rarely seen today, but modern pocket-sized adaptations have been made for river runners. Today's maps still use the same mileage designations, with Lee's Ferry shown as Mile Zero.

Since large dams on the Colorado were at last believed feasible, politicians in the

---

4. See Sheet A, Plan and Profile of Colorado River from Lees Ferry, Ariz. to Black Canyon, Ariz.-Nev. and Virgin River, Nev., U.S. Geological Survey, 1924.

Human muscle assists an underpowered truck move the scow *Navajo* through some soft terrain near Lee's Ferry. The boat was used from 1921 to 1923 in the investigation of a damsite in lower Glen Canyon.                                                    *U.S. Geological Survey*

seven Colorado Basin states began the long "War for the Colorado," the outwardly polite, but sometimes bitter struggle to obtain water developments for their respective areas.

In this "war," California held the best hand, for its rapid industrial growth greatly increased its appetite for both water and electric power. California's large population and high tax base provided that state with greater political power as compared to the other states in the basin. Of even greater concern, however, was the doctrine of "first in time, first in right," which meant that if California actually diverted and used all the water in the river, it would have the right to use all of it thereafter–forever!

To somewhat forestall California, representatives of the other states proposed a compact that would apportion the waters equitably. As the first big step toward that objective, the Colorado River Compact was signed in late 1922 in Santa Fe. The Compact has been the virtual law of the river ever since.

In the Compact, Lee's Ferry again played a significant part. Since the states could not agree on a formula to apportion the water state-by-state, they divided the water in what they believed were nearly equal amounts between an arbitrary "Upper Basin" and a corresponding "Lower Basin." The dividing point between the basins was designated as Lee's Ferry. (Actually the "Compact Point" was set one mile below the mouth of the Paria River or about two miles below the ferry crossing. In official water matters, the Compact Point is called "Lee Ferry.")

In the Compact the Upper Basin agreed to release 75 million acre-feet of water every 10 years, or an average of 7.5 million acre feet per year. And the flow would be measured at Lee's Ferry. To accomplish this, the U.S.G.S. was directed to build and permanently-staff a gauging station at Lee's Ferry. In July, 1921, the Southern California Edison Company, anticipating that it might succeed in building its own hydroelectric generating dam and powerplant in Glen Canyon, sent a crew to Lee's Ferry to help the U.S.G.S. set up a gauging station and to begin surveying damsites.

Necessary installations for the gauging station included a cable hung on towers across the river, a recorder well and shelter, and living quarters for a resident operator. The largest of Charlie Spencer's old rock cabins was remodeled into a residence, while another was converted into a warehouse. Water measurements were first made in August 1921 and have been recorded daily ever since.[5]

---

5. Records of the U.S. Geological Survey, Denver Colorado.

The first proposed dam site in Glen Canyon was about four miles above Lee's Ferry. Looking downstream, 1922. *U.S. Geological Survey*

Bureau of Reclamation camp at Lee's Ferry, 1948. This camp was used during the investigation of possible dam sites in lower Glen Canyon.                           *Bureau of Reclamation*

When the gauging station was established, the official in charge was U.S.G.S. hydrologist E.C. LaRue. After writing the 1916 survey report on the river, LaRue had participated in the 1921 mapping survey expedition of Cataract and Glen Canyons, and was busily examining potential damsites. He concluded that the best damsite on the entire Colorado River was at a point only four miles above Lee's Ferry. The river, just before it reaches the ferry, and while still deeply entrenched in Glen Canyon, makes a five-mile loop. But the straight-line distance from Lee's Ferry through the gooseneck would be less than a mile.

A dam at Mile 4, LaRue stated, could take advantage of a natural spillway location through the gooseneck. Water from the reservoir could also be conveyed, by tunnel and penstock, through the rock neck to operate a hydroelectric generating plant at Lee's Ferry.[6]

Impressed by LaRue's findings, the Southern California Edison Company worked at Lee's Ferry and at the Mile 4 damsite from 1921 to 1923, collecting data needed for design specifications. A drill crew, using a barge, obtained a number of core samples from the river bed and from the abutments.

In 1925 the U.S.G.S. published an impressive report by LaRue in which he detailed his findings at damsites all along the river. He reported on a damsite in Black Canyon (present site of Hoover Dam), for instance, but concluded that Glen Canyon's Mile 4 was superior.[7]

As the decade of the 1920's wore on, however, arguments prevailed for the building of a dam closer to the southern California electric power market. For one thing, transmission lines would be shorter. In 1928 the Boulder Canyon Project Act, which authorized construction of Hoover Dam, was passed, ending the argument.

Crews from the Southern California Edison Company filed away their drill logs from Glen Canyon and turned their attention elsewhere. At the Lee's Ferry gauging station a succession of operators worked and lived beneath the cliffs, measuring the daily flow of the muddy river.

---

6. E. C. LaRue, *Water Power and Flood Control of Colorado River Below Green River, Utah* (Washington: Government Printing Office, 1925) U.S. Geological Survey Water Supply Paper 556.
7. Ibid.

Most water experts agreed, however, that if the Upper Basin was to have its share of water development projects, a huge storage reservoir had to be built somewhere to even out the erratic river flows. Since the 1922 Compact was quite specific that deliveries of water would be measured at Lee's Ferry, the big reservoir had to be above that point.

It was also apparent that only one potential reservoir site was large enough. A reservoir in Glen Canyon could hold sufficient water from wet years to meet annual Compact requirements for water releases to the Lower Basin, even during a sustained drought. Water projects further upstream would not have to be shut down in dry years to allow the deliveries past Lee's Ferry.[8]

In September 1946, the Bureau of Reclamation sent a field team to Lee's Ferry to make a reconnaissance of potential damsites. A temporary camp and headquarters was set up near the Lee's Ferry Fort. For months, these men spent almost every day in lower Glen Canyon.

---

8. U.S. Bureau of Reclamation, *The Colorado River: A Comprehensive Report on the Development of the Water Resources of the Colorado River Basin for Irrigation, Power Production, and Other Beneficial Uses in Arizona, California, Colorado, Nevada, New Mexico, Utah and Wyoming* (Washington: Government Printing Office, 1946).

Bureau of Reclamation surveyors on the rim of Glen Canyon, Mile 15.3, where Glen Canyon Dam stands today. Photo taken in 1947.                    *Bureau of Reclamation*

Starting at the old Mile 4 damsite located by LaRue in the 1920's, the BuRec crew, led by engineer Vaud Larson, quickly found some basic flaws. The cliffs on either side were badly fractured–poor places to anchor a dam. Also drilling disclosed that the slippery Chinle shale was close to bedrock–obviously a dangerous foundation for a massive dam. In 1947 and 1948 Larson and his men moved their investigation farther upstream and found a much better damsite at Mile 15.3, where Glen Canyon Dam is now located.

Several writers have erroneously concluded that when the plan to build Echo Park Dam (in Dinosaur National Monument), was defeated by Congress in 1955, Glen Canyon Dam was proposed as the substitute major dam of the Colorado River Storage Project. Actually, Glen Canyon Dam, with both its huge holdover water storage in Lake Powell and its immense power generation capacity, was *always* the key unit of the CRSP plan. The CRSP could have been built without Echo Park Dam–but not without Glen Canyon Dam.

Soon after Glen Canyon Dam was authorized in 1956, roads were cut across the mesas to the damsite and to the new town of Page. Lee's Ferry was little touched by the building of the dam which was completed in 1964.

A proposal to build Marble Canyon Dam was seriously discussed in the late 1960's. See Chapter 18, Gateway to the Canyons.

# LAST DAYS OF THE FERRY

**B**y 1918 automobiles were a fairly common sight at Lee's Ferry, but wagon travel still predominated. Roads south to Flagstaff and northwest to Kanab were extremely bad, even by the standards of the day; surfacing, either with pavement or with gravel, was practically nonexistent. Even main roads were only tracks through the desert.

Under these conditions, a trip through Lee's Ferry was not something to be undertaken lightly. Since few autos then had luggage compartments, drivers wise to desert travel quite liberally festooned their cars with water bags, tools, spare parts, and emergency survival gear. In reporting an official trip by Coconino County employees in 1919, one participant wrote:

> *Stuck in sand at Bitter Springs... Reached ferry next noon. River low. Waded and pushed car halfway across to get on ferry boat, and but for a horse hitched on front of car, that vehicle and driver would have been immersed on farther side, as car kicked boat backward when it started for shore. Stuck in sand 10 miles beyond the ferry. Broke gear pinion. Camped there [two days] trying to fix car. All grub gone but sardines and one cracker... Cowboy appeared at camp. Sent him to ranger station to telephone Fredonia for relief. Buckboard and horses appeared. Abandoned car.*[1]

Traffic was usually light. At intervals, many days would pass without a single traveler wanting to cross the river. Coconino County nevertheless maintained a strong interest in keeping the ferry in operation, since it provided the only direct link with a big portion of the county as well as with the state of Utah.

---

1. *Coconino Sun*, Flagstaff, Arizona, 21 November 1919, from file at Northern Arizona University, Flagstaff.

The ferryboat at Lee's Ferry was often used to transport men and horses across the Colorado River.                                                                                       *Utah State Historical Society*

Early automobile travel utilizing the ferry at Lee's Ferry.

Two men prepare to test their Model T Ford across the mud bank after crossing the river on the ferry. Photo taken about 1922.
*Dock Marston Collection, Huntington Library*

Sharlot Hall, Arizona Territorial Historian, in 1911, made an epic wagon trip from her home in Prescott, north to Tuba City, Lee's Ferry, Fredonia, the North Rim, then west and south to Kingman, and return. Her purpose was to write about the Arizona Strip, that cut-off portion of the State lying between the Colorado River and the State of Utah. She described her arrival at Lee's Ferry:

> *The fields that John D. Lee had planted were green under the beetling walls of the Vermillion [sic] Cliffs and the house he had built showed through the orchard he had grown from seeds. But the quarter mile of liquid-copper river was between and a scrap of board beside the road said in pencil, "Fire a gun here if you want to cross."*
>
> *As we reached the bank where the road ended in a sort of beaver slide down to the edge of the water, a gasoline boat about as big as a bath tub began to crawl across like a water bug.*

The ferryboat at Lee's Ferry. Photographed and captioned by Charlie Spencer. The date shown, "1908", should probably read *1909*.
*Charles H. Spencer*

*Ferry Boat at Lees Ferry*
*1908        CHS*

The "Louse House," where travelers, probably reluctantly, slept at Lee's Ferry. At right is a ramada used for sun shade.

> *It drew up on our bank and I and the camera and a suit case were loaded*
> *in and away the little vessel slid into the copper-red, swirling water and*
> *presently pulled again to shore and I jumped out on the southern edge of*
> *my Promised Land–in the "Arizona Strip" at last.*[2]

During this period the ferry operators were sons of Warren M. Johnson, principally brothers Jerry, Frank, and Price, who all lived at the ranch. Most of their income was derived from the ranch and not from the meager revenue incident to the infrequent ferryboat operation. County officials wanted to improve the roads on either side of Lee's Ferry, but they were faced with the difficult fact that the ferry itself would still be the weakest link in the road system. Every few years a serious accident occurred at the ferry. Frequently men drowned. Often an accident would take the ferry out of service for days or even months.

In July 1923, for instance, an accident occurred when a wheel on the forward trolley split, dropping its axle onto the main cable and stopping the boat, which began to pitch violently. On board at the time were four men (including the ferryboat operator), and five boys.

Irving G. Cockroft, resident engineer at the water gauging station, watching from the bank, quickly comprehended the situation and launched his canoe. When he reached the ferryboat he yelled to the passengers to join him in a dilapidated rowboat being towed behind the ferryboat. The five boys and two of the men quickly complied.

Atherton Bean, one of the five boys, wrote:

> *Cockroft felt that he could steer the boat into an eddy on the north shore*
> *of the river and that all would be well. Suddenly, however, he looked up*
> *with concern saying, "We missed the eddy!" With that he took the rope*
> *of the boat in his mouth and swam ashore where the rope was just long*
> *enough for him to hold it in his left hand and to just reach the branch of*
> *a willow on the shore. To be dramatic it could easily be said that had*

2. Sharlot M. Hall, *Sharlot Hall on the Arizona Strip: A Diary of a Journey through Northern Arizona in 1911,* (Flagstaff: Northland Press, 1975), ed. by C. Gregory Crampton, pp. 46-47.

Two 1920's vintage automobiles cross the Colorado River at Lee's Ferry during high flows of spring, probably June.                                    *Museum of Northern Arizona*

*that difference been 6" more we would have gone down into the rapids. Cockroft pulled us into shore and we arrived as "residents" of Lee's Ferry with two virtually naked men, five boys and no equipment of any kind. Then, as we saw when we looked back to the ferry, it was pitching heavily and soon turned over and deposited our cars in the river where presumably at some point between Lee's Ferry and the first rapids they still lie well imbedded in the river silt... The ferryman, whose name I do not remember, and Amos Bjork had stayed on the ferry, and when it became apparent that it was going to turn over, the two of them swung hand over hand ashore on the ferry's cable.*[3]

By 1923 almost everyone realized that the only acceptable alternative to periodic accidents like this one was to build a bridge. Construction of Navajo Bridge began in 1927 and continued until January, 1929. (See Chapter 15, Navajo Bridge and Marble Canyon Lodge)

Construction crews completed the bridge in phases, working first on one side of the canyon, then crossing at Lee's Ferry with their tools and material to work on the other side. Many such ferry crossings were necessary.

Heavy trucks and even heavier loads of bridge steel caused considerable strain on the ferryboat, on the track cable, and on the attaching cables and pulleys. As stated in a 1929 issue of Arizona Highways, "This ferry boat, in all probability, would have lived its allotted three score years and ten and now be resting peacefully in some museum instead of on the bottom of the river if the construction of the new bridge had not thrown extra burdens upon the already decrepit ship."[4]

3. *Coconino Sun*, Flagstaff, Arizona, 20 July 1923, McClintock file, Phoenix Public Library, with more details in a letter from Atherton Bean of Scottsdale, Arizona to C. Gregory Crampton, dated 18 February 1989.
4. W. R. Hutchins, "Hardships Encountered In Bridging The Grand Canyon," *Arizona Highways* 5 (1929).

# The Last Days of The Ferry

The end came on June 7, 1928. With spring runoff swelling the river, the flow was measured at 85,600 cubic feet of water per second—only a moderately high flow, yet dangerous to an already weakened ferryboat and cable system. On that day an Indian trader named Royce Dean, with a Navajo passenger, Lewis Nez, drove a Model T Ford onto the boat from the north shore. Dean and his companion were returning from Kanab, where they had been trading, to Cedar Ridge, Arizona, their home base.

Jerry Johnson, the regular ferryman, was away working on the bridge construction. In his place was his young nephew, Adolph Johnson. With his two passengers and the Model T on board, Adolph set the cables and started across the river. When the boat touched the south shore, Johnson jumped out and attempted to snub the bow line to a post. Before he could tie the rope, however, the boat began to drift upstream, caught in an unusual eddy current caused by the high river flow. Johnson dug in his heels and tried to hold the boat, but he was dragged down the slope and into the water. He swam to the boat and climbed aboard.

By this time the boat was drifting upstream under its track cable. Attaching cables became slack. Then the eddy current pushed the boat further out into the river where it was caught by the fast downstream flow. Johnson could not work quickly enough adjusting the cables to angle the craft properly to the current. Reaching the end of the slack with a violent jerk, the boat nosed under and began taking water.

A traveler wishing to cross the river rings the bell to signal the ferryman. This bell was later mounted over the gate at the Lonely Dell Ranch, but it was stolen by a former owner in 1974.

*Dock Marston Collection, Huntington Library*

This cabin at the main ferry site was used by ferryman, by visitors, and by U.S. Geological Survey employees. Photo taken by Charles Kelly in 1932. The cabin was deliberately burned to the ground in 1959 by the U.S.G.S. "to prevent vandalism."
*Utah State Historical Society*

In June, 1928, the ferryboat capsized with three men and a Model T Ford aboard. All the men were drowned and the boat was lost. Since Navajo Bridge was then nearing completion, the ferryboat was never replaced.
*Museum of Northern Arizona*

Within a few moments it capsized and the track cable snapped. All three men were drowned. Young Johnson's wife was watching from shore.

An attempt was made to save the boat, which had hung up on the bank some distance below the ferry site. No one could reach it, however, before it drifted on down into Marble Canyon.[5]

This accident was the worst ever to happen at Lee's Ferry. It was also the final run of the ferry. For fifty-five years, ferryboats had traveled back and forth across the muddy Colorado at Lee's Ferry. Now they would cross no more. An era of pioneering had come to an end.

Since the new bridge was nearing completion, county officials declined to spend the funds necessary to put the ferry back into operation. Thus from June 1928 to January 1929, highway travelers could not cross the river anywhere between Moab, Utah, and points below the Grand Canyon. When the bridge contractor had to move equipment or materials to the other side of the canyon, he had to send his trucks on a circuitous eight hundred-mile trip through Needles, California–to a destination only eight hundred feet from the starting point![6]

---

5. Interview with Frank Johnson, 28 October 1962.
6. Hutchins, "Hardships Encountered In Bridging The Grand Canyon."

With the ferryboat sunk and with Navajo Bridge not yet finished, desperate measures were needed. The car is shown being lifted, in 1928, across the river on the U.S.G.S. river gaging cable.

*U.S. Geological Survey*

# NAVAJO BRIDGE

# AND

# MARBLE CANYON LODGE

## NAVAJO BRIDGE - THE ORIGINAL

**B**ridging Marble Canyon had been contemplated even before ferry operations began in 1873. In 1870, Major John Wesley Powell was reported to have found a place–undoubtedly the upper part of Marble Canyon—where a suspension bridge for a railroad could be built.[1] In 1881 the Arizona Northern Railway Company, a company associated with the Denver and Rio Grande Western Railway, had its engineers examine possible bridge sites near Lee's Ferry. A site was selected and approaches were graded before the work was suspended. The projected rail line, of course, was never built.[2]

By the 1920's, when new highways were being built across the United States, a fast, reliable road link between Arizona and Utah was given high priority, but funds were not easily found. Finally, the U.S. Bureau of Indian Affairs pledged $100,000 to build a bridge that would connect the Navajo Reservation with country to the north. The State of Arizona agreed to pay the remainder, or $290,000.[3]

Although the original plan called for a suspension bridge, it was redesigned as a steel arch bridge that would be anchored to the canyon wall. The contract was let to

1. *Daily News*, Denver, 19 November 1870, from files of Otis Marston, San Francisco, California. After the death of Marston in 1979, his files were transferred to the Huntington Library, San Marino, California.
2. Chief Engineers Report, signed by M. T. Burgess, Chief Engineer, Arizona Northern Railway, 21 December 1881. From files of Denver & Rio Grande Western Railroad, Colorado Historical Society, Denver.
3. Ralph A. Hoffman, "Bridging the Grand Canyon of Arizona," *Arizona Highways* 3, no. 8 (November 1927).

Twin arching segments of Navajo Bridge approach closure 467 feet above the Colorado River in Marble Canyon–or, more properly, the Marble Gorge of the Grand Canyon. It was opened to traffic in 1929, and until 1935, was known as "Grand Canyon Bridge." *U.S. Geological Survey*

Navajo Bridge approaches completion in 1928. (Above & Right) *Jane Foster, Marble Canyon Lodge*

the Kansas City Structural Steel Company, and work began in June 1927, at a point about six miles downstream from Lee's Ferry. The site was identical to the place selected by the Rio Grande Railroad surveyors forty-six years earlier.[4]

Due to its isolation and the rugged terrain, the logistics of bridge construction were a constant problem. To transport the heavy steel and other material from Flagstaff required traversing one hundred and thirty miles of almost totally unimproved road that led through sand washes, up and down steep grades, and over rolling and uneven rocky hills.

In 1928, only a week after the ferry accident, a spectacular mishap occurred at the bridge when an ironworker named Lafe McDaniels lost his footing and fell four hundred sixty feet to the Colorado River.[5] No net was being used for fear that hot rivets might start a fire. As it was, McDaniels was the only workman killed during the bridge building.

For much of the construction, the contractor used the ferry at Lee's Ferry to cross trucks, heavy steel, and other supplies from one side of the canyon to the other. After the ferry accident of June 5, 1928, the contractor had to send his trucks on a circuitous 800-mile route through Needles, California, to a destination only 800 feet from the starting point.

All during construction, and even through the dedication, the bridge was called the Grand Canyon Bridge. Many people in northern Arizona, however, wanted to commemorate the old ferry by calling it "Lee's Ferry Bridge," and a bill to this effect was introduced in the Arizona legislature. Opposition to the bill was not long in coming. Notified of the bill to name it Lee's Ferry Bridge, Mormon President Heber J. Grant wrote to the Arizona State Historian, "I think it would be an outrage on the Mormon people, who were among the first and most substantial settlers of Arizona, to have this bridge named the Lee Bridge."[6] At that time Grant and the other church authorities still believed--or wanted to believe--that Lee was almost solely responsible for the Mountain Meadows Massacre.

President Grant carried his appeal directly to the Arizona legislature, addressing them in person. He suggested that the bridge be named Hamblin Bridge, for Jacob

4. Ibid. Also, Frank Johnson interview 28 Oct 1962. Johnson stated that he located the Arizona Northern R.R. stakes on the rim of the canyon, that he showed these to the Arizona Department of Transportation, and that Navajo Bridge was built squarely on the same point.
5. *Coconino Sun*, Flagstaff, Arizona, 15 June 1928, from file at Northern Arizona University.
6. Heber J. Grant to James H. McClintock, 15 February 1929, McClintock file, Phoenix Public Library.

Part of the huge crowd that assembled for the dedication of Navajo Bridge on June 14 and 15, 1929. Photo taken by Barry Goldwater.

*Arizona Historical Foundation*

Hamblin, or "Hamblin-Hastele Bridge," for both Hamblin and Navajo Chief Hastele, who had been a friend to the Mormons.[7]

None of the suggested names, however, could avoid factional argument. As a compromise, an amendment was finally submitted to the effect that the bridge be called Navajo Bridge, a non-controversial name that was adopted in 1934.[8]

In spite of difficulties, work progressed on schedule through the closing of the steel arch, installation of vertical piers, and placement of the concrete deck. On January 12, 1929, the bridge was opened to traffic.

In what the *Coconino Sun* in Flagstaff headlined as the "Biggest News in Southwest History," the new bridge was dedicated on June 14 and 15, 1929. Governors of Arizona, Utah, New Mexico, and Nevada, and Mormon Church President Heber J. Grant made speeches. Since it was still the time of prohibition, a bottle of ginger ale was used to christen the bridge. In spite of the bad roads, an almost incredible crowd of five thousand was reportedly on hand. The Flagstaff newspaper added that two thousand Indians were also present.[9] Indian dances were held in the evening. For many spectators, however, the biggest thrill came when Jack Irish of Flagstaff flew his airplane, an American Eagle 110, down the canyon and under the bridge. (See Tour Site #21)

## BUCK LOWREY AND MARBLE CANYON LODGE

Opening simultaneously with Navajo Bridge was Marble Canyon Lodge, located about one-half mile away on the northwest side of the canyon. The Lodge was built, owned and operated by Buck Lowrey, described as a "John Wayne" type, tough man of the West.

7. Unidentified newspaper account, McClintock file, Phoenix Public Library.

8. Lee's Ferry file, Arizona Library, Archives, and Public Records Division, unidentified newspaper clipping dated 17 November 1935.

9. *Coconino Sun*, Flagstaff, Arizona, 21 June 1929, from file at Northern Arizona University.

Home for Buck Lowery and his family at Lee's Ferry, from 1927 to 1929, was the largest of the Spencer mining buildings, originally built about 1911. At his wife's insistence, Buck put a wood floor over the formerly dirt floor. *Jane Foster, Marble Canyon Lodge*

David "Buck" Lowrey had been raised in Texas, but moved to the Navajo Reservation about 1918 to become a trader. Employed by the famous Navajo trader, Lorenzo Hubbell, Lowrey was first assigned to Kaibito Trading Post, then one of the most remote posts in the Reservation. He later worked at The Gap and at Cedar Ridge Trading Posts.

Sometime during the mid-1920's, having heard about the future Navajo Bridge across the Colorado, Lowrey determined that the north side of the river, by the bridge, would be an ideal place for a lodge and store. It would undoubtedly have considerable traffic in future years, and, equally important, it was just off the Reservation, where the land could be homesteaded from the Federal Government.

After applying for the homestead, Lowrey and his family moved to Lee's Ferry. Why Lee's Ferry? Because Lee's Ferry was established, it was close to Navajo Bridge, it had water, and it had a place to live—at least temporarily. Around 1927, Buck moved his family into the largest of the Spencer buildings, where—at his wife's insistence—he laid a new wood floor over the former dirt floor.

Lee's Ferry even had a school, established and regulated by Coconino County. Lowrey's two oldest children, Mamie and David, Jr., were sent to a distant city to attend school, but Virginia, being only seven, attended school at the Lonely Dell Ranch. About 10 to 12 other children also attended, and all of them, except Virginia, were children of two polygamist families, the Johnsons and the Spencers (no relation to Charlie Spencer, the miner-promoter), who lived at Lonely Dell.

About a year after the Lowrey family moved to Lee's Ferry, Virginia Lowrey, then age 8, was playing beside the river when the ferryboat capsized and three men were drowned (See Chapter 14). When she saw the upside down ferryboat float by, Virginia thought it was a large driftwood log, but it frightened her, so she ran to tell her mother. Only later did Virginia learn the details of the tragedy.[10]

When she could, Virginia also watched the workmen build Navajo Bridge. They were all from Kansas City, she said, and so rough a bunch that Florence wanted Virginia to stay away from them. But they were fun to watch, for they put on a marvelous show of daredevil agility over the depth of the gorge. Virginia would often eat lunch with the bridge crew, about 35 to 40 men at any one time. Separate crews

---

10. Interview with Virginia Lowrey Greer, Orem, Utah, March 12, 1991. Most of the details about the construction and early operation of Marble Canyon Lodge were obtained from Virginia.

followed each other depending on their specialties, whether drillers, highscalers, concrete men, or riveters.

When the bridge lacked only the main deck, Virginia held the hand of her father, Buck, as they walked across the canyon on two 18-inch wide boards laid side by side! Both Buck and Virginia knew full well that they should never mention this adventurous incident to Florence—and they never did.

Buck Lowrey, meanwhile, had to build a trading post on the south side (the Navajo side) of the canyon, which would provide him with a livelihood. Locating the post on a hill just upstream from the bridge, he soon had it in operation. Almost every day he traveled up and down the narrow dugway in his small truck and crossed the river by boat to his home at Lee's Ferry.

To Florence Lowrey, each day that Buck had to cross the river and travel the dugway to tend the trading post was a worry, especially when Buck returned after dark. Nora Cundell, a frequent guest of the lodge and friend of the Lowrey family wrote:

> *Mrs. Lowrey has told me how, night after night, when the river was running high, she'd stand and watch the headlights as they came winding along the track, far away up on the mountain. Slowly, they would descend, and as soon as they were extinguished, she'd know that the far shore had been reached. After that there would be a sickening wait, during which time she could see nothing and hear only the roar of the rapids, until a welcome voice would tell her that the crossing had been made safely.*[11]

While tending the trading post on the south side, Buck had to simultaneously build Marble Canyon Lodge on the north side and have it ready to open when the bridge was finished. To finance it, Buck scraped together what money he had, but he

Buck Lowrey (right), points out the favorable filming possibilities of Marble Canyon—directly below—to a probably nervous visiting location man from a Hollywood studio. Photo taken about 1927.

*Jane Foster, Marble Canyon Lodge*

11. Nora Cundall, *Unsentimental Journey,* (London: Methuen & Co., Ltd., 1940), p. 78

David "Buck" Lowrey on the steps of Marble Canyon Lodge, 1935     *Jane Foster*

ran short, and on March 16, 1929, before the lodge was yet opened to the public, he borrowed $10,000—at 10 percent interest—from Lorenzo Hubbell.

Lowrey could have built the lodge of wood, or even of commercial brick, but he chose instead the much more difficult material—native rock, quarried from the nearby cliffs. Since he could not afford to hire skilled workmen from Flagstaff, he virtually did everything himself, occasionally making trips to the Flagstaff Library to read books on carpentry, plumbing, electrical work, or rock work. He employed 2 or 3 Navajo men as assistants, while his son, David Jr. helped during the summer months.

Marble Canyon Lodge (first named Vermilion Cliffs Lodge), opened its doors to the public on the date Navajo Bridge was dedicated, June 14, 1929. With thousands of people present for the occasion, the lodge was, of course, filled even beyond its capacity— but only for a few days. Regular business was less lucrative, since the unpaved highway and distances were intimidating to many potential patrons. Expenses were also high, and when Buck and his wife, Florence, served a large steak dinner, their guests were shocked to learn that it cost them the high price of $1.75 each. Of course, the lodge had no air conditioning, but Buck had built the walls quite thick as a form of insulation. All power was obtained from diesel generators.

Obtaining water for the lodge was an achievement in itself. Buck located a small spring at the base of the Vermilion Cliffs, but on the distant side of the high rock bench that looms over the valley floor. He and his temporary assistants cleaned out the spring, got the water flowing as much as possible, then ran pipe for 3 1/2 miles, first to a storage tank, and then to the Lodge. For almost 40 years, this small spring

Buck Lowrey's Marble Canyon Lodge, originally called Vermilion Cliffs Lodge, looks much the same in this 1930 photograph as it does today.     *Jane Foster, Marble Canyon Lodge*

was the sole source of water for the lodge, the restaurant, and, later, the motel. (See Tour Site #23)

## MURDER AT MARBLE CANYON

Late Saturday evening, June 22, 1935, all was quiet at the lodge. The only one at Marble Canyon still on the job was George Wilson, a 65-year old man hired by Buck to keep the lonely gas station open all night. Just then a car drove up, bearing three young men, Albert and Carl White, age 19 and 17, and a young hitchhiker named Carl Cox.

After looking around the store for a minute, Albert White pulled a gun on Wilson and demanded the cash box, but Wilson, instead of complying, tried to hit White with a flashlight. White fired, and Wilson went down, with a bullet in his abdomen. When Wilson, despite his injury, struggled into the back room to get his rifle, White fired again, but missed. Panicked by what they had done, the young men jumped into their car and sped off in the darkness to the west. Wilson managed to fire once at the fleeing car, but without effect.

Buck heard the shots, dressed quickly, and ran to the filling station. Finding Wilson wounded, he told his wife, Florence, to care for Wilson until a doctor arrived. Then Buck, a deputy Sheriff of Coconino County, drove off toward the Kaibab Plateau in pursuit of the outlaws.

When he reached Jacob Lake, Buck telephoned Dr. Aiken in Kanab and asked him to hurry to Marble Canyon. He also called Dickie Lewis, a deputy sheriff at Fredonia, and advised him to set up a road block. Within a few minutes, Lewis had the Arizona-Utah border sealed off. When the outlaw trio arrived at the small town, the deputies fired, causing the White brothers and Cox to make a screeching U-turn and head back to the Kaibab Forest. Although they easily outran the pursuit, the outlaws were trapped.

On Sunday morning a squadron of deputies began searching dirt roads leading off the highway into the Kaibab Forest. At Pine Flat, they spotted the car. The boys were asleep. At the lawmen's command to come out, the boys jumped from the car and fled into the woods. Carl White was hit in the elbow by a bullet, but his brother, Albert, helped him temporarily elude the posse.

Not until late afternoon did the deputies find the three teenagers, asleep near a

The original gas station, on the north side of the highway at Marble Canyon Lodge, photographed about 1930. The fatal shooting of George Wilson at this station in June, 1935, began a dramatic episode that was climaxed by the killing of the gunman by Buck Lowrey and Buck's son, David Jr.

*Jane Foster, Marble Canyon Lodge*

spring. Approaching cautiously, they surrounded them before the boys awoke. All three gave up without a struggle.

The wounded gas station attendant, George Wilson, however, was in great pain. Dr. Aiken, with his wife, arrived from Kanab, but he could only give Wilson a shot of morphine to help kill the pain. Aiken advised that Wilson be rushed to the nearest hospital, which was the Indian hospital at Tuba City. Florence Lowrey and her daughter, Virginia, age 15, placed the suffering man in their car and drove south toward Tuba City. Virginia had to drive.

At the Tuba City Indian Hospital, the administrator in charge refused to admit Wilson because he was not an Indian. So Florence and Virginia were forced to take him on to Flagstaff. But too much time had elapsed. Peritonitis set in and Wilson died on Wednesday night, three days later. Just before Wilson died, however, the Sheriff and Buck Lowrey took the handcuffed Albert White to the hospital, where Wilson identified White as the killer. "That's the baby that shot me!" Wilson exclaimed.

When Wilson died, Buck vowed that if he could, he would administer quick justice to the murderer–with a bullet.

No one ever knew how Albert White obtained a hacksaw blade, but he used it to cut his way out of the Flagstaff jail, on July 21, 1935, just a day short of a month after he had shot Wilson. A short distance from town, White stole a car, headed north, but ran out of gas. He stopped a motorist, offering to trade a spare tire for some gasoline, but the motorist refused and drove on.

White's escape from jail was, by this time, known to lawmen in all directions. Buck Lowrey heard about it, advised his son, David Jr., and the two of them set up a road block near Bitter Springs, 14 miles south of Marble Canyon Lodge. When the motorist who had refused White's offer to trade gas for a tire stopped at the road block and told Buck the story, Buck realized that White was probably headed his way.

Somehow, White obtained gasoline, for it wasn't long until Buck and David Lowery saw a car approaching them from the south at high speed. David signaled the car to stop, but White, who was driving the stolen car, turned directly toward David. David jumped clear, but Buck, who was on the other side of the car, fired his rifle twice at the driver's door. David also fired as the car careened off the highway and into a dry wash. White offered no further resistance; he was dead, with three bullets in him.[12]

A frightening incident occurred when Buck and David, Jr. brought the dead man back to Marble Canyon Lodge. Before he left to set up the road block, Buck had told "Peaches" Beard, the cook, that if the fugitive got through the road block, Buck and David would chase him, honking their horn continuously. When Peaches heard the horn, he was supposed to position himself beside the road at Marble Canyon and "shoot to kill" as the first car approached.

In their excitement of killing White, however, Buck forgot his instructions to Peaches. As a signal of their success, Buck and David crossed Navajo Bridge with the horn blaring. Peaches took careful aim and was about to fire, when he suddenly recognized Buck at the wheel. It was a close call.[13]

12. Kel M. Fox, "Murder at Marble Canyon," *Journal of Arizona History,* 24-4 (Winter, 1983). Also interview with Virginia Lowrey Greer, 12 March 1991.
13. Interview with Merle "Peaches" Beard, Kanab, UT 13 June 1991.

With military precision, tents to house visitors are staked behind the Lee's Ferry Fort for the 1935 reunion of pioneers and their descendants who had crossed at Lee's Ferry to settle in Arizona. Sharlot Hall, former Arizona Territorial Historian, gave a speech. Nora Cundell, (from England), also attended this celebration, but remained in some confusion over what it was all about.

## NORA CUNDELL

Marble Canyon Lodge has seen its share of outlaw transients. But it has also been visited by fine writers, such as Zane Grey and J.B. Priestly, by outstanding photographers, such as Joseph Muench, by colorful river runners, such as Georgie White Clark and Martin Litton, by movie actors, such as Gary Cooper, and by several prominent American industrialists. None of these visitors, however, has loved the Lodge, the Vermilion Cliffs, and Lee's Ferry quite as much as Nora Cundell, an artist from England.

Nora Cundell, who apparently heard about the canyon country from J.B. Priestly, made her first visit about 1934, then came again for a few months during each of the next three years. She was in her forties, well-educated, a bit homely, and had never been married. But she had energy to burn, with an indefatigable desire to see every red cliff and canyon, to learn the mysterious ways of the Navajos, and to join with the Lowreys in their day-to-day activities. And always she could contrast the proper customs and mores of her small English home village to the tough life in the Arizona canyon country.

Describing a celebration at Lee's Ferry that she attended:

> I've since learnt that we were supposed to be celebrating the first crossing of the Colorado by the Mormon pioneers, but, at the time, had no more idea than the Navajos what it was all about and I attended in much the same spirit–that of not wanting to miss anything... (Navajos will celebrate anything with anybody. If a party of Old Etonians should unexpectedly find itself stranded in the middle of the seemingly empty desert, on the fourth of June, and decide to mark the occasion with a suitable display of fireworks, I will guarantee that, before they have let off half a dozen squibs, a bunch of Indians will have materialized from nowhere, and started to make coffee, all ready to join in the fun.)

Then to sum up the day:

> But Mormons, Indians or white men, they all seemed to join in the festivities that day. There was hymn-singing in one booth, and a lot of speeches, in the course of which the orators announced pridefully

114

*that they came of "good polygamous stock." There were sideshows; a tent full of poisonous snakes, a rifle range, where I watched some wonderful plain and fancy shooting, and a dance floor, so that "a good time was had by all." But unlike the placid Navajos, I couldn't help wishing that I really knew what it was all about.*[14]

Concerning the Lowreys, Nora had only the highest praise. To her, Buck was the toughest, most courageous man alive. Even young Virginia, who was still in grade school, was complimented on her piano playing. For David Jr., however, who took her to Indian dances, camping, and exploring, her account glitters with overtones of pure, passionate love, unrequited and very proper, never mentioned directly, but nonetheless fully evident. Of Florence Lowrey, (and perhaps, while thinking of David), Nora wrote:

*It's one of the most charming and admirable characteristics of the best types of Southern and Western men–their respect for women. By them one is treated as a fragile flower that must be shielded, as far as possible, from all roughness and brutality. In the West, of course, it has to be the sort of fragile flower that can sew, cook, launder, ride horseback, change the wheel on a car and, if necessary, handle a gun; but apart from these few little things, the more delicately feminine the better. Mrs. Lowrey is that kind of a fragile flower and such, in time and with a little more practice, I hope some day to be.*[15]

14. Nora Cundell, *Unsentimental Journey*, pp. 65-66
15. Ibid., p. 101.

David Lowrey, Jr., portrait painted by Nora Cundell about 1936. David was killed in one of the last few days of World War II while serving on a U.S. Navy mine sweeper off the coast of the Philippines.

*Virginia Lowrey Greer*

The small plaque placed in memory of Nora L.M. Cundell, who died on the Isle of Wight in August, 1948, but who had requested, in her will, that her ashes be scattered near Marble Canyon and the Vermilion Cliffs, in the land she loved more than any other.

Nora Cundell's ashes are distributed in a simple ceremony at the base of the Vermilion Cliffs in May, 1949. At right is "Preacher" or "Shine" Smith, friend to virtually all the Indians and non-Indians in northern Arizona. In front of the large rock, holding the box of ashes, is Buck Lowrey, and next to him is Florence Lowrey.

*Joseph Muench*

Time was running out for the Lowreys and for Nora. Eventually, Buck could keep Marble Canyon Lodge open no longer. It was 1937, Depression time, and tourist travel, as well as every economic activity in America, was at a low ebb. Lorenzo Hubbell wanted his $10,000 back that he had loaned Buck in 1929, plus $3,000 accrued interest, but Buck simply could not pay. Furthermore, Buck and Florence were worn out; the constant hard work of trying to keep the Lodge in operation had adversely affected their health. The Lowery's packed up and prepared to leave.

Nora Cundell, who was living at the Lodge on that last day, wrote:

> *I slept badly and was awake before it was light, so I got up*
> *and dressed. In the half darkness of the passage I met Mrs.*
> *Lowrey, already with her coat on. "I guess we're going now."*
> *she said. I choked down a cup of coffee that scalded my throat...*
> *and climbed into the Ford.*
>
> *Behind me, I felt that the whole, vast Vermilion Cliffs, and all*
> *that they had stood for, were crumbling and dissolving, as in a*
> *dream that is past. I know, of course that they must still be*
> *standing there, solid and impregnable, and as nearly eternal*
> *as anything in this world can be–and yet, somehow, I can't*
> *believe it. To me it is as though, on that morning, like a mirage,*
> *they faded forever over the desert sand.*[16]

David Jr. was the first to die, killed in action at the very end of World War II—or even a few days after–when his ship hit a Japanese mine off the coast of the Philippines. Florence Lowrey died in Flagstaff about 1949, while Buck lived until 1963. Daughters Mamie and Virginia are now becoming elderly, but have many stories to tell about their youthful days along the desert river.

When Nora Cundell died in England, she was, according to her wishes, cremated, and her ashes taken to Marble Canyon. Beside the road to Lee's Ferry, up against the cliffs, on a sunny day in early May, 1949, a simple commemorative ceremony was held. Buck and Florence Lowrey attended, as did a handful of friends who had known Nora in years past. Preacher "Shine" Smith, beloved friend of the Navajos as well as all the whites in this part of Arizona, scattered her ashes. Today, the spot is marked by a small, inconspicuous plaque on a sandstone boulder.

## MARBLE CANYON LODGE, 1937–1959

With the departure of Buck Lowrey and his family, Lorenzo Hubbell assumed ownership of the Lodge. Hubbell was located in distant Ganado, in the middle of the Navajo Indian Reservation–too far away to exercise active management–so he employed a series of managers. Then, in 1943, Hubbell hired Art Greene as manager, and Greene remained for about six years. Greene's river running business and Wahweap Lodge are discussed in the next chapter.[17]

In 1949, in a creditors proceeding against Ramon Hubbell, a son of the late Lorenzo Hubbell, an engineer turned real estate developer named Kyle Bales purchased Marble

---

16. Nora Cundell, *Unsentimental Journey*, pp. 243-244
17. Interview with Jane Foster, 5 March 1991. Most of the details in this section are taken from that interview.

Canyon Lodge (along with several other properties in Albuquerque, New Mexico, and in St. Johns and Winslow, Arizona). Bales moved to Winslow, but made only occasional visits to Marble Canyon Lodge. About 1957, Bales leased the lodge to a man named Ewell Moore, who built the long building just east of the gas station, and used it as a restaurant, bar, and package liquor store. This was during the early stages of Glen Canyon Dam construction, and considerable traffic passed the Lodge. But patronage fell off when businesses in Page were developed about 1958.

While Moore ran the Lodge, the owner, Kyle Bales, died, and the Administrator of Bales' estate, the Valley National Bank, made a holding operation of the Lodge until 1961, when it, along with all the other Bales property in Arizona, was given to Bales' three daughters, Doris, Pat, and Jane.

Their three-sister partnership, trying to administer property in several states, proved too difficult, so Jane proposed a split that would assign to her any 1/3rd of the total properties that the other two sisters wanted to give her. This proved acceptable, and Jane became the full owner of Marble Canyon Lodge.

## MARBLE CANYON LODGE - 1959 TO DATE

Jane Bales Foster was trained as an attorney, and worked in that capacity for several years after college. Her husband, Robert Foster, also an attorney, was employed by Walt Disney Production from 1954 to 1973 and was instrumental in the purchases of land for Disney World in Florida, 1969–1971. Jane and Robert had two sons, Graham David Foster and Stewart Donald Foster. Jane had a son, Steven Knisely, by her first husband, Harry Knisely, also a lawyer. Jane and the three boys spent most of their summers at the Lodge during the 1960's. When the youngest boy entered college in 1979, Jane moved to the Lodge to take over active management and to supervise many planned improvements that had not been possible with absentee ownership.

Over the years, Jane Foster has attacked the principal problems faced by Buck Lowrey back in 1929–a reliable water supply, a power supply, and a telephone.

The far distant spring used since 1929, the Lowrey Seeps, supplied too little water for the growing business. And, in winter, the above ground supply pipe had to be drained to prevent it from freezing. Jane supplied details:

> *When I first took over, we were often out of water, and I would have traded Coke for water. Sometimes the pipe freezes. Each spring we would have to send someone up there and bring the water down. Frank Black used to have what he called his "water line kit," including bailing wire, inner tube, and other things. The deal always was that every spring we would leave a case of wine at the bottom of the line. So Frank would work with his kit until the water came over the hill. And then he got the case of wine as a reward.*[18]

Most of the culinary water now used by the Lodge comes from a nearby well, but the Lowrey Spring still supplies a portion of the needs.

In 1968, electric power was brought in over the Echo Cliffs, principally for the Lee's Ferry area, but partly a result of Jane's urging, a line was brought up the hill to

---

18. Interview with Jane Foster, 5 March 1991

serve Marble Canyon Lodge. Telephone service was established by an independent company, also by virtue of Jane's urging and the help of an important lawyer friend, in 1971.

Jane Foster revels in the history of Lee's Ferry and of Marble Canyon Lodge. In 1986, for instance, she and Robert decided to refurbish the main Lodge building, which had not been used for several years. Simultaneously with its reopening, Jane proposed to hold a "re-birthday party, with old-timers invited to come and tell stories about earlier days in the land. When she mentioned this proposal to a National Park Service Ranger, the NPS seized the idea and turned it into a "Lee's Ferry Reunion," an event that was held in September 1986, and repeated in 1987 and 1988. [19]

Jane said that while she and Robert were working in the Lodge, Jane felt the presence of a ghost, probably that of Buck Lowrey. The ghost did not make her uncomfortable, and it did not seem to be threatening, she said, but she could tell it was definitely there. The contractor she employed to work on the building also felt that "someone else was in the room." But when the building was finished and ready for guests, Jane said, the ghost suddenly disappeared. It may occasionally return, for a woman staying alone in the Lodge reported on one occasion, hearing footsteps in

The Navajo Bridge Interpretive Center, constructed by the Arizona Department of Transportation, is sponsored by the National Park Service (GCNRA), and is operated and maintained by the Glen Canyon Natural History Association. The Center was dedicated 17 June 1997. Carole Rusho at left.

---

19. Interview with Jane Foster, 5 March 1991.

the night, and, on another occasion, a door closing. She did not get up either time to investigate![20]

Marble Canyon Lodge is now the gathering place for Elderhostel groups, who, in groups of about 35 persons, spend about a week at the lodge during the fall and spring months. Instructors are hired by Yavapai College of Prescott, Arizona, the sponsoring institution. At the lodge and on field trips the participants learn about history, archaeology, geology, biology, Glen Canyon Dam, Lake Powell, Grand Canyon, and other subjects in a wide and diverse program. Each year over 500 Elderhostel guests enroll in the program.

## THE SECOND NAVAJO BRIDGE

Navajo Bridge was sensational in 1929, for it connected areas long separated by the Grand Canyon, and previously linked only by the ferryboat at Lee's Ferry. But, as a bridge, it was inadequate, almost from the day it opened. The bridge deck was only 18 feet wide, it had no pedestrian walkway, and its structural strength was not adequate for modern truck traffic.[21]

Workmen gather to help install a final pin in the new Navajo Bridge during construction in 1995.

20. Interview with Carol Sue Vann, 5 March 1991.
21. Interview with Jerry A. Cannon, Cannon & Associates, Tucson. 7 March 1991. Also *Final Environmental Assessment–U.S. 89A Bitter Springs to Fredonia–Navajo Bridge,* (Phoenix: Arizona Department of Transportation, June 1990)

The Arizona Department of Transportation began to study a possible replacement for Navajo Bridge in the mid-1980's, and they engaged engineer Jerry A. Cannon of Tucson as a Consultant and Project Manager.

First, Cannon and his assistants looked at the possibility of widening the existing bridge, but a widened, old bridge deck would remain supported by a substandard arch structure. Also, simple widening was not cost effective.

Several people who would like to shorten the drive from Fredonia to Flagstaff expressed a preference for a bridge site closer to the Kaibab Plateau, where Marble Canyon is very wide. A number of possible locations for a new bridge across lower Marble Canyon were examined, and cost estimates were prepared, but all of the sites were simply too expensive in terms of bridge length, and in terms of additional highway required to reach the sites. The cost estimate for one site, for instance, far down Marble Canyon, would be $127 million.

The preferred alternative, by a matter of elimination, turned out to be a new bridge one-hundred fifty feet downstream from the old one. At that point the bridge would cost , only $15 million.

A number of public meetings were held on the preferred, as well as all the other alternatives, in Flagstaff, in Marble Canyon Lodge, in Fredonia, and at one of the Navajo Chapter Houses. Cannon states that much opposition was initially evident, but when it was explained, everyone seemed to agree with the preferred alternative.

Navajo Bridge II, the new bridge, designed by Cannon & Associates, matches the old bridge in general appearance, even though structurally, the two bridges are quite different. In 1928, the Kansas City Structural Steel Company used 1,200 tons of structural steel to build the historic Navajo Bridge. Construction of the second bridge used 1,900 tons of steel. The new bridge is 44 feet wide, 909 feet long, with a 726 foot-long steel arch main span. Although the depth and rise of the main span match the older bridge, the new span is 110 feet longer, and the deck is 2.5 times wider. The arch rib is constructed from high strength structural steel that is three times stronger than the steel usually used on bridges of this type. It is capable of carrying the wider, longer bridge deck, and it allowed reduction of the weight of the structural members from 168 pounds per square foot to 90 pounds per square foot. This meant that the massiveness of the new arch could be reduced, and the visual impact of the second bridge could be minimized. Because the high-strength steel weighs relatively less, it can carry the heavier loads of modern-day traffic without visually overwhelming the old bridge.

The new bridge was constructed by contractor Edward Kraemer & Sons, Inc., during a nineteen month period from February 1993 to September 1995. Approaches to the bridge were carefully cut so that the rock resembles nearby natural formations. To comply with laws limiting the amount of material falling into the river, the contractor, when excavating the bridge foundations, used precise blasting and steel nets to contain 95 percent of the loose rock.

Rather than use rivets, as was done in the 1920's, the new bridge is held together with high strength bolts. A safety net under the new bridge was credited with saving the life of an Arizona Department of Transportation inspector, who slipped and fell after unhooking his safety belt so that he could move around a vertical framing member.

The bridge was dedicated in a ceremony held September 14, 1995, with representatives of Arizona, Utah and the Navajo Nation providing remarks.

The "twin" Navajo Bridges, as seen from river level, 470 feet below. The new bridge, completed in 1995, is in the foreground.                                        *Cannon & Associates*

The 1929 bridge was preserved as a pedestrian footbridge, while an interpretive area, a visitor center and parking lot were constructed on the north side. The old observation shelter, built by the Civilian Conservation Corps in the 1930's was also preserved.[22]

As part of the expenditure for the new bridge, Arizona Department of Transportation constructed a visitor center complex on the right abutment between the two bridges. Named the Navajo Bridge Interpretive Center, the establishment features exhibits and audio-visual displays of interest to visitors. The Center, staffed by personnel of the Glen Canyon Natural History Association, was dedicated in June 1997.

---

22. Written details from Cannon & Associates 2 June 1997

# LONELY DELL
# RANCH

Lonely Dell Ranch was always part of the Lee's Ferry scene. No matter who was the designated ferryman, operating the ferry could never be a full time job. Conveying wagons, livestock, and people across the Colorado River, maintaining the boats, sweeps, ropes and pulleys, and repairing dugways and roads could often require a man to work from dawn to dark, perhaps for several days in succession. Grown, or nearly grown, children could also help with these duties. But the ferryman, whoever it was, and his children, always had time for farming at the Lonely Dell Ranch. It was a matter of survival.

Lonely Dell Ranch made the whole operation feasible, for without it, the people assigned to the ferry would have had very little to eat, especially in the many years of extreme isolation before the arrival of automobiles. These Lee's Ferry residents, who lived on the edge of poverty, could afford neither the time nor the money for shopping trips to the distant towns.

Raising edible crops or livestock was made especially urgent by the presence of large numbers of children in the polygamous families of Lee, Johnson, Emett, and of others who came later. In 1881, for instance, Warren Johnson, his two wives, their eight children, David Brinkerhoff, (Johnson's brother-in-law), Brinkerhoff's wife, and their three children—a total of six adults and eleven children—all lived at the ranch.[1]

Lonely Dell Ranch was where people lived, where some were born, where several died, where the joys and the sorrows of family life in an outpost of civilization were felt most acutely, particularly by the women. The men could work outside, could operate the ferry, could meet and talk with travelers, and could farm. Young children, when they weren't called upon to perform chores or attend a one-room school, could hike the trails, go fishing, or wade the Paria. But the women, confined to the farm, with an endless abundance of tedious toil that had to be performed without benefit of plumbing or electricity, and with little or no social life, were often frustrated and resentful.

A woman who lived at the ranch in 1913 stated that the presence of three other wives helped, but "for six solid months I saw no other white women. It about drove me frantic."[2]

In terms of chronology, Jacob Hamblin was the first "farmer" at Lee's Ferry. Hamblin and some Paiute helpers tried to farm a small plot of ground at Lonely Dell in 1870, but Jacob spent too much time in the Indian country, and too little on the

---

1. P.T. Reilly, "Warren Marshall Johnson, Forgotten Saint", *Utah Historical Quarterly* 39, no 1 (Winter 1971) p.15.
2. Interview with Mary Harker, Salt Lake City, 18 March 1965

Emma Batchelder Lee, seventeenth wife of John D. Lee, the first woman to live at Lee's Ferry, is generally credited with naming the place "Lonely Dell." She was known for her stamina and firm character.                                    *Utah State Historical Society*

farm, which was apparently abandoned. John D. Lee, who arrived in December, 1871, made no mention in his diary, of seeing any evidence of prior farming.

For Lee, carving out a farm and constructing buildings and roads was a monumental task. Confined by steep hills and cliffs, the useable flat land consisted of about 40 acres along a meandering bend of the Paria River.

Lee spent many days putting in a diversion dam on the Paria and digging a long canal to the farm. He probably knew from experience that desert streams like the Paria often flood violently after summer rains. But he had no choice; the Paria was his only source of water.

For a few months, all went well, but in early June, 1872, a flash flood washed out the dam. Informed of the disaster by a son, James, who walked about 20 miles through the hot desert to find him, Lee hurried back to Lonely Dell. His diary entry:

> *Now begins the Tug of War. A Dam 8 foot deep & 7 Rods long to make, besides heavy repairs on the ditch, before the water can be brought to revive the now dyeing crops, vines and trees. However imitedely we went to work. This Point Must not be abandoned. The proboble Salvation of Iseral depends on it, temporal if not Spiritual. I with my 4 litle Boys & what assistance Emma could render with a young Babe at her Breast, we continued our exertions for 21 days, watering the fruit Trees and some vines by hand and by the grace of god we finally conquered & brought the water & began to revive our dying crops...*[3]

Just a month later, the dam washed out again, but this time Lee had the assistance of a few of Major Powell's men, who were waiting at Lee's Ferry for Powell to arrive for the forthcoming boat trip down the Grand Canyon.

After repairing the dam and digging out the mud in the ditch, Lee and Emma had "our generous friends of Maj. Powel's Expedition to spend the glorious 24th with us."[4] Lee also recorded on this day that "In return for the kind reception & affable Manner in which they had been entertained since their arrival at this place, they & Maj. Powel adopted My Name for the place, Lonely Dell & so ordered it to be p[r]inted U.S. Maped."[5]

One of Powell's men, a photographer named James Fennimore, only employed a month, was weak and sick from exposure, and required rest. Having resigned from the Powell Expedition, and at Lee's invitation, Fennimore remained in Lee's home for three weeks. When Fennimore left, he told Lee that "Its like leveing the House of my Father. Your kindness to me has Made an impression that will long be remembered with grateful acknowledgment."[6]

In what must be the supreme irony, just before John D. Lee was executed by a firing squad at Mountain Meadows on March 23, 1877, he was photographed sitting on his coffin. The photographer was James Fennimore.

---

3. Cleland and Brooks, *A Mormon Chronicle*, 2:202
4. Ibid. 2:206. July 24 is the anniversary of Brigham Young's arrival in the Salt Lake Valley in 1847. It is today an official Utah holiday.
5. Powell was not present at this dinner. Furthermore, "Lonely Dell" is always labeled as Lee's Ferry (or Pahreah Crossing), on Powell's maps.
6. Cleland and Brooks, *A Mormon Chronicle*, 2:207.

The "Emma" cabin at Lonely Dell, photographed by Charles Kelly about 1932. This cabin was probably built by John D. Lee.                                                    *Utah State Historical Society*

Just what kind of a domicile Lee and Emma and their children lived in when they first moved to Lee's Ferry is uncertain. Lee recorded that on Dec. 28, 1871, "Now my energies was turned to building a couple of Houses, for Emma was still in suspense [expecting a baby]." And on January 12, 1872, he states that the houses were finished.

Obviously, if one man could build two houses in 15 days, then the structures were certainly more like cabins, and simple ones at that. Probably, the small cabin with a porch that remains at the ranch is one of those that Lee built. Although no one can date it precisely, it fits the situation. Furthermore, Frank Johnson, who was born at Lonely Dell Ranch in 1878, stated that today's cabin was there when he was born.[7]

On January 17, 1872, Emma gave birth to the first baby to be born at Lonely Dell, a baby girl named Frances Dell, "after the Place of our location," Lee wrote.[8] She was probably born in the cabin that still remains at the ranch. This was Emma's fifth child, the other four being aged 11, 9, and 5 (twins).

Lee spent much of 1873 away from Lee's Ferry, hiding out from a reported group of soldiers coming to arrest him, and developing his ranch in Moenave. Emma and her older children, plus Rachel's daughter, Nancy, and Nancy's husband, Heber Dalton, had to perform most of the farm chores as well as operate the ferry.

In December 1872, a young man named James Jackson was sent to help, but Jackson's weak physique and inexperience were ill-suited to the demands of the assignment. Jackson made a valuable contribution by teaching school to Lee's children, but he could not work effectively on either the ranch or the ferry. Jackson lived in a small cabin on ten acres of sandy soil along the Paria just north of Lee's ranch.

On February 28, 1874, on his return portion of a solitary trip to Kanab, Jackson was found almost dead from exposure. Taken to Lee's Ferry by the company headed for Arizona, Jackson was only home for four hours before he died. A coffin for him was made from the door and the table of his small cabin and he was buried nearby. Although his was the first burial in what became the Lee's Ferry Cemetery, his grave is today marked only by a collection of loose stones (see Tour Site No. 10).[9]

7. Interview with Frank Johnson, 28 October 1962.
8. Cleland and Brooks, *A Mormon Chronicle*, 2:181.
9. Jackson's death is in Bleak, "Annals of the Southern Utah Mission."

Lee spent the last five months of 1873 at Moenave. During that time his wife Emma carried on at Lee's Ferry with her small children. In November Emma gave birth to another child, without benefit of a midwife, nurse, or doctor. Appropriately, she named her daughter Victoria in memory of her personal victory over isolation and hardship. Three days after this blessed event, Lee arrived.

An often repeated Lee family tradition says that in November, 1874, a group of Navajos, knowing that Lee had been captured, crossed the river at Lee's Ferry one evening and camped not far from Emma's house. Emma's son, Billy, alerted Emma that the Indians were acting as though they intended to raid the house, or at least steal a cow. Emma too, thought that the Navajos, by not begging, were acting in a suspicious manner. Instead of locking her door and hiding, she gathered her six children in prayer, then collected blankets and pillows, and marched outside. They walked directly to the Indian camp, where Emma told the chief that she was afraid, and asked for the chief's protection. Surprised and impressed, the chief pointed to a clearing where Emma and her children could bed down for the night.

The next morning, when Emma awoke, the Indians were gone. She caught sight of them briefly in the distance, climbing out of the Paria Valley and heading toward Kanab. A few days later the Chief recounted the story to Jacob Hamblin in Kanab, stating that Emma was a "heap brave squaw."[10]

Jacob, however, was alarmed at the story, for it emphasized Emma's precarious isolation at the Lonely Dell Ranch. First he alerted church officials that a replacement for Lee was urgently needed. Then Jacob himself and his son, Lyman Hamblin, traveled to the Colorado River to tend the ferry until the replacement could arrive.

Lee's replacement was Warren Johnson, a hard-working, dedicated man who had worked both as a farmer and as a school teacher. When Johnson arrived on March 30, 1875, his first task was to fix up the James Jackson cabin so that his first wife, Permelia, and her baby, Mary, could have a place to live. Then he had to repair the diversion dam across the Paria and clean the ditches.

Lee had built a large diversion dam only about a mile upstream, but it had repeatedly washed out. To reduce the size of the dam required, Johnson extended the ditch upstream for almost another mile. Around the rock points that jutted out from the west bank he built wooden flumes, held up by cantilever supports.

About 1900, James S. Emett and his sons, using only hand tools, slowly excavated a tunnel for the ditch through one of these rock points.

Lonely Dell Ranch was originally about one-third larger than it is today. Until the flood of 1917, the Paria River passing the ranch meandered toward the east side of the river bottom all the way to its confluence with the Colorado. In 1917, the high water caused the Paria to cut diagonally across the lower part of the ranch, and since then, it has emptied into the Colorado on the west side of the river bottom.

Until the National Park Service installed the bridge over the Paria in 1963, the usual route from Lonely Dell Ranch to the upper ferry was diagonally across the fields to a ford of the Paria, then under the low cliff to the Colorado River, and then upstream to the ferry site. The route to the lower or winter ferry site did not require crossing the Paria.

In May 1891, a family traveling from Richfield, Utah, to Tuba City paused for a night at the Johnson house. They told Johnson that one of their children had suddenly

---

10. Brooks, *John Doyle Lee.*

The Warren Johnson family at Lee's Ferry in 1891. They are (l to r), Mary, Jonathan, Polly, wife Pemelia holding Roy, Jerry, Millie, Frank, Warren, Laura Alice, Nancy, and Melinda. Shortly after this photograph was taken, Jonathan, Millie, Laura Alice, and Melinda, died of diphtheria and were buried in the Lee's Ferry Cemetery.                                    *Ena Johnson Spendlove*

died on the way and that they had buried the child in Panguitch. Cause of death was then unknown.

About four days later, Johnson's five-year-old boy, Jonathan, was suddenly stricken with sore throat and fever. Then two daughters, Laura Alice and Permelia "Millie," ages seven and nine, fell ill. Jonathan choked to death in his father's arms. Then both of the girls died. Finally, fifteen-year-old Melinda caught the disease and died. A son and three daughters had thus died between May 19 and June 5. The four children were buried side by side in the Lee's Ferry Cemetery.

The disease was diphtheria. The passing family, after burying their child in Panguitch, had not realized the need to disinfect themselves, their clothing, or their wagon. Three of Johnson's other children caught the diphtheria, but eventually recovered. Fortunately, some of the children were spared because they were attending school in Kanab.

In 1895, Johnson and the LDS Church authorities reached a mutual conclusion that Johnson's mission at Lee's Ferry had ended. He prepared to move to Kanab to take up a new life. While inspecting a ranch for prospective purchase, a hay rack he was riding upset, throwing him to the ground. Johnson landed on his spine and was paralyzed from the waist down for the rest of his life.

Undeterred by his handicap, Johnson changed his plans and moved his family to Wyoming in 1896 to set up a ranching operation. The difficult life, however, proved too much for him, and during the severe winter of 1902 he died. He was buried at Byron, Wyoming. An unspectacular man, Warren Johnson nonetheless deserves tribute for the time he spent personally educating his children, for his steady competence, and for the great amount of physical labor he applied to his mission at Lee's Ferry.[11]

Johnson was replaced by James S. Emett, who moved to Lee's Ferry with his three grown sons and their wives and children. (See Chapter 11, Jim Emett and Zane Grey).

11. Reilly, "Warren Marshall Johnson" *Utah Historical Quarterly*, Winter 1971. Also, interview with Frank Johnson, 28 October 1962.

Attractive school teacher Sadie Staker (left) watches her pupils at the Lee's Ferry School about 1898. Children are members of the Jim Emett and Bill Lamb families. *Cora Brown*

In 1909, when the Grand Canyon Cattle Company, the Bar Z, bought the ferry and the farm land from the LDS Church, Jim Emett, his wives and sons moved away, leaving the ranch in the custody of ranch hands. The sale price, for about 200 acres, was $1,750.[12] As the company ranged about eight or nine thousand cattle on a section of House Rock Valley about the size of Connecticut, the management treated the Lonely Dell Ranch as their eastern outpost. After a short period of haphazard ferry operation by inexperienced cowboys, the Bar-Z turned the ferry over to Coconino County. A county official, in 1910, summoned Jerry Johnson, son of Warren, from his home in Wyoming, to run the ferry. Jerry, his wife and children moved into the two-story house on the ranch. A few months later, he was joined by his brother, Frank.

For the children, Lonely Dell education was uncertain, intermittent, and short. As mentioned earlier, Warren Johnson, educated in New Hampshire and Massachusetts, had been a school teacher (as well as a farmer), before coming to Lee's Ferry. He therefore undertook to give his children a basic education, but he could do this only during the winters, when he was not busy with ferryman or farming chores. Occasionally, other families would come to Lonely Dell, and would stay a few months to a year, and Johnson would also teach visiting children.[13]

---

12. Scamehorn, H. Lee, *Historic Structure Report Lee's Ranch, Historic Data*, unpublished report prepared for the National Park Service, 15 August 1976, p. 15
13. Letter from Mary E. Judd, daughter of Warren Johnson, to Bessie Kidd Best, Coconino County Superintendent, dated January 26, 1938.

At Lonely Dell Ranch stands the "Emma" cabin (left), and what is called the blacksmith shop. During the late 1920's, the blacksmith shop was also used as a school.

An unofficial school operated at Lonely Dell during the late 1890's, using a teacher hired by residents of the ranch. An official Lee's Ferry School District, with the teacher hired by the Coconino County, operated from October 7, 1900 until 1910, when it was discontinued. It was reestablished on June 1, 1925, and continued functioning regularly until January 7, 1935, when the District was ordered lapsed by the County School Superintendent.[14]

When Virginia Lowrey attended the Lee's Ferry School in 1927, the "schoolhouse" was the tiny wooden building, presently called the "blacksmith shop," near the larger log building. Both of these structures were probably built by John D. Lee.[15] Later, about 1930, a small wooden school house, painted white, was built about 100 yards north of the Emma cabin.[16] This school house, apparently used until 1935, was torn down or removed before the author first visited the ranch.

The Grand Canyon Cattle Company did use Lonely Dell sufficiently to assign two or three men and their wives to live there indefinitely. They resided either in the old cabins, or they shared the large, two-story, frame house with Jerry and Frank Johnson and their families. In 1916, the Bar-Z built the long, rock building to function as a range sub-headquarters. This structure remains at the Ranch.

Main headquarters for the Bar-Z was located about 30 miles west of Lee's Ferry, in House Rock Valley on the north side of U.S. 89a and just east of the Kaibab

---

14. Letter from Bessie Kidd Best, Coconino County School Superintendent, 25 April 1962.
15. Interview with Virginia Lowrey Greer, 12 March 1991.
16. Statement of Hal Nelson, Lee's Ferry "Old-timer" meeting, 19 September 1986.

The Warren Johnson home at Lonely Dell, built about 1887, accidentally burned to the ground in December 1926.

*Frank Johnson*

Plateau. The Bar-Z ranch house, now abandoned, still stands, as do some of the corrals.

In mid-December, 1926, Jerry Johnson, then the ferryman, was working for a road crew about twelve miles to the south. As he left camp one morning, he noticed a large column of smoke rising from the direction of Lonely Dell Ranch, although the ranch itself was hidden by hills. The road foreman, Chester Moon, shouted to Jerry, "Go at once to the ranch. Your large frame house is the only thing on the ranch that could make such a smoke as that!"

Jerry Johnson drove his truck to Lee's Ferry, as fast as the rough, narrow dugway would permit, becoming more convinced as he drove that his house had indeed been consumed by fire. When he reached the river he learned that his fears were indeed fact. Johnson said later that he was only concerned about his family, who were all found scared, hungry, and homeless, but uninjured. Clothes drying over a stove had ignited and the fire had quickly raced out of control. The family lost most of their clothes, furniture, some of the stored food, and other possessions. Contributions from friends in Kanab, Flagstaff, and elsewhere helped sustain the family over the winter.[17]

After the demise of the ferryboat and the drowning of three men, including Jerry Johnson's nephew, Adolph, on June 5, 1928, the Johnsons remained for a few years. Jerry himself worked on the construction of Navajo Bridge, and later served as a maintenance man for the Highway Department.

During these early years of the 1930's, families living at the ranch included those of Jerry Johnson and his wives, Clive LeBaron and his wives, a man named Spencer (no relation to Charlie Spencer, the miner-promoter), and a non-Mormon, non-polygamist named Johnson.[18]

---

17. Written statement by Jeremiah Johnson, no date. Typescript copy owned by Ena Johnson Spendlove, Page, AZ, and loaned to the author 9 August 1974.
18. Statement of Hal Nelson, 19 September 1986.

Hal Nelson, who lived at Lee's Ferry as an 11-year old boy in 1931 and 1932, stated that the Johnsons, LeBarons, and Spencers were certainly poor, but they could always buy fabric for clothes and food staples on their infrequent trips to Kanab or Fredonia. Furthermore, Nelson says that the Johnsons and other families at Lonely Dell were the most generous and sharing people that he has ever known.[19]

Generous they might have been, but most of them were polygamists, excommunicated from the LDS Church and violating Arizona law by their multiple marriages. They had discovered in both Lonely Dell and in Short Creek, Arizona, havens of remoteness where they could practice polygamy without fear of arrest, and they moved back and forth between these two places. Most of the older residents in Kanab, Fredonia, and Flagstaff were aware that polygamists lived at Lee's Ferry and at Short Creek, but the people in larger cities seemed to share a philosophical reluctance to stir up trouble without provocation. The polygamist men, however, tried to avoid travel to these cities where they might be arrested.

Dr. George Russell Aiken of Kanab, in his memoirs, tells of having been summoned to Short Creek in 1928 to treat a pregnant, young wife of Price Johnson (one of the sons of Warren Johnson). Fearing arrest for polygamy, Johnson had resisted taking the woman to a city until she became desperately ill, when he finally called the doctor for emergency treatment. To save the mother, Dr. Aiken, without adequate facilities in Short Creek, had to force a premature delivery, but the baby died.[20]

In 1932, Jerry Johnson secured a homestead patent for 160 acres, encompassing the Lonely Dell dwellings and related structures, reservoir, ditches and tillable land.[21] Johnson's homestead, however, was apparently only a means of obtaining clear title so that he could sell the ranch back to the LDS Church, which he did that same year, for $4,100.

By the early 1930's, Lonely Dell Ranch at Lee's Ferry was losing its attraction as a haven for polygamists. Lee's Ferry was no longer as remote as it had been, due to the increasing number of visitors brought about by the openings of Navajo Bridge and Marble Canyon Lodge, only six miles away. The Johnsons, LeBarons, and Spencers all moved to Short Creek (now called Colorado City), where many of their descendants live today.

Lonely Dell Ranch passed through a number of owners from the mid-1930's to the 1960's. In February, 1936, the LDS Church sold the ranch to a couple from Flagstaff, Leo and Hazel Weaver, who intended to turn it into a dude ranch. The Weavers, using the rock house built by the Grand Canyon Cattle Company in 1916 as a base, added a wood frame wing on the east end to contain rooms for their guests. The Weavers also attempted to raise Anglo-Arabian horses. But their dude ranch attracted few customers, and the Weavers fell behind in their mortgage payments and tax payments.

In 1939, a woman owner named Edith Bowers, a widow from Los Angeles, bought the ranch by paying the mortgage payments and back taxes. Mrs. Bowers soon had all the fragrant almond trees at the ranch removed because, she said, these trees

---

19. Ibid.
20. George Russell Aiken, M.D., *The Doc Aiken Story, Memoirs of a Country Doctor*, (Kanab, Utah, Southern Utah News: 1989), p. 42-43.
21. Scamehorn, op.cit. p. 15

harbored a number of owls that, during each night "sounded like the ghost of John D. Lee."[22]

Only a little over a year after she had purchased the ranch, in October, 1940, Edith Bowers sold it to C.A. Griffin, a retired employee of the Bureau of Indian Affairs. The Bureau of Reclamation had a chance to inexpensively purchase the 160 acres from Griffin when Reclamation withdrew land for the Glen Canyon National Recreation Area in the 1950's, but since the ranch was not needed for Glen Canyon Dam or Lake Powell, Reclamation declined to purchase it. Years later, however, this was seen to be a shortsighted and expensive omission.

In 1964, before the National Park Service administration had made much impact on the area, C.A. Griffin sold Lonely Dell Ranch to several speculators from Phoenix,[23] who first planned to farm the land. About 1967, these owners began to realize that the ranch had potential as a tourist-oriented recreation site. Their plans to subdivide and put in a resort alarmed National Park Service officials, who soon announced their intention to purchase the property, but could not say when. Negotiations continued for several years, but the NPS offer was always far below the figure asked by the owners. Then in April, 1971, the U.S. Attorney, acting for the NPS, filed condemnation proceedings in the Federal Court in Phoenix. This legal action had the

---

22. Interview with Frank Johnson, 28 October 1962.

23. They were listed in the Coconino County Recorder records as D&J Evans, Luhrs, R&C Brown, E&I Fryer, J. Refnes, and J&F Whiteman.

Lonely Dell Ranch, photographed in 1910 from the ridge just north of Lee's Lookout. Except for the few acres near the ranch house at upper right, most of this flat land is now barren of vegetation. Note that in 1910, the Paria River curved east before emptying into the Colorado. In 1917, the Paria cut through the sharp bend and across the sandbar at upper center and now reaches the Colorado at upper right.

*A.H. Jones*

effect of preventing the owners from making any alterations in the buildings or of selling the ranch to anyone else. Yet the condemnation suit dragged on for two and a half years, a delay that greatly embittered the owners. The suit was finally dismissed for lack of action. In April, 1974, not wishing to return to court, the NPS and the owners agreed on a price of $300,000, and on July 11, 1974, Lonely Dell Ranch was transferred to the United States.[24]

When they departed for good, in July, 1974, the former owners stripped the ranch house of valuable furniture. They even removed the old bell, once used to summon the ferryman from across the river, from its mounting over the ranch gate. Neither the bell nor the furniture has ever been returned.[25]

Today the NPS administers Lonely Dell Ranch along with the remainder of Lee's Ferry. Occasionally, NPS employees or volunteers conduct living history demonstrations where men and women dress and act the part of John D. Lee and his wife, Emma.

During the last few years, fruit orchards at the ranch grew very poorly, a result of many years of being watered by the alkali-laden Paria River. An analysis showed that the soil had become so impregnated with salts that plant growth was inhibited. In 1989, the NPS switched its water pumps from the Paria over to the Colorado River, now flowing clear and cold from Glen Canyon Dam. The apricot, pear, peach, and plum trees have responded quickly to this clean water, and produce abundantly.[26]

Present orchards, gardens and lawns at Lonely Dell Ranch are maintained for demonstration only, and therefore cover but a small percentage of the land formerly irrigated by Lee, Johnson, Emett, and others. A view from Lee's Lookout, for instance, discloses that less than 10 percent of the available land is currently used for any kind of agriculture.

Yes, the Colorado River *did* occasionally freeze over! Here Christina Klohr (wife of USGS river gauger Jim Klohr), stands on the frozen river at Lee's Ferry in January, 1925. Beside her is her young son, Jimmy, while at right is her daughter, Helen.       *Jim Klohr*

Today, Lonely Dell Ranch often exhibits a peaceful, summer afternoon tranquillity that belies the hardship, toil and tragedy that were constant companions to the people who lived there. Such ordeals were hardly unique to the early American West, but unlike most of the West, Lonely Dell has changed very little. Here, the past, and the landscape, are essential parts of the present. The arid hills and forbidding cliffs, ever changing in light and shadow, continue to loom high above the ranch, continue even to shape the lives of those who come here. And on moonlit nights, from beneath dark silhouetted fruit trees, the soft hooting of owls can be heard, an echo perhaps of voices from the past, like a whispered cry of Lonely Dell's ghosts.

---

25. The author actually witnessed the bell, loaded on a flatbed truck, ready to be hauled away to an unknown destination.
26. Interview with John Lancaster, Superintendent, Glen Canyon National Recreation Area, 6 March 1991

# THE VERMILION CLIFFS BIG HORN and CONDORS

**A** first time visitor descending the Kaibab Plateau by automobile is usually struck by the enormous landscape that opens up onto House Rock Valley and its surrounding rugged topography—a seemingly barren emptiness of red and brown, an overarching, limitless sky, a land devoid of water, perhaps of life itself, a scene that one might expect on the planet Mars. Yet of course, water is present, especially in the Colorado River gushing unseen down the deeply entrenched Marble Canyon, sliced and meandering into the valley floor.

House Rock Valley has always been an integral part of the Lee's Ferry story. For travelers seeking to cross the Colorado River, the valley, lying between the Vermilion Cliffs to the north and the Echo Cliffs to the south, functions as a giant funnel that directs all traffic toward Lee's Ferry. Dominguez and Escalante, in 1776, were the first non-

Indians to travel down this funnel only to arrive at the mouth of the Paria, then to gaze up at the nearly vertical cliffs with a feeling of being trapped. Eventually, these padres escaped, but only after an adventurous ascent of the perilous Echo Cliffs.

Later travelers had the advantage of a ferryboat to cross the river, yet most horseback and wagon travelers, when traversing House Rock Valley, kept close to the base of the huge cliffs, where some small water seeps could be found, including House Rock Spring, Two-mile Spring, Jacob Pool, Soap Creek, and Navajo Spring. These small springs were also the key to the ranching that began late in the 19th Century. Cattlemen generally kept their stock close to these springs, where the animals could find grazing and water.

136

Vermilion Cliffs rise 3,000 feet above the valley floor, presenting the most imposing vertical rock face in the United States.

Dominating the scene are the massive Vermilion Cliffs, a 3,000 vertical foot escarpment rising in giant domes, jagged rock teeth, and small, rolling benches. Cut by innumerable crevices, the cliffs display what is arguably the largest, the highest, and the most awesome barren rock face in America.

As noted in chapter one, Anasazi Indians did construct small dwellings on the dry, sandy Paria Plateau, on top of the cliffs, but they undoubtedly had difficulty procuring water. One archaeologist reported that, for some of the dwellings, the nearest water was a spring located several hundred feet down the precipitous Vermilion Cliffs. When she tried to reach this spring from the top she got close enough to see petroglyphs near the spring, but she could not descend any closer. It was simply too dangerous. One wonders how many Anasazi set out for the spring but never returned.[1]

John Wesley Powell reported that he named the cliffs in 1870. He writes:

*Starting, we leave behind a long line of cliffs, many hundred feet high, composed of orange and vermilion sandstones. I have named them "Vermilion Cliffs." When we are out a few miles, I*

---

1. Personal communication. Bureau of Land Management Archaeologist Aileen LaForge to the author. November 1995

*look back and see the morning sun shining in splendor on their
painted faces; the salient angles are on fire and the retreating
angles are buried in shade, and I gaze on them until my vision
dreams and the cliffs appear a long bank of purple clouds piled
from the horizon high into the heavens.*[2]

## DESERT BIG HORN SHEEP

Desert big horn sheep were plentiful on the Vermilion Cliffs and the Paria Plateau for
many thousands of years. Before the arrival of Europeans, Indians for many millennium
used the big horn as a prominent symbol on petroglyphs and pictographs, and several
fossil remnants have been found.

Domestic sheep brought in by settlers, however, spelled the demise of the big horn.
Biologists are virtually certain that diseases and insects, to which the domestic sheep
had become immune, were fatal to the wild variety. During the 20th Century, no big
horns were sighted in the area until 1982, when a hiker chanced upon one in the Paria
Canyon and took its picture. Still, they were extremely rare. During the 1960's the
Bureau of Land Management banned all domestic sheep from the Arizona Strip,

---

2. Powell, John Wesley, *Exploration of the Colorado River of the West, 1869-1872. (Ibid.*

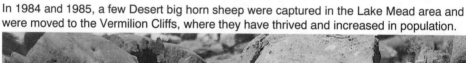

In 1984 and 1985, a few Desert big horn sheep were captured in the Lake Mead area and
were moved to the Vermilion Cliffs, where they have thrived and increased in population.

declaring it to be a cattle grazing only area. Yet the big horn population could not recover without restocking.

In July, 1984, Arizona Game and Fish Department biologists captured 37 Desert big horns near the shore of Lake Mead, conveyed them by truck to House Rock Valley, then lifted them by helicopter sling high up side canyons of the Vermilion Cliffs where they were released. One year later, in 1985, another 15 big horns were similarly moved.

Of the 52 big horns, one-third were equipped with radio collars, so that their movements could be tracked. They were followed for three and one-half years and periodic censuses were taken. During the monitoring period the mortality was about 10 percent, mostly due to the sheep falling from snow and ice crusted cliffs. Since the big horns had been raised in the Lake Mead area they had no previous experience with snow. Bob Lemons, Wildlife Manager for the Arizona Game and Fish Department, says that "Once they learned to ice skate and ski they did pretty good."

These big horns range all over the Vermilion Cliffs, but about 40 percent are usually near the rim, while 60 percent and on the cliffs and benches. For water, they usually use natural springs, which are of better quality than the Paria River. Several springs exist on the cliffs, including the Lowery Spring used by Marble Canyon Lodge. Where springs are far apart, however, wildlife managers have placed water catchment basins, so that water is available at about five-mile intervals.

In spite of the initial accidents, the reproduction rate during the late 1980's and early 1990's was very high, so that by 1993, the population of big horns was 170. Lemons says that the population in 1997 is about 125, having declined due to a state-wide drought.

Hunting of the big horns is allowed on a very limited basis, usually only three to four permits per year. Cost of each permit is $153 for Arizona residents and $753 for non-residents. Furthermore, a permittee who succeeds in a kill is never allowed another permit; it's a once-in-a-lifetime event. Hunter success has been an amazing 100 percent, with hunting days per kill only half the state average.[3]

## CONDORS: FORMER RESIDENTS RETURN

California condors are one of Nature's most dramatic creatures—not for beauty, but for sheer size—the B-52 of the avian world. With a wing span of up to 10 feet, they soar on warm thermal updrafts, their keen eyesight ever alert for carrion, their next meal. They are, of course, vultures, with bald orange heads, fierce curved beaks, and black feathers that combine into a image of sublime, fascinating ugliness. But they are not mean and aggressive; they are in fact very timid.

Condors are survivors of the distant past, having been on earth for many thousands of years, especially in the American West. Fossil evidence shows that they once inhabited the Grand Canyon. Yet outside of California, none have been spotted since the early 1920's. Even in California they were almost wiped out, victims of DDT, poisonous lead shot from hunters, and lost of habitat. Biologists of the U.S. Fish and Wildlife Service and the Peregrine Fund then rescued what few still survived, about 20 individuals, and placed them in pens. Through captive breeding fledglings were raised and successively released back into the wild. Today about 120 captive and wild condors live in southern California.

In 1996, the U.S. Fish and Wildlife Service, the Arizona Game and Fish Department,

---

3. Telephone interview with Bob Lemons, Wildlife Manager, Arizona Game and Fish Department, Page, AZ, 29 April 1997

A young, male California condor perches on the brink of the Vermilion Cliffs. The huge condors, with a wing span of up to 10 feet, were moved to the cliffs as part of a release program begun in late 1996.

*David Clendenen,*

*U.S. Fish and Wildlife Service*

and the Peregrine Fund made a decision to introduce condors into northern Arizona. On 28 October 1996, six young condors were taken by Bureau of Land Management aircraft, then lifted by helicopter to a lofty point on the Vermilion Cliffs, high above House Rock Valley, where they were kept in a fly pen until 12 December, when they were released. Testing their wings, the birds gradually extended their range, day by day, until they now fly from the Vermilion Cliffs up to 40 miles and back, into Glen Canyon, over Lake Powell, and into the Grand Canyon. Each condor is fitted with two radio transmitters that constantly send signals to biologists using direction-finding receivers.

Wildlife biologist Bill Heinrich of the Peregrine Fund in Boise, Idaho states that they feed the birds periodically with dead animal carcasses. Heinrich and the other five biologists in the field are encouraged, however, by their discovery that a few of the condors have found carrion on their own, leading them to believe that eventually the condors can be freed of human feeding assistance.

Unfortunately, fatalities are inevitable. Early in 1997 one condor was forced from the air by a belligerent golden eagle, then attacked on the ground. The eagle apparently killed the condor by a puncture wound to the head. Then in late May, another condor struck a one-inch thick aluminum power line leading south from Glen Canyon Dam to Flagstaff. He was not electrocuted, but died of hemorrhaging in the brain caused by the collision. In view of the condor's exceptional eyesight, this accident must have occurred after sunset.

On 29 April 1997, nine additional two-year old condors were brought out from the Los Angeles Zoo and the San Diego Wild Animal Park. After a conditioning period in the fly pen, these birds were also given their freedom. In future months and years, the Peregrine

Fund plan calls for transporting many more condors to northern Arizona until a stable population of 150 is established. Since the breeding age of the birds is about five to six years, it will be some time before fledglings are hatched on the cliffs. Barring accidents and given a stable food supply, condors are known to live up to 60 years.

The release site for the condors is located on the southwest bend of the Vermilion Cliffs, about 26 miles west of Marble Canyon Lodge. Although the actual "home", the aerie, of the condors is remote and almost inaccessible for humans, the huge birds can often be seen soaring along the cliffs from auto turnouts along U.S. 89a. Binoculars are essential.

Using private contributions, the Peregrine Fund provides complete financing for the condor release program. For more information contact The Peregrine Fund, 566 West Flying Hawk, Boise, ID 83709, telephone (208) 362-3716.[4]

A condor takes to the air from his aerie perch on the Vermilion Cliffs. Note the number and the radio transmitter on his wing. Biologists carefully monitor the movements of all the newly released condors.                    *George Andrejko, Arizona Game and Fish Department*

---

4. Telephone interview with Bill Heinrich, Project Manager, Peregrine Fund, Boise, ID, 22 May 1997

# GATEWAY TO
# THE CANYONS

**M**ajor Powell was the first to discover how useful Lee's Ferry could be as an access point to the Colorado, for it enabled him to break his second voyage into two segments. Then came Robert B. Stanton, with his railroad surveys in 1889 and 1890, who found Lee's Ferry indispensable as a supply point. Powell and Stanton embodied the roles of explorer, scientist, and engineer; they were not boating for adventure.

The first of a new breed of river boatmen then appeared in 1896, when George F. Flavell and Ramon Montez passed by Lee's Ferry on their way through the Colorado River's principal canyons. They were followed the next year by Nathaniel T. Galloway and William Richmond. Although Galloway and Richmond did some trapping, both teams ran the Colorado primarily for sport.[1]

Few would follow, however, until a number of articles and books appeared that publicized the adventure awaiting a canyon voyager. Noteworthy were the books of Frederick S. Dellenbaugh, who, in *A Canyon Voyage* (1908), wrote a colorful account of his experiences with Major Powell on the 1871-72 voyage. Another influential book was Ellsworth L. Kolb's *Through the Grand Canyon from Wyoming to Mexico* (1914), a detailed and accurate account of the movie making trip Ellsworth and his brother Emery made in 1911-12.

Even with the publicity the sport took hold slowly, for it was not only arduous, it was downright dangerous. The river flowed in canyons far from large cities, and it was reached only by way of difficult roads. Few guides were available, adequate maps were non-existent until the 1920's, and navigational techniques as well as boat designs had not advanced far enough to insure anything but a hazardous, uncertain

In 1932, an early-day river runner, writer Hoffman Birney, prepares his gear at Lee's Ferry for his departure on a boat trip down the Grand Canyon.

*Utah State Historical Society*

---

1. David Lavender, *River Runners of the Grand Canyon,* (Grand Canyon: Grand Canyon Natural History Association, 1985). Also Otis Marston, "River Runners: Fast Water Navigation," *Utah Historical Quarterly* 28, no. 3 (July 1960).

Off to a rendezvous with destiny. Glen and Bessie Hyde in their homemade scow, pause at Lee's Ferry in October, 1928. A month later, their boat was found at Mile 222 in the Grand Canyon, but the Hydes were never seen again.     *Glen Canyon Natural History Association*

ride through the rapids. During the first decade of the twentieth century, only three trips were made through the Grand Canyon. One took place in 1912, two in the 1920's, four in the 1930's, and six in the 1940's. Many of these trips, especially the later ones, used Lee's Ferry as a starting point.[2]

Norman D. Nevills was the first to undertake commercial boating through Marble and Grand Canyons for paying passengers. After a trip through Glen Canyon, Nevills first reached Lee's Ferry in 1936. In 1938, he made his first trip past Lee's Ferry, carrying passengers, including the first women to boat through the Grand Canyon. On a similar trip in 1940, one of his passengers was the future U.S. Senator from Arizona, Barry Goldwater. Goldwater's interest in these canyons, and in Colorado River history, continues strong to this day.

Glen Canyon, which lies upstream from Lee's Ferry, was not initially popular for boating because the early sporting emphasis was on running rapids, of which Glen Canyon had none of any consequence. With but a few exceptions, most travelers, such as Powell's men in 1869 and 1871, noticed little of Glen Canyon's beauty and only expressed impatience at the slow, meandering current. It was not until after World War II that the expanded use of color photography made people see the dazzling spectrum of sunlight and shadow in this intricate sandstone gorge.

In Glen Canyon some of the earliest paying passengers were customers of Art Greene, who began making occasional boat trips from Lee's Ferry to Aztec Creek, the access point for Rainbow Bridge. Greene had boated on the San Juan River and was

2. Barry M. Goldwater, *Delightful Journey Down the Green & Colorado Rivers* (Tempe, Arizona: Arizona Historical Foundation, 1970). Senator Goldwater's book includes a listing by Otis Marston of the first hundred persons to traverse the Grand Canyon by boat.

In 1938, Norman Nevills pauses at Lee's Ferry on the first commercial trip ever to carry paying passengers through the Grand Canyon.
*Utah State Historical Society*

A passenger on a Norm Nevills trip in 1940 was Barry Goldwater, later to become U.S. Senator from Arizona. In this photograph he appears to be operating a short term—and obviously small scale—laundry service along the river bank.

*Arizona Historical Foundation*

The first Grand Canyon motorboat trip was conducted in 1949, here photographed just before departure from Lee's Ferry on June 12, 1949. The party was headed by Otis "Dock" Marston (left) and Ed Hudson (second from right). In their boat, named the Esmeralda II, they reached upper Lake Mead in five days.     *Dock Marston Collection, Huntington Library*

well acquainted with the canyon country and the Navajo Reservation. In 1943 he became manager of Marble Canyon Lodge (at Navajo Bridge) and soon thereafter began his sporadic tours to Rainbow Bridge.[3]

Greene's early trips were made in a tiny, thirteen-foot rowboat powered by a twenty horsepower outboard. After the war he increased the size and the number of his boats, but he kept his operations simple. If a motor developed bad trouble he simply drifted back to Lee's Ferry. Whenever he chanced upon another river runner, all of whom were well-known to Greene and his family, it was common to make camp then and there, so that the friends could "swap lies." Schedules were almost non-existent. Art just told his customers that he would take them to Rainbow Bridge and back and that it would take "up to a week."

To avoid trouble caused by hidden sandbars and rocks, Greene experimented with an air-driven boat powered by an airplane engine and propeller mounted on the top deck. After trying a few smaller engines he finally settled on a huge 450-horsepower Pratt & Whitney "Duster" engine that he put on the boat in 1952.

One big problem was that the engine burned great quantities of gasoline, so much that cans of gasoline had to be placed in advance at certain places beside the river. From the visitor's point of view, however, the major drawback was the terrible noise of the engine. Earplugs and cotton were standard issue to all guests and crew. To communicate while enroute, Art tried a hose with funnels at each end, but that didn't work. He finally gave everyone a pencil and note pad for important messages. As Art "Bill" Greene, Jr. said, "You couldn't hear for a week after one of those trips!"

In spite of its drawbacks, Art's air boat performed beautifully. In very shallow water, for instance, it seemed to rise up on its own "pressure wave." Frequently the

3. Interview with Art "Bill" Greene, Jr., Wahweap Lodge, Lake Powell, 5 October 1973.

Art Greene, former cowboy and Indian trader turned riverman, beside his unique aluminum boat propelled by an airplane engine, used to take visitor excursions up Glen Canyon to Rainbow Bridge. The boat could handle the sandbars and shallow water of the Colorado River, but the frightful noise of the engine temporarily deafened everyone on board. Photo taken in 1953. Greene and his family later built Wahweap Lodge on the shore of Lake Powell.          *Joseph Muench*

boat would lurch slightly and those on board could look back and see grooves cut through a sandbar. In optimum conditions the boat could reach a speed of fifty-five miles an hour. Greene operated the air boat until 1960.

Throughout these years, Greene was also developing general tourist accommodations. About 1949, he began building Cliff Dweller's Lodge on U.S. 89a, a few miles from Navajo Bridge. Formerly he and his family had lived in the strange cabins built under, around, and over some balanced rocks just west of Soap Creek. These rock cabins had probably been built by a man named Bill Russell, who lived at Soap Creek around 1927.[4]

---

4. Statement of Cecil Cram, Lee's Ferry "Old-timers meeting," 19 September 1986.

A scenic view of Art Greene's air-propelled boat at Sentinel Rock, at the mouth of Wahweap Creek in Glen Canyon. Photo was taken in 1953. This area, just upstream from the present Glen Cnayon Dam, now lies under several hundred vertical feet of Lake Powell water.

*Joseph Muench*

From Bureau of Reclamation engineers who stayed at Marble Canyon Lodge during the 1940's and at Cliff Dweller's Lodge during the early 1950's, (successively managed by Greene), Art learned many details about the future Glen Canyon Dam and reservoir. Using this base of knowledge, Art examined much of the shoreline of the planned lake by airplane, four wheel drive vehicle, and horse, until he at last pinpointed the best site for a lodge—on a hillside above Wahweap Creek. Art leased his chosen land first from the State of Arizona and then from the U.S. Government. On this land, now the shore of Lake Powell, stands Wahweap Lodge.

During the 1940's, while Art Greene was running his earlier trips from Lee's Ferry upriver to Rainbow Bridge, Glen Canyon was "discovered" by Boy Scouts and many others. Mostly untrained as boatmen, these people floated the easy waters of the Colorado from Hite, near the head of the canyon, down to Lee's Ferry. Using war surplus neoprene rafts, canoes, kayaks—almost anything that would float—they journeyed through magnificent Glen Canyon. First hundreds, then thousands, made the trip, and all of them left the river at Lee's Ferry. As a result of their traffic through Glen Canyon from 1946 to 1956, Lee's Ferry was visited by far more people that at any other time in its history.

After 1956 boating through the damsite was prohibited, so Glen Canyon voyagers left the river at Kane Creek where a graded road reached the river bank. After this Lee's Ferry faded somewhat from public view, but Art Greene continued to run short trips from Lee's Ferry up to Glen Canyon Dam until 1963. In the early 1960's, Lee's

Ferry was, of course, the starting point for the increasing number of river running trips through Grand Canyon.

Lee's Ferry was included in the lands either acquired or withdrawn for the Glen Canyon National Recreation Area. The only exception was the one hundred sixty-acre homestead at the Lee's Ferry Ranch, or Lonely Dell, which continued as private property until July 1974, when it was purchased by the U.S. Government. (See previous chapter)

In 1963 the National Park Service moved into Lee's Ferry to establish a recreation site. As an access point to the river the place was essential, since only at Lee's Ferry could tourists and boaters reach the clean, cold tailwater that was discharged from the dam. Short trips could be made upriver through Glen Canyon to the dam. Even more important, however, was that Lee's Ferry was the only launching site for commercial river trips down Marble and Grand Canyons.

To the National Park Service Lee's Ferry has been something of an enigma. Its importance as a recreation site was undeniable, yet it was also a historic site. Any action to put in boat ramps, motel, store, parking lots, or access roads was likely to interfere with the historical integrity of specific points. Still, Lee's Ferry could not be maintained solely as an open air museum. The NPS destruction of the Spencer buildings in 1967 could certainly be attributed to confusion about the dual nature of Lee's Ferry. In contrast to the 1960's, officials of the Glen Canyon National Recreation Area now appear to be more cognizant of the history of the area and the need for historical preservation. The Glen Canyon Natural History Association has published brief historical summaries, in pamphlet form, for distribution to tourists.

In 1967 the Fort Lee Company was granted a concession at Lee's Ferry and operated it for several years before the NPS discontinued the concession, thus closing the store, the restaurant, and the trailers used for guest lodging.

## PROPOSED MARBLE CANYON DAM

During the late 1960's, Commissioner Floyd E. Dominy of the Bureau of Reclamation pushed hard to convince Congress, and whatever "publics" he thought necessary, that two dams were needed for the Central Arizona Project, both in Grand Canyon—one, called Bridge Canyon Dam, in the lower part of the canyon, and another, Marble Canyon Dam, at Mile 40 (below Lee's Ferry). The primary purpose of both these dams was to generate cheap hydroelectric power to power huge pumps that would suck water out of Lake Havasu and send it on to Phoenix and Tucson. If built, the reservoir behind Marble Canyon Dam would, when full, back all the way to the foot of Glen Canyon Dam. And it was going to flood most of what we know as Lee's Ferry.

For about two years, it appeared that Marble Canyon and Bridge Canyon Dams would actually be built. In fact, National Park Service planning for Lee's Ferry was predicated on that probability. But slowly, almost imperceptibly, Dominy's influence with Congress began to wane. Simultaneously, concern for the environment, throughout America, steadily gained adherents. David Brower and the Sierra Club certainly deserve much credit for their intensive campaign to alert citizens to the potential environmental losses that the two dams would cause.

In 1969, the plan for the dams was finally crushed, hopefully forever. In the same year, Congress passed the National Environmental Policy Act, the law that now forces agencies that seek to alter Federal lands to investigate and evaluate the environmental consequences, to make disclosures, and to seek public involvement.

The boat launching ramp at Lee's Ferry is a busy place on summer mornings, as private and commercial river-running companies assemble their passengers and load the necessary equipment for the trip down the Grand Canyon. All permits and equipment are checked by National Park Service Rangers.                                                                    *Don Cecala*

Also in 1969, President Johnson signed an Executive Order that created Marble Canyon National Monument, further protecting the canyon from dam builders. Grand Canyon National Park was enlarged (absorbing the National Monument), in 1975 so as to contain all of the canyon between Lake Mead and the Paria River at Lee's Ferry. The canyon above the Paria River remains part of the Glen Canyon National Recreation Area. Since two National Park Service units adjoin at Lee's Ferry, both the Park and the Recreation Area have Rangers on duty.

## GLEN CANYON, GRAND CANYON AND THE RIVER

Whitewater boating has changed considerably since the early rough and adventurous trips in wooden boats through the Grand Canyon. Of significance has been new boating equipment-first rubber rafts, then eventually twenty-eight-foot long bridge pontoons, often called "baloneys." The switch to motor power greatly changed methods of running the rapids and permitted use of the big baloneys. Several companies feature smaller rubber rafts, usually oar-powered, that provide a more intimate, as well as adventuresome, contact with the river. At least one company uses wooden boats called dories, flat bottom boats that curve upward at each end, which can be maneuvered rapidly by a skilled boatman.

Boating downriver from Lee's Ferry grew substantially in volume after Glen Canyon Dam was built. Undoubtedly, the dam construction coincided with a nationwide increase in river boating and with improvements in boating equipment and techniques of river running. The longer boating season allowed by regulation of seasonal flows through the dam has also permitted a dramatic increase in Colorado River boating. Undoubtedly, the controversy over whether or not to build Marble Canyon Dam and Bridge Canyon Dam in Grand Canyon stimulated much interest in the downstream river run. The number of boaters through the Grand Canyon, controlled by the National Park Service on a visitor-day basis, rose from about two hundred eighty in 1962 to nearly sixteen thousand in 1973, and is now about twenty-two thousand each year.

Lee's Ferry is the key to all boating through the Grand Canyon, for it is the only place above the canyon where trucks, buses, and cars may drive to the bank of the river. It became even more important by the construction of Glen Canyon Dam, which sealed off river boating through Glen Canyon. .

During the decade from 1982 to 1992, the entire 285 mile stretch of canyon between the dam and Lake Mead was exhaustively examined by biologists and geologists to determine the environmental effects of fluctuating clear water flows from the dam. Although they had no authority or mandate to recommend removal of the dam and a return of the river to its historic warm, muddy flows, the scientists did determine that the clear, fluctuating, cold water had severely eroded sandy beaches and had almost wiped out all native fishes. An Environmental Impact Statement was issued in 1994 that recommended a reduction in both the maximum flows and the "ramping rate" (speed of change), of the flows. Later the Secretary of the Interior Bruce Babbitt signed a Record of Decision putting this recommendation into effect.

To rebuild beaches, the scientists recommended periodic "spike flows," that is, minor flood releases from Glen Canyon Dam to churn up low lying sand in deep pools and deposit it on river banks. In March 1996 the first spike flow of 45,000 cubic feet per second was released over a two-week period. Beaches were quickly expanded, leading researchers to hope that an even higher flow, but over a shorter period, can be released during the spring of some coming year.

Lee's Ferry is also the access point for boating and fishing on the 15-mile stretch of Glen Canyon that lies upstream to the dam. Sightseers may ride a commercial raft on a magnificently scenic and leisurely half-day trip from the dam down to Lee's Ferry, where they will be met by bus and returned to the town of Page. During most months one or two daily float trips are conducted from the dam down to Lee's Ferry by a NPS concessionaire, Wilderness River Adventures, a division of ARA Leisure Services.

Fishing for trout has been exceptional on the river upstream from Lee's Ferry, especially during the cooler months of the year. Adequately equipped private boats are allowed. Commercial fishing guides can also be hired on a daily basis. An Arizona fishing license is required. One of the best books about local fishing is *The Lee's Ferry Angling Boating Guide,*, by Dave Foster.

During the winter months, the canyon can be quite cold, so that except for a few hardy fishers, Lee's Ferry is again fairly lonely. But on a typical day between March and October, one will see all manner of boating tourists, from bikini-clad college girls to grizzled river veterans, from high school boys drinking their first beer to thoughtful retired couples videotaping the scenery. All find their place at Lee's Ferry and on the Colorado River. Once in the canyons a boating tourist usually discovers that his customary identity has little importance and that he or she becomes one with the crew, with fellow passengers, with the canyon, and with the river.

As a gateway across the river, Lee's Ferry's days ended in 1928, but as a gateway to the Colorado River, Lee's Ferry's days have only just begun.

If Emma Lee could return on a busy summer day, she would undoubtedly look around at the boats and all the river runners, at the fishermen, at the camera laden tourists walking about her former home. These she would view with amazement, then she might exclaim, softly, and with a smile,

"And this Dell <u>used</u> to be <u>so</u> Lonely!"

From Lee's Ferry, the river plunges into the scenic depths of Marble Canyon, and then into Grand Canyon. Each year about 20,000 people make a memorable boat trip through these canyons.

*Bureau of Reclamation*

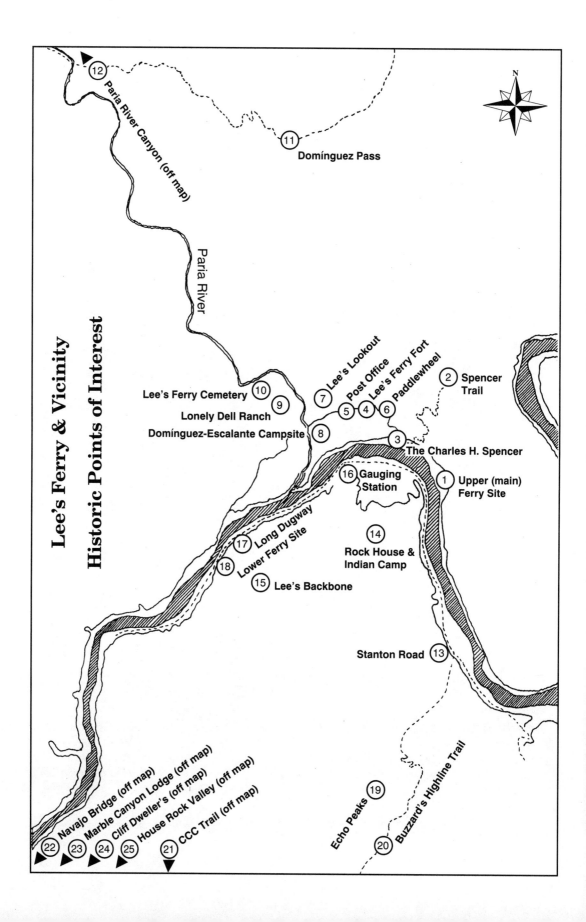

# Lee's Ferry & Vicinity

# Historic Points of Interest

Paria River Canyon (off map)

(12)

(11)
**Domínguez Pass**

Paria River

Lee's Lookout

Post Office

Lee's Ferry Fort

Paddlewheel

(2) **Spencer Trail**

Lee's Ferry Cemetery (10)

(9)

(7)

(5) (4) (6)

**Lonely Dell Ranch**

**Domínguez-Escalante Campsite** (8)

(3) **The Charles H. Spencer**

(16) **Gauging Station**

(1) **Upper (main) Ferry Site**

Long Dugway

(17)

(14)

**Lower Ferry Site**

(18)

**Rock House & Indian Camp**

(15) **Lee's Backbone**

**Stanton Road** (13)

**Navajo Bridge (off map)**

**Marble Canyon Lodge (off map)**

**Cliff Dweller's (off map)**

**House Rock Valley (off map)**

**CCC Trail (off map)**

(19)

**Echo Peaks**

Buzzard's Highline Trail

(20)

(22) (23) (24) (25) (21)

# TOUR SECTION

## A GUIDE TO HISTORIC SITES AND PLACES AT AND NEAR LEE'S FERRY

Lee's Ferry is rich in visible traces of history, yet the spectacular desert landscape is apt to dominate, even to overawe; historic sites tend to be inconspicuous and need to be pointed out. All of the more important accessible sites are listed in this Tour Section, together with brief descriptions and some photographs. These sites are also shown on the accompanying map. Many sites are clustered near the present boat ramp and may be visited within a short time. National Park Service Rangers offer further sources of assistance and directions.

A *warning*: None of the old trails or abandoned roads is maintained, and all have some hazards. A few are dangerous. Before hiking any of them, check with the District Ranger.

The south side of the river is Navajo Indian Reservation. If you plan to hike extensively on the Reservation, you should obtain a permit or official permission from the Navajo Tribe.

1. **UPPER (MAIN) FERRY SITE.** The most important ferry crossing site was upstream about half a mile from the boat ramp. Here ferryboats operated continually from 1873 to 1878, during the spring and early summer from 1873 to 1896, and continually from 1896 to 1928. It was at this upper ferry site that most of the early Mormon emigrants from Utah crossed the river as they heeded the "call" to settle in Arizona. Most emigrants considered the river crossing as the one real danger on the long trip (see Chapter 8). In 1896 a heavy track cable was hung across the river at this site to hold the boat. From then until 1928, this site was used throughout the year.

Ferry accidents at the various crossing sites caused drownings in 1876, 1880, 1884, 1899, 1911 and 1928. In the last accident, June 7, 1928, three men drowned. It was a tragic finale to ferry operations at Lee's Ferry. Since Navajo Bridge was then under construction, the ferryboat was never replaced (see Chapter 14). Although little evidence of former activity remains at the upper ferry site, some rock foundations of cabins used by ferrymen and travelers are visible. Nearby is a section of heavy cable used to hold the ferry.

Across the river the old approach road to the ferry, dug out of the steep river bank, leads downstream. The landing on the opposite shore was at the low point in the road. Extending upstream from the ferry site is another dugway, the Stanton Road (see Site No. 13).

A powerboat cruises past the old ferry site and up into Glen Canyon. Here the fishing is good and the scenery superb.

2. **SPENCER TRAIL**. The Spencer Trail climbs the steep slope east of the Fort to the canyon rim, 1500 feet above the river. Switchbacking ingeniously around sheer ledges, the trail even today seems a marvel of engineering. It was built in 1910 by a mining company headed by Charles H. Spencer. Spencer himself reported that it was laid out, at least in part, by a clever mule named Pete (see Chapter 12). Spencer intended to pack coal by mule train from Warm Creek Canyon over the trail. Although the Spencer Trail was little used for coal transport, for other travelers it was a decided improvement over the Domínguez Pass Trail (see Site No. 11), two and one-half miles up the Paria.

The Spencer Trail is not maintained, but it is still passable to hikers who exercise care and good judgment. Hikers on this historic route are rewarded with magnificent views of the canyon, the plateau country, and the Colorado River. Before setting out check trail conditions by consulting the National Park Service office.

3. **THE *CHARLES H. SPENCER***. In the mud of the riverbank lies the hulk of a stern paddle wheel steamboat know as the *Charles H. Spencer*. This steamer, twenty-five feet wide and ninety-two feet long, was the largest craft ever floated on the Colorado River above the Grand Canyon. It was built in San Francisco in 1911, dismantled, and shipped by rail and wagon to the mouth of Warm Creek, in Glen Canyon, where it was reassembled. The company headed by Charles H. Spencer, mining entrepreneur at Lee's Ferry, brought the boat to the Colorado River to haul coal from the Warm Creek mines to Lee's Ferry. The coal was to be used to fire steam boilers for sluicing gold particles from the abundant outcropping of Chinle shale located about two hundred yards north of Lee's Ferry Fort. One of the big steam boilers still remains near the spot where Spencer centered his mining operations.

During 1912, the *Charles H. Spencer* made about five one-way trips, largely of an experimental nature, ending up at Lee's Ferry. The steamboat could probably have

154

The incredible Spencer Trail climbs 1,500 vertical feet up the Echo Cliffs.

The remains of the *Charles H. Spencer* partially buried by mud in 1962. This mud has since been scoured out by the clear water flowing from Glen Canyon Dam. The ruin of the steamboat, however, has suffered from exposure and from "tourist erosion."

been adapted to carry considerable coal, but the mining venture failed because of other factors and the coal was not needed (see Chapter 12). The *Charles H. Spencer* remains a visible artifact that illustrates one of the more dramatic chapters in mining along the Colorado River.

4. **LEE'S FERRY FORT**. Near the boat ramp and parking lot, and quite obvious to visitors, is Lee's Ferry Fort. Built primarily as a trading post–not as a fort–its construction in 1874 was a means of keeping peace between the Navajos of Arizona and the whites of southern Utah. Trouble erupted in January 1874, when three Navajos were killed and another wounded by white men while the Indians were on a trading trip into south-central Utah. The wounded Navajo, who managed to struggle back to Arizona Territory, precipitated demands for revenge, if not outright war, against the white settlers. The incident threatened to engulf the Mormon-Navajo frontier in further bloodshed, but the situation finally cooled. As a means of keeping Navajos out of southern Utah, the Mormons decided that a post at Lee's Ferry would be helpful. In July 1874, a construction crew from the L.D.S. St. George Stake built the trading post (see Chapter 7). No evidence exists that the building was ever under attack. It was used only intermittently as a trading post, but was used in later years as a residence, a school, and a mess hall.

Note the name "J. Hislop 1889" pecked into the stone at the side of the right doorway. John Hislop was with Robert B. Stanton on a railroad survey down the Colorado. Stanton and his men had Christmas dinner beside the fort in 1889 (see Chapter 11). John D. Lee had no connection with the building or operation of the Lee's Ferry Fort, and it is inappropriate to call it "Lee's Fort." East of the Fort are two rock buildings used by the U.S. Geological Survey. The older of the two was one of several buildings built by Charles H. Spencer around 1911. All the other Spencer buildings, except for the ruins of a rock chicken coop, have been removed.

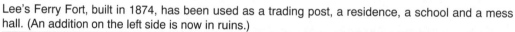

Lee's Ferry Fort, built in 1874, has been used as a trading post, a residence, a school and a mess hall. (An addition on the left side is now in ruins.)

5. **POST OFFICE**. The small rock cabin located a short distance west of the fort was used as a post office. An official post office was maintained at Lee's Ferry from 1879 to 1923.

The Post Office, in use in 1923. In front are Jim Klohr, USGS river gauger, Margie Jean Wilson and Mary Wilson.                              *National Park Service*

6. **PADDLEWHEEL OF THE NAVAJO**. Located on the trail beside the two USGS buildings is an remnant of an old paddle wheel. Originally this was attached to the *Navajo*, a scow or barge used by the Southern California Edison Company during their dam site investigations in Glen Canyon from 1921 to 1923.

7. **LEE'S LOOKOUT**. The round knob of Shinarump conglomerate rising about 175 feet above and northwest of Lee's Ferry Fort is Lee's Lookout. From it can be seen the lower Paria, the Vermilion Cliffs, lower Glen Canyon, and upper Marble Canyon—in fact, the entire Lee's Ferry area. Rumors that John D. Lee, as a fugitive, actually used this height for a lookout point led to the present name, but there can be little truth to the story. In his short time at Lee's Ferry, Lee was far too busy working on the ranch or tending to ferryboat duties to have time for standing around on high ledges.

Atop the knob is a low circle of rocks about twenty feet in diameter. This circle was there before Lee arrived, for a member of the 1869 Powell expedition, Jack Sumner, made a note of it. Still, the origin of the rock circle is a subject of conjecture. Prehistoric Indians probably laid up the stones, but archaeologists have found no evidence to confirm or deny it. The Lookout is an easy hike from the parking lot.

Otis "Dock" Marston, famed Colorado River historian, on February 8, 1957, checks the stern paddlewheel of the motorboat *Navajo*, used from 1921 to 1923. Since this photograph was taken, the paddlewheel has suffered 40 additional years of exposure to the elements and is now a mere remnant.                          *Dock Marston Collection, Huntington Library*

8. **DOMÍNGUEZ-ESCALANTE CAMPSITE**. From October 26 to November 1, 1776, the Spanish padres and their entourage camped on the bank of the Colorado near the mouth of the Paria River. In their diary Escalante reports that the campsite was beside the river near a high rock. They were obviously camped at the base of the Shinarump ridge along the present paved road between the Paria River and Lee's Ferry Fort. Naming their campsite San Benito, the Spaniards gazed at the great cliffs facing them on every side, then with a touch of humor added the name "Salsipuedes," meaning "get out if you can" (see Chapter 2).

In 1869 when a group of Mormon men were sent to the Paria River to guard against marauding Navajos, the Mormons camped under the same rock. They dubbed

Lee's Lookout, looking northwest.

Domínguez-Escalante campsite at Lee's Ferry was on the river bank below this rock prominence.

their small enclosure "Fort Meeks" (see Chapter 3).

9. **LONELY DELL RANCH**. The ranch lies on the nearly flat valley floor within a large meander of the Paria River. Crops and livestock grown here provided economic support for the ferry operators, their families, and others from 1872 to the 1940's. The ranch is referred to as "Lonely Dell" because it was Emma Lee's description of the entire Lee's Ferry setting when she first saw it in late December 1871. Although the soil was fair, the task of maintaining a constant water supply, particularly in the hot summer months, was often beyond human capability. Flash floods on the Paria repeatedly wiped out diversion dams and either destroyed irrigation ditches or filled them with silt. Work was grueling and virtually unending. When John D. Lee, as a fugitive, left Lee's Ferry to go into hiding, no one remained who was capable of maintaining the irrigation system. Without water in blistering summer heat, Lee's crops soon withered and died. When Lee returned he found all crops dead except a single apricot tree that Emma Lee had hand-watered with a bucket.

After Lee was executed in 1877 and Emma Lee and her children had departed, the

Lonely Dell Ranch in 1969

new ferry operator, Warren Johnson, built a large, two-story home on the ranch for his two wives and their growing families. Johnson's wooden home lasted through changes in ferry operators until December 1926, when it accidentally burned to the ground.

In 1916, the Grand Canyon Cattle Company built the long rock bungalow that still stands on the ranch. In the 1930's, it was used as a dude ranch by Leo Weaver, who added the wooden rooms to the east end. Weaver's business was poor, and the ranch traded hands several times before the U.S. Government purchased it to be part of the Glen Canyon National Recreation Area.

On this ranch are a one-room cabin and a log shed, both probably built by John D. Lee. One of the Johnson boys, born at Lee's Ferry in 1878, recalls that the two structures were almost certainly there when he was born. In later years the log shed was used as a schoolhouse. Two small, indistinct structures at the ranch are visible on an 1873 photograph taken from across the Colorado River. (see page 35).

During the many years of irrigating with the poor-quality, alkali water of the Paria River, the soil of the Lonely Dell Ranch has lost its fertility. The National Park Service now irrigates with the high-quality, clear water from the Colorado River. Early reports are that the orchards of pear, apricot, peach, and apple are responding favorably.

10. **LEE'S FERRY CEMETERY**. Located about one-quarter mile northwest of Lee's Ferry Ranch, the cemetery contains possibly twenty graves, the oldest dated 1874 and the latest dated 1928. Over half of the graves are either poorly marked or bear no marking at all. The earliest grave, that of James Jackson who died in March 1874, is marked only by a pile of loose stones. Among the tragic deaths were four Johnson children who contacted diphtheria from a passing traveler and who died within a period of four weeks during May and June 1891. (see Chapter 16). The

At the Lee's Ferry Cemetery, the marker for the Johnson children who died in 1891.

Johnson children graves have been marked with a single large gravestone.

11. **DOMÍNGUEZ PASS**. This pass and the steep trail up to it were discovered by the Domínguez-Escalante expedition in 1776. After spending a futile week at San Benito Salsipuedes (Lee's Ferry) trying to cross the Colorado, the priests and their men located this pass. They apparently blazed a new trail from the Paria River up to the pass (see Chapter 2).

Mormon missionaries enroute to the Hopi villages in 1858, 1859, and 1860 also used this route. John D. Lee and others of his day traveled it often, while in later years cowboys, outlaws, and miners occasionally traversed the trail.

Today this historic trail across the Echo Cliffs is unmarked and all but forgotten. The trail is traceable only in part, but the entire route is generally apparent. It begins beside the Paria River about two and one-half miles above Lee's Ferry, winds through bleak hills of Chinle shale, then up long slopes of shifting sand, angling southeastward toward a low point in the cliffs–Domínguez Pass. The pass is some two thousand feet above the Paria River.

The Domínguez Pass route can be followed today by well prepared hikers willing to exert strenuous effort and carry ample water. Midway up, the trail crosses a long, steep pitch of soft sand, while near the crest it is extremely steep and angles across narrow sandstone ledges. Any one planning to make the hike should notify the Park Ranger at Lee's Ferry.

12. **PARIA RIVER CANYON**. One of the more spectacular, narrow, rocky canyons in the West channels the Paria River as it knifes its way through the Paria Plateau and on to Lee's Ferry. John D. Lee and his son, on their first trip into the area, had an eight-day, agonizing ordeal, trying to herd a few cattle down this canyon to Lee's Ferry in December, 1871. In 1984, Congress established the 112,000 acre Paria Canyon-Vermilion Cliffs Wilderness Area, a roughly horseshoe-shaped area bordering the Paria Plateau on three sides. The area also includes the lower portion of the Buckskin Gulch, an extremely narrow, (in some places less than 2 feet wide), winding

The trail to Domínguez Pass

In the depths of the Paria River Canyon

*Bureau of Land Management*

defile that joins the Paria 1,000 feet below the canyon rims.

All hikers must register in advance with the Bureau of Land Management in Kanab or at the Paria Ranger Station near U.S. 89. While the canyon floor hike is only 37-miles long, the BLM recommends allowing 4 days for the trek, since hikers will probably encounter such difficulties as pools, rough, wet, foot-bruising rocks, and even quicksand. Dangerous flash floods can occur in mid to late summer, especially in Buckskin Gulch. Yet the trek through the deep and winding Paria River Canyon is, for most people, a unique and awesome experience, as well as a photographer's bonanza.

13. **STANTON ROAD**. On the south (left) bank of the Colorado River, extending upstream from the upper ferry site about one and one-half miles, is the Stanton Road. It terminates just below the first big bend of the river. This road was put in during 1899 by Robert B. Stanton, railroad promoter turned mining engineer. At the time Stanton was preparing to place a huge gold dredge on the Colorado in upper Glen Canyon. Confident that the dredge would successfully extract gold particles from the river sands, Stanton staked mining claims up and down both sides of the river. The "road" at Lee's Ferry was simply assessment work required to keep some of these claims valid. Stanton's dredge was big and expensive, but it was incapable of capturing the flour-fine gold from the river bed. The entire enterprise soon collapsed (see Chapter 11).

14. **ROCK HOUSE AND INDIAN CAMP**. On the south side of the river, located at the base of an alternate wagon road around Lee's Backbone, an abandoned one-room rock house stands beneath the cliffs. Although the origin and purpose of this house have not been determined, it has been used as a camp by Navajo Indians, who have also built a number of small stone corrals near by. At Lee's Ferry, all of the area south of the river is part of the Navajo Reservation, and the river bottom land is frequently used by these Indians as grazing land for their animals.

15. **LEE'S BACKBONE**. What was known as Lee's Backbone is the relatively flat but steeply inclined surface of Shinarump conglomerate on the south side of the river. Over this rock surface, Mormon emigrants took their wagons south from the ferry crossing. It was used continually from 1873 to 1878, when the lower ferry site and dugway were constructed for use during periods of low river flow (see Site No. 18). Still in use during times of high river flow, the Backbone was partially bypassed by a slightly better road over high terrain in 1888. In 1898, when the long dugway was opened (see Site No. 17), Lee's Backbone was completely abandoned.

Lee's Backbone is covered by numerous rock gullies and boulders that brutally pounded wooden wagons and straining animals. Some travelers claimed it was the worst piece of land ever crossed by wagons (see Chapter 8).

Today hikers may follow the old wagon road over Lee's Backbone. In places, grooved wagon ruts can be seen in solid rock. At its highest point, where the road ran literally on the edge of the cliff, evidence of much road work can still be seen. At the extreme southwest end, the roads switchbacked down some four hundred feet over a steep talus slope to the fairly level terrain of the Marble Platform.

The alternate route, built in 1888 over higher terrain, was not much of an improvement. This bypass can be followed only with difficulty today since much of it has been washed out.

Lee's Backbone (center), as seen from the Spencer Trail. The first road to the south traversed this steep and rough rock incline.

16. **GAUGING STATION**. Operated by the U.S. Geological Survey, the essential structure of the station is the narrow concrete water recorder well beside the river at the base of Lee's Backbone. This gauging station is the most important one on the entire Colorado River, since it measures the amount of water passing from the Upper to the Lower Basins in fulfillment of the 1922 Colorado River Compact–the "law of the river." The dividing or "Compact" point between the basins is set at one mile below the mouth of the Paria.

One reason for building Glen Canyon Dam was to provide a huge storage reservoir (Lake Powell) that could be used to meet down stream commitments. Whether or not these commitments are met is determined by measurements taken at the Lee's Ferry Gauging Station.

On Grand Canyon river maps the gauging station is marked Mile Zero, the reference point from which distances downstream are measured (see Chapter 13).

17. **LONG DUGWAY**. The long dugway on the south side of the Colorado was built in 1898 so that travelers could bypass the arduous route over Lee's Backbone. Carved from the soft, brown Moenkopi formation, the road follows the contour of the slope and ascends about three hundred feet in a mile. For thirty years it carried all the traffic to and from the upper ferry site—horses, mules, bull teams and wagons, and finally early-day automobiles (see Chapter 10).

Although it is now greatly eroded away, the dugway, when in use, was kept wide enough for one wagon or automobile. But it was none too wide. Sharlot Hall, Arizona Territorial Historian, who traveled this dugway by wagon in 1911, wrote of it, "The road looked as if it had been cut out of the red clay with a pocket knife. Sometimes it hung out over the river so we seemed sliding into the muddy current and again the cliffs above hung over till one grew dizzy to look."

The dugway is boldly visible from a number of points on the north side of the river. Hikers, using care at places where washouts have occurred, may walk the entire dugway.

The Dugway, main road to Lee's Ferry from the south from 1898 to 1928.

18. **LOWER FERRY SITE.** Ferryboats crossed the river at this lower site during low flow stages of the river from 1878 to 1896. The advantage of crossing here was that the road over Lee's Backbone was avoided; on the south side wagons had only to climb the short dugway out of the inner canyon to strike the main road to the Arizona settlements. This crossing was used each year between August and May. During the spring high water made a crossing here dangerous, if not impossible, so travelers had

ferry was finally anchored to a track cable at the upper site, this lower site was abandoned. The short, steep dugway on the left side of the river at this site may be seen from the campground and from a number of points on the north side of the Colorado.

A short dugway from the Lower Ferry site, used from 1878 to 1896, but only during periods of low river flow.

19. **ECHO PEAKS**. Across the river to the south rising 2500 feet above Lee's Ferry, the jagged Echo Peaks dominate the horizon. In October 1871, some of Major Powell's men climbed the peaks, and, for amusement, shot a pistol at the river, far below. The sharp report was followed by a twenty-four second silence, then came the echoes, as "the sound waves were hurled back... with a rattle like that of musketry" (see Chapter 4).

On a warm June day some years ago, the author, W.L. Rusho, climbed the peaks and attempted to duplicate the long-delayed echo by firing an 1860 model cap and ball revolver, but without success. It was probably too hot. Apparently fairly low air temperatures and an absence of wind are necessary to obtain the echo effect described by Powell's men.

The Echo Peaks are the high point in the seventy-five-mile line of Echo Cliffs extending from Lee's Ferry south almost to Tuba City, nearly paralleling U.S. 89. The cliffs also extend north of the Colorado along the east side of the Paria River canyon.

20. **BUZZARD'S HIGHLINE TRAIL.** An important Indian trail once descended the Echo Cliffs through rough, broken terrain on the south and east sides of the Echo Peaks, then down a long sand slope to the river. It was reportedly part of a major system of Indian trading trails and may have been used for centuries.

Where a northbound traveler on this trail crosses the ridge and obtains his first view of Lee's Ferry, there he will see a large pile of stones. Many years ago a battle was reported to have occurred here between Navajo and Ute Indians. Subsequently every Navajo who passed threw a rock onto the pile. (See photo, p. 144)

This difficult trail was used on occasion by white men coming into Lee's Ferry from points east. For instance, mining man Charles H. Spencer and some of his men were guided over the trail in May 1910 by a Navajo Indian. It was one of Spencer's men who suggested the name Buzzard's Highline Trail.

Except for a small section near the high ridge overlooking Lee's Ferry, the Buzzard's Highline Trail is extremely faint and difficult to follow. In summer the terrain is oppressively—even dangerously—hot and arid. Consequently, the trail is not recommended for hikers.

Buzzard's Highline Trail around the Echo Peaks

Monument to an Indian Battle, Buzzard's Highline Trail.

CCC Trail up to the Echo Cliffs.

ECHO PEAKS

CCC TRAIL

21. **CCC TRAIL**. Cresting the Echo Cliffs southwest of the Echo Peaks is the so-called CCC Trail, which was reportedly constructed by Civilian conservation Corps workmen during the 1930's. A CCC camp definitely did operate in House Rock Valley for some time, but records of that camp have not yet been located. The CCC Trail was apparently built so that Navajo Indians could more easily take their livestock to the river and bottom lands at Lee's Ferry. It was probably a replacement for the Buzzard's High line Trail (see Site No. 20).

A traveler approaching the river from the south on the CCC Trail crosses the ridge at the head of a side canyon, then switchbacks down talus slopes to the Shinarump ledge. From there, he may traverse across to Lee's Backbone or he may descend further to the level of the Marble Platform. The CCC Trail is an easy hike, but the access road from U.S. 89a to the base of the trail is suitable for four-wheel drive vehicles only. In the vicinity of the base of the trail are numerous uranium prospecting roads and test pits.

22. **NAVAJO BRIDGE**. Although located six road miles downstream from Lee's Ferry, Navajo Bridge represents a vital part of Lee's Ferry history. In 1928, during construction of the bridge, the ferryboat was lost in a tragic accident (see Site No. 1). The boat was not replaced because completion of the bridge would put the ferry out of operation.

Work began in June 1927 and was completed January 12, 1929, when the bridge was opened to traffic. It was dedicated in June 1929. A proposal to name it "Lee's Ferry Bridge" led to a spirited controversy in the Arizona State Legislature. The

The "old" Navajo Bridge, completed in 1929.

name "Navajo Bridge" was the result of compromise.

Until the highway bridge at Glen Canyon Dam site was completed in 1959, Navajo Bridge was the only bridge crossing of the Colorado from Moab, Utah, to Hoover Dam, a distance of almost six hundred miles (see Chapter 15 for further details).

A new, much wider, Navajo Bridge was designed and constructed by the Arizona Department of Transportation as a replacement for the old one. The older, 1929 bridge, only 19 1/2 feet wide will continue to be maintained, but only as a footbridge for pedestrians. A visitor center, built on the north abutment of the older bridge, was opened to the public during the spring of 1997.

The new bridge, 47 feet wide, matchs the old one in general appearance. It was built 120 feet downstream is over a two year period, concluded by a dedication ceremony on September 14, 1995.

Two Navajo Bridges span Marble Canyon of the Grand Canyon six miles downstream from Lee's Ferry. The older bridge, now a pedestrian footbridge, is at left. At far right is the Navajo Bridge Interpretive Center, opened to the public in 1997.

**23. MARBLE CANYON LODGE.** This lodge, about one-half mile from Navajo Bridge, was constructed by David "Buck" Lowrey from 1927 to 1929, with the opening coinciding with the completion of the bridge. Before it was finished, Lowrey operated a small trading post, also near the bridge, but on the Navajo Reservation side of the canyon, while Lowrey and his family lived at Lee's Ferry. He also built 14 rock cottages behind the lodge. Water was obtained from a small spring, high on the Vermilion Cliffs, 3 1/2 miles away. Lowery left in 1937. Art Greene, who managed

Marble Canyon Lodge, built by Buck Lowrey, opened for business the same day Navajo Bridge was dedicated, June 14, 1929.  *Jane Foster, Marble Canyon Lodge*

Marble Canyon Lodge from 1943 to 1949, left to build Cliff Dwellers Lodge. In 1959, the present owner, Jane Foster, began active management of the enterprise. In 1985 and 1986 she restored the lodge, and now rents it out for group meetings or to visiting tour groups. The motel, restaurant, and store across the highway were built, building by building, from 1959 to 1991.

24. **CLIFF DWELLER'S LODGE**. About nine miles west of Navajo Bridge is Cliff Dweller's Lodge, a delightful oasis of cabins, restaurant, a new lodge and service station nestled at the foot of the spectacular Vermilion Cliffs. Just east of the modern buildings are the unoccupied, but still curious rock cabins built under and around huge balanced rocks during the 1930's by a man named Bill Russell. Art Greene built the lodge and restaurant in 1949, and he and his son and daughters owned and managed it until February, 1979, when it was sold to Chuck and Vivian Dewitz, Coni Gilmore, and Roger Dewitz. Hatch River Expeditions maintains a large outfitting warehouse and headquarters adjacent to Cliff Dweller's.

25. **HOUSE ROCK VALLEY AND THE MARBLE PLATFORM**. If an entire valley can be a tour site, this is a good one. For visitors, its chief attractions are broad views of the valley floor, of the incredible Vermilion Cliffs, of the jagged deep gash of Marble Canyon, of clouds scudding across a deep blue sky, even of occasional pounding torrents of rain falling in black sheets onto the desert floor. House Rock Valley proper is the western section, the land drained by House Rock Wash. The valley does not cross the Colorado River. Those valley floor areas at the foot of the Vermilion Cliffs that drain into Soap Creek, Badger Creek, and the Paria River are more properly on the Marble Platform. The distinctions, however, are admittedly subtle and somewhat meaningless.

During the early years of the twentieth century, the Grand Canyon Cattle Company

Unique cabins were built around and under balanced rocks at Soap Creek, adjacent to Cliff Dweller's Lodge, during the 1930's.

(Bar-Z), grazed thousands of cattle, first in House Rock Valley itself, then after 1909, all the way east to Lee's Ferry. The Bar-Z headquarters was at the foot of the Kaibab Plateau, just north of the present U.S. 89a. The headquarters building still stands. The Buffalo Ranch, operated by Arizona Division of Wildlife, lies on the rim of Marble Canyon, 22 miles south of U.S. 89a. Visitors are welcome, but the road is unpaved.

Historic sites in House Rock Valley, such as Jacob's Pools and House Rock Spring,

Cliff Dweller's Lodge appears dwarfed by the 3,000 foot high Vermilion Cliffs.

are difficult to find, and land owner permission is required.

The Vermilion Cliffs in this area are included in the Paria Canyon-Vermilion Cliffs Wilderness Area, administered by the Bureau of Land Management. Information on trails and possible climbing routes can be obtained from the BLM in Kanab, Utah.

From turnouts on U.S. 89a near the western side of House Rock Valley, visitors may be fortunate enough to sight one of the condors soaring along the Vermilion Cliffs or sailing on its great black wings across the valley. Binoculars are highly recommended.

Marble Canyon cuts deeply and colorfully through the strata along the southern border of House Rock Valley. Photograph taken about 41 river miles below Lee's Ferry, looking upstream, to the east.

# READING LIST

A SHORT LIST OF BOOKS AND ARTICLES THAT TOUCH ON LEE'S FERRY

Several books touch upon Lee's Ferry, but the book you are reading was the first to trace the basic historical facts of this important crossroads. Many events that touch on Lee's Ferry, however, have been discussed more fully in other published books and articles. If not still in print, these titles may be found in any good-sized library or university collection.

W.L. Rusho's "Living History at Lee's Ferry," *Journal of the West* 7 (January 1968): 64-75, describes the many reminders of the ferry's rich history. Two books by C. Gregory Crampton, *Standing Up Country, the Canyon Lands of Utah and Arizona* and *Land of Living Rock, the Grand Canyon and the High Plateaus, Arizona, Utah, Nevada* (New York: Alfred A. Knopf, 1964 and 1972 respectively), place Lee's Ferry in its regional setting and historical perspective. Edwin Corle's *Listen Bright Angel* (New York: Duell, Sloan & Pearce, 1946) is entertaining but somewhat inaccurate. A more authoritative book by J. Donald Hughes, *The Story of Man at the Grand Canyon* (Grand Canyon: Grand Canyon Natural History Association, 1967), touches a wide area but concentrates on the National Park. Works by F.S. Dellenbaugh, *The Romance of the Colorado River* (New York and London: G.P. Putnam's Sons, 1902), Lewis R. Freeman, *The Colorado River, Yesterday, Today, and Tomorrow,* (New York: Dodd, Mead & Co., 1923), Frank Waters, *The Colorado,* (New York: Rinehart & Co. 1946), and David Lavender *Colorado River Country,* (New York: E.P. Dutton, Inc., 1982) treat Lee's Ferry briefly in the perspective of Colorado River history.

After the book you are reading was originally published in 1975, a small book that also deals with Lee's Ferry directly, Evelyn Brack Measeles, *Lee's Ferry–A Crossing on the Colorado* (Boulder, Colorado: Pruett Publishing, 1981) was published. Mrs. Measeles's book contains some interesting historical photographs, but the text has many errors of fact and/or omission.

On local geology, a report by David A. Phoenix, *Geology of the Lee's Ferry Area, Coconino County, Arizona* (Washington: Government Printing Office, 1963) U.S. Geological Survey Bulletin 1137, emphasizes stratigraphy, but does touch on commercial mining. Theodore Roosevelt's description of the Vermilion Cliffs is in his article about his pack trip, "Across the Navajo Desert," *Outlook* 105 (October 1913).

Abundant technical literature can be found on the prehistoric Indian cultures of the canyon country, but no archaeological study has yet concentrated on Lee's Ferry and its environs. In an article entitled, "The Canyon Dwellers," *The American West 4,* (May, 1967), Robert C. Euler discusses the split twig figurines and the prehistoric life in the Colorado River Canyons. Evidence of the Desha Complex found near Navajo Mountain is in Alexander J. Lindsay, Jr., et al, *Survey and Excavations North and*

*East of Navajo Mountain, Utah, 1959-1962*, (Flagstaff: Museum of Northern Arizona, 1968), Bulletin No. 45, Glen Canyon Series No. 8. A summary of successive Indian cultures is found in Robert C. Euler, *Southern Paiute Ethnohistory*, (Salt Lake City: University of Utah, 1966), Anthropological Papers 78, Glen Canyon Series 28. Navajo history and expansion are covered by James J. Hester, *Early Navajo Migrations and Acculturation in the Southwest*, (Santa Fe: Museum of New Mexico, 1962), Papers in Anthropology 6. The historical importance of the Navajo Trader is detailed by Frank McNitt, *The Indian Trader*, (Norman: University of Oklahoma Press, 1962).

For tracing the Dominguez-Escalante Expedition trail, nothing compares with *The Route of The Dominguez-Escalante Expedition 1776-1777*, (Salt Lake City: Utah State Historical Society, 1976), edited by David E. Miller, a study printed in only a few spiral bound copies, and by now, quite rare. The most recent translation is by Fray Angelico Chavez, *The Dominguez-Escalante Journal* (Provo: Brigham Young University Press, 1976), edited by Ted Warner, which also has numerous footnotes that help to identify the route. An excellent general narrative and delineation of the route, is Walter Briggs, *Without Noise of Arms–The 1776 Dominguez-Escalante Search for a Route from Santa Fe to Monterey.* (Flagstaff: Northland Press, 1976). Of the older studies of the D-E Expedition, the best is Herbert E. Bolton, *Pageant in the Wilderness*, (Salt Lake City: Utah State Historical Society 1950). A good translation is Herbert S. Auerbach, *Father Escalante's Journal, 1776-1777*, (Salt Lake City: Utah State Historical Society 1943).

The mountain men who trapped the Colorado River canyons left few records, and only scattered reference to their activities are extant. See James Ohio Pattie, *The Personal Narrative of James O. Pattie*, (Cincinnati: John H. Wood, 1831), ed. by Timothy Flint, and Robert Glass Cleland, *This Reckless Breed of Men–The Trappers and Fur Traders of the Southwest*, (New York: Alfred A. Knopf, 1952). The overland caravan trade between Santa Fe and Los Angeles on the Spanish Trail and variants is in LeRoy R. and Ann W. Hafen, *The Old Spanish Trail, Santa Fe to Los Angeles, with Extracts from Contemporary Records, and including Diaries of Antonio Armijo and Orville Pratt* (Glendale, California: Arthur H. Clark Co., 1954)

Early Mormon explorations and expeditions to the Indian country across the Colorado River are narrated in an autobiographical account by Jacob Hamblin, taken down by James A. Little, entitled *Jacob Hamblin Among the Indians* (Salt Lake City: Juvenile Instructor Office, 1881). Two biographies, Pearson H. Corbett, *Jacob Hamblin, the Peacemaker* (Salt Lake City: Deseret Book Co., 1952), and Paul Bailey, *Jacob Hamblin, Buckskin Apostle* (Los Angeles: Westernlore Press, 1948), give the explorer-Indian missionary a stature bordering on the heroic.

John Wesley Powell's voyage down the Colorado River and his attendant land explorations are surely the most written-about episodes in Colorado River history. Lee's Ferry and environs figure prominently in Powell's second expedition of 1871-1872, reported in detail by the youngest of its members, Frederick S. Dellenbaugh, in *A Canyon Voyage* (New Haven: Yale University Press, 1962). A number of diaries kept by members of Powell's first and second expeditions were published in special issues of the Utah Historical Quarterly, 1947-1949. An excellent biography of Powell is W.C. Darrah, *Powell of the Colorado*, (Princeton: Princeton University Press, 1951). A treatment of Powell's role in the opening of the West and as a Government science administrator is Wallace Stegner, *Beyond the Hundredth Meridan*, (Cambridge, Mass.: Riverside Press, 1954).

Juanita Brooks, *The Mountain Meadows Massacre*, 2nd ed. (Norman: University of Oklahoma Press, 1962), although not a complete story of the tragic event, presented many of the facts for the first time. Especially valuable for John D. Lee's activities before and during his years at Lee's Ferry is Robert G. Cleland and Juanita Brooks, eds., *A Mormon Chronicle, the Diaries of John D. Lee, 1848-1876*, (San Marino, Calif.: Huntington Library, 1955). Drawing on other sources to help round out the Lee's biography is Juanita Brooks, *John Doyle Lee, Zealot-Pioneer-Scapegoat* (Glendale, Calif.: Arthur H. Clark Co., 1972). A small book by Juanita Brooks, *Emma Lee* (Logan, UT: Utah State University Press, 1975) is a semi-novelized story of John D. Lee's 18th wife, and is based on folklore and family tradition.

The history and early use of Lee's Ferry by Mormons, as well as the colonization of the Little Colorado River country, may be found in James H. McClintock, *Mormon Settlement in Arizona: A Record of Peaceful Conquest of the Desert* (Phoenix: Manufacturing Stationers, 1921). A highly readable, scholarly work based on original documents is Charles S. Peterson, *Take Up Your Mission: Mormon Colonizing Along the Little Colorado River, 1870-1890* (Tucson: University of Arizona Press, 1973). A valuable article on the role of Warren M. Johnson at Lee's Ferry was written by P.T. Reilly as "Warren Marshall Johnson, Forgotten Saint," *Utah Historical Quarterly* 39 (Winter 1971): 3-22.

Probably the best account of the 1874 shooting of Navajos in Grass Valley appeared in Peter Gottfredson, *History of Indian Depredations in Utah* (Salt Lake City: Skelton Publishing Co., 1919): 330-332.

Only a few scattered references are found concerning visits of outlaws to Lee's Ferry. Matt Warner's autobiography was entitled *The Last of the Bandit Riders* (New York: Bonanza Books, 1940). Ralph Keithley, in *Buckey O'Neill* (Caldwell, ID: Caxton Printers, 1949), details the exploits of one of Arizona's most colorful lawmen.

Zane Grey has portrayed Buffalo Jones in *Last of the Plainsmen* (New York: Outing Publishing Co., 1908), and James Emett in "The Man Who Influenced Me Most," *American* 102 (August 1926), and in *Tales of Lonely Trails* (New York and London: Harper and Bros., 1922). More detail on Buffalo Jones and on the "cattalo" experiment in House Rock Valley is in Robert Easton and Mackensie Brown, *Lord of Beasts: The Saga of Buffalo Jones* (Tucson: University of Arizona Press, 1961). Zane Grey's writing and movie-making at Lee's Ferry and the Arizona Strip are summarized in Candace C. Kant, *Zane Grey's Arizona*, (Flagstaff: Northland Press, 1984). A colorful description of the Lee's Ferry country in the early Twentieth Century is Sharlot Hall, *Sharlot Hall on the Arizona Strip: A Diary of a Journey Through Northern Arizona in 1911*, (Flagstaff: Northland Press, 1975), ed. by C. Gregory Crampton.

Robert B. Stanton's own writings are in Robert B. Stanton, *The Colorado River Survey: Robert B. Stanton and the Denver, Colorado Canyon and Pacific Railroad*, ed. by Dwight L. Smith and C. Gregory Crampton, (Salt Lake City and Chicago: Howe Brothers, 1987); and in Robert B. Stanton, *Down the Colorado*, ed. by Dwight L. Smith (Norman: University of Oklahoma Press, 1965), both of which detail the dramatic story of the railroad survey through the Colorado River Canyons, including the long stop at Lee's Ferry. Stanton's record of his mining venture in Glen Canyon has been edited by C. Gregory Crampton and Dwight L. Smith, *The Hoskaninni Papers: Mining in Glen Canyon, 1897-1902* (Salt Lake City: University of Utah, 1961), Anthropological Papers 54.

A good study of Charles H. Spencer's Lee's Ferry operations, including the mining activities, the construction of buildings, and, particularly, the building and operation of the steamboat, *Charles H. Spencer*, was conducted by the National Park Service in 1986. The NPS report is Toni Carrell, James E. Bradford, and W.L. Rusho, *Submerged Cultural Resources Site Report: Charles H. Spencer's Mining Operation and Paddle Wheel Steamboat*, (Santa Fe: National Park Service, 1987), Glen Canyon National Recreation Area. The story and photographs of the steamboat, *Charles H. Spencer*, are included in Richard E. Lingenfelter, *Steamboats on the Colorado River, 1852-1916*, (Tucson: University of Arizona Press, 1978).

The merits of building a dam in lower Glen Canyon and an eye witness account of the investigation were discussed by Lewis R. Freeman in *The Colorado River, Yesterday, Today, and Tomorrow* (New York: Dodd, Mead and Co., 1923), and in *Down the Grand Canyon* (New York: Dodd, Mead and Co., 1924). Frank Waters, in *The Colorado* (New York and Toronto: Rinehart & Co., 1946), reviews the history of dam construction on the Colorado up to that time. An account of the Congressional battles preceding authorization of Glen Canyon Dam is John Upton Terrell, *War for the Colorado*, Volume 2 (Glendale: Arthur H. Clark, 1965). Philip Fradkin, in *A River No More: The Colorado River and the West*, (New York: Knopf, 1981) tells the story of water development in the Upper Colorado River Basin, pointing out unfavorable environmental consequences. An excellent account of the actual building of the Glen Canyon Dam, as well as the associated environmental controversy, is Russell Martin, *A Story That Stands Like A Dam: Glen Canyon and the Struggle for the Soul of the West*, (New York: Henry Holt and Co., 1989).

Because of its vital importance as a supply point or as a  launching point, Lee's Ferry is mentioned in practically all written accounts of river running through the Grand Canyon. In these accounts, however, Lee's Ferry is never the principal location of the action. The best account of Grand Canyon river running is David Lavender, *River Runners of the Grand Canyon*, (Grand Canyon: Grand Canyon Natural History Association; Tucson: University of Arizona Press, 1985). Otis "Dock" Marston, in "River Runners: Fast Water Navigation, *Utah Historical Quarterly* 28 (July 1960) lists the Green and Colorado River boating parties through Utah after the Powell expeditions. The Kolb brothers ran the Colorado in 1911 and provided a good picture of Spencer's operations at Lee's Ferry and at Warm Creek. See Ellsworth L. Kolb, *Through the Grand Canyon from Wyoming to Mexico* (New York: Macmillan Co., 1914). Barry M. Goldwater, who made the Colorado run in 1940 with Norman Nevills, provides a short history of Lee's Ferry, as well as personal observations, in *Delightful Journey Down the Green and Colorado Rivers* (Tempe, AZ: Arizona Historical Foundation, 1970). Art Greene was the subject of a brief biography by Frank Jensen, "Riverman" *Desert Magazine* (July 1961). Other references to Greene and his river operations have appeared in numerous regional travel magazines and in newspapers. Excellent guidebooks include:  Larry Stevens, *The Colorado River in Grand Canyon: A Guide* (Flagstaff: Red Lake Books 1983), Buzz Belknap, *Grand Canyon River Guide* (Evergreen, CO: Westwater Books, 1989),  Kim Crumbo, *A River Runner's Guide to the History of the Grand Canyon* (Boulder, CO: Johnson Books, 1981).

For hikers and amateur explorers, see Michael R. Kelsey, *Hiking and Exploring the Paria River*, (Provo, UT: Kelsey Publishing 1987), for description of trails up the Paria Plateau, for a history of ranches found in upper House Rock Valley and along the Paria River, and for a hiking guide to the Paria Canyon and tributary canyons. Kelsey also has a good description of Lee's Ferry, as well as a summary history of

John D. Lee.

Marble Canyon Lodge, David "Buck" Lowrey and his family figure prominently in Nora Cundell, *Unsentimental Journey*, (London: Methuen & Co. Ltd., 1940), a charming book by a woman artist from England who was captivated by the colorful country during the mid-1930's and who often returned for long visits.

The 2nd Navajo Bridge, constructed from 1993 to 1995, is discussed thoroughly in *Final Environmental Assessment, U.S. 89A Bitter Springs to Fredonia, Navajo Bridge*, (Phoenix: Arizona Department of Transportation, 1990), and in *Navajo Bridge, Bridge Design Report* (Tucson: Cannon & Associates, Inc., 1990)

# INDEX